# DOUBLEBORN

# THE FLAXFIELD

# QUARTET:

# VOLUME THREE

## Doubleborn

## TOBY FORWARD

WALKER
BOOKS

This is a work of fiction. Names, characters, places and incidents are either the product of the author's imagination or, if real, are used fictitiously. All statements, activities, stunts, descriptions, information and material of any other kind contained herein are included for entertainment purposes only and should not be relied on for accuracy or replicated as they may result in injury.

First published 2012 by Walker Books Ltd

87 Vauxhall Walk, London SE11 5HJ

2 4 6 8 10 9 7 5 3 1

Text © 2012 Toby Forward
Illustrations © 2012 Jim Kay

The right of Toby Forward and Jim Kay to be identified as the author and illustrator respectively of this work has been asserted by them in accordance with the Copyright, Designs and Patents Act 1988

This book has been typeset in Historical

Printed and bound in Great Britain by Clays Ltd, St Ives plc

British Library Cataloguing in Publication Data:
a catalogue record for this book is available from the British Library

ISBN 978-1-4063-2045-9

www.walker.co.uk

*A man that looks on glasse,*
*On it may stay his eye;*
*Or if he pleaseth, through it passe,*
*And then the heav'n espie.*

From "The Elixir", by George Herbert

---

I had good teachers, bad teachers, terrible teachers and wonderful ones. Don't we all? This book is dedicated to all my good and wonderful teachers.

Part One

# DOUBLEDEALING

# "Well what am I?"

asked Tamrin.

No one could have called her tidy at the best of times, and when she was cross, which was a lot of the time now, she looked more dishevelled than ever.

She waited for Vengeabil to answer. Either he didn't hear her or he was pretending he didn't, and she knew that he heard everything.

"I mean it," she said. "What am I?"

Vengeabil put a piece of thread in his mouth. He was sewing up a stuffed dragon that had fallen from a high shelf and come undone. It was a Small Tortoiseshell, very rare, about the size of a cat, with a tail that ended in three points. He pointed to the thread and shrugged his shoulders, indicating that he couldn't talk.

Tamrin jabbed her pen on her exercise book. The nib splayed out, ink sprayed over the page and on to her hands. When she brushed it away she just smeared it more.

"Blotting paper," said Vengeabil.

"Hah!" she pointed her pen at him. "I knew you could talk with that thread in your mouth. What am I? Really. I mean it."

"I know you mean it," he said, taking the thread out of his mouth now that it no longer protected him from talking. "But I don't know what you mean. They're not the same thing."

Tamrin had ink up to her elbows now and a smear of it on her cheek.

"I'm not a real apprentice, am I?" she said. "Not really."

Vengeabil put the last stitch in and tied up the end. He examined the stuffed dragon from every side.

"And I'm a twin," she continued. "But I don't know what sort of twin and I never see my twin. I never even met him until a year ago, and then he was gone almost as soon as he was here."

"This dragon," said Vengeabil, "is the only one ever seen anywhere by anyone."

"How do you know?"

"Because the book of dragons says there are seventeen varieties of dragon and eight of them have never been seen by anyone, and the Small Tortoiseshell is one of the eight."

Tamrin peered across the kitchen at it.

"How did you get it?"

"There's a story attached to that," said Vengeabil.

Tamrin rolled her eyes. With Vengeabil there was a story attached to everything.

"That's what I mean," she said. She clenched her fists and knuckled her forehead. It was difficult to sort things out in her head. "You never teach me anything, not really. You just tell me stories. Not proper lessons, like in the college."

The kitchen they were sitting in was in the cellars of Canterstock College, the oldest, biggest, and, if you really admitted it, the only college for wizards. Above their heads nearly two hundred pupils were studying magic. Tamrin had been one of them once, as a little girl, but it hadn't worked out and she was sort of expelled and she sort of just left. After a while, Vengeabil took her on as his apprentice, to make her a wizard that way.

"Stories are how you teach an apprentice," he said. "It's how my old master taught me." He stroked the dragon and looked into the distance. "Flaxfield. There was a wizard for you. He never went to the college. Proper wizards don't; they pass it on to their apprentices. Your people upstairs, they'll never be the sort of wizard he was. Not the sort of wizard I am. Not the sort of wizard you can be."

This was Vengeabil's story. Tamrin loved to hear him tell it. Every time it was just a little different. Every time there was just a little something new that he hadn't told before. Every time she understood something better than she had the last time.

She pushed her books aside.

"Tell me," she said.

Vengeabil moved across and sat next to her. He looked at

her work. Despite her complaints about only hearing stories, Tamrin had filled many exercise books with notes and diagrams and drawings, lists and recipes, maps, names of herbs, and tables of figures. The pages were creased and blotched. The corners buffed and ragged. The covers, and more than the covers, were smeared with butter and wax and soot and grease. Any teacher upstairs would have refused to mark them, they were such a mess. Vengeabil marked them though, and he never found a mistake in the spelling or the calculations or the facts. Never. Tamrin had cried once because she couldn't be neat and Vengeabil had said, "I remember Flaxfield saying to me something about the comfortable tidiness of the small mind."

A bell rang high above them. Hundreds of feet thudded down the corridors.

"Lunch time. Lessons are finished for the morning," said Vengeabil. "And it's gloomy in here."

He leaned over and pulled a candle towards them. He pinched the wick between his finger and thumb, and a flame was born, tiny, then small, then strong and blue with a yellow beating heart.

"Shouldn't really," he said. "I should get a light from the range, but there you are, there you are. Are you ready?"

Tamrin nodded.

"I was Flaxfield's apprentice," he began. "All in the proper way. Left home at six years old and went to learn from him. Signed my indentures when I was twelve. It was all going smoothly. And then there was the incident."

This was the part that Tamrin wanted him to talk about. Sometimes he called it an event, sometimes an incident, once he called it a disaster, sometimes it was a chapter of occurrences.

"Anyway, after the — incident — everything changed."

"What was it?" she said. "The incident."

Vengeabil sighed. "You know, Flaxfield told us all never to talk about it. He said if we forgot all about it then we might be safe."

"And did you forget? Is that why you never tell me what it was?"

"No. No, I never forgot. Still, after it happened, nothing was the same and I had to leave Flaxfield and come here."

"Did you hate it?"

Vengeabil looked shocked. "Hate it? No. Not at all. Part of me wanted to come here. You have to remember, it was a different sort of place then. We had a good principal. A very good principal."

Tamrin couldn't stop herself from hitting the table with her knuckles, which hurt, but was worth it.

"I know," he agreed. "Not like now. And I was apprenticed jointly to Flaxfield and to someone here. First time it's ever happened. I didn't go to lessons. Just learned," he gave her one of his looks that made him look like a naughty twelve-year-old, "by stories. So I'm sort of half an apprenticed wizard and half a college wizard. Just like you."

"Who was your master here?" she said. Not for the first time.

"So you see, to answer one of your questions — who am I? — you're my apprentice and I like to think that's not a bad thing."

Tamrin felt ashamed.

"It's a good thing," she said. "I love it. But there are the other questions."

She didn't like to say that a question she hadn't said out loud to him was, "And what are you?" She knew whatever answer he gave it wouldn't be enough of an answer. And if she didn't know what he was how could she know what she was?

"There's someone coming," said Vengeabil.

They paused and listened.

"I'd better go and see what they want," he said.

Tamrin waited for him to leave the kitchen, then as she usually did, she followed him, silently.


"Mr Masrani," said Vengeabil. "What can I do for you, young sir?"

Tim Masrani grinned at him.

"Did you want a new pair of shoes?" the man asked.

"No. Er, no, thanks."

"No?"

Vengeabil lifted the counter top and stepped out to stand next to Tim.

Vengeabil's storeroom supplied everyone in the college with books, uniform, equipment and ingredients for experiments and spells, paper, ink, games, toys, bandages, rubber bands, pens and anything else he thought they might need. He was the storekeeper, which was just about the lowliest job in the college. The pupils treated him as a bit of a joke. The better ones felt sorry for him. The others would have made fun of him if they weren't just a little bit scared of the scruffy old man who lived in the dark passages under the college.

"No," said Tim. "I haven't come for new shoes."

"Well you ought to. Look at the state of them. They're all scuffed and dusty."

Tim looked down at his feet. His shoes weren't really in any worse state than the rest of his uniform — trousers baggy at the knee, jerkin just too small, with a hole in the left elbow and reminders of meals down the front, hair not combed for a week. He brushed himself down with his hands, achieving no improvement at all, and said, "I've come to take Tamrin to Professor Frastfil. He wants to see her."

"What if she doesn't want to see him?" said Vengeabil. "What if she's not here?"

A jerkin slid down from the counter and wrapped itself around Tim's leg, turning into a small octopus and winding itself round him.

"Oh, not that again," he complained, shaking his leg. "Why do you always do that? It's wet, and slimy."

"I'll go and see him," said Tamrin, stepping out from the shadows. "What does he want?"

Vengeabil nodded to the octopus and it slithered off Tim's leg and turned back into a jerkin.

"Don't know," said Tim. He grinned at her. "You don't think he'd tell me anything, do you?"

"Come on," said Tamrin.

"Come straight back," Vengeabil called after her. "You've got work to do."

They climbed the stairs and made their way along the corridor toward the principal's room.

Tamrin looked up at the globes that bobbed above their heads, casting dim light on the corridor.

"This place is sick," she said. "Look at them. They should be bright as day. We crouch around in here, dodging from place to place, never doing anything useful. It's rotting."

Tim gave her a worried glance. She knew he quite liked her and she knew he was quite frightened of her. Not as frightened as the other pupils. To them she was a half-hidden secret, the girl who didn't belong, the girl who had been thrown out of college and never left. Not a pupil, not a servant, not a cook or a cleaner or gardener. She was nobody. Just a girl who'd been left at the college by some poor tailor. Except when she was with Vengeabil in his storeroom, as his apprentice. But no one knew that either. As far as they knew he had just given her somewhere to live after she'd been expelled, and she tidied the stores and helped around the place in return. Her magic was still there, but it was uncontrolled, untutored.

They reached Frastfil's door and Tim gave a hesitant

knock. Before anyone could call them to come in Tamrin banged her fist on the wood, turned the handle and stomped in. She closed the door on the boy's astonished face.

The three faces that looked at her now were even more astonished. Frastfil himself, the principal, was sitting behind his desk. His thin face, hooked nose and dishevelled clothes made him look more like a shopkeeper who sold damaged goods than the head of a great college.

"That door had a locking spell on it," he protested.

Tamrin smiled.

"Did it?" she said, in a voice that made it clear she was not telling the truth. "I didn't notice."

"You must have done. You're lying."

The accusation was made by the other adult in the room, Dr Duddle, recently appointed as vice-principal. Tamrin was turning thirteen and Duddle was not much taller, though a lot heavier. And he had a fat smirk. As though he liked you, when Tamrin knew that the smile really meant that he liked himself. He carried his little round tummy in front of him, smiling all the time at how pleased he was to be Dr Duddle.

"If Professor Frastfil put a locking spell on the door, I wouldn't have been able to open it, would I?" she asked Duddle. "After all, he's a powerful wizard and I'm just, well, I'm nothing, am I? Either he's not good or there was no spell."

The third face in the room sucked its cheeks in at this. Smedge nodded and looked from Duddle to Frastfil and back to Tamrin. Tamrin saw him considering the third possibility, that she could break any spell Frastfil set. Tamrin glared at him.

"What are you staring at?" she said.

"You see?" Smedge said to Frastfil, and the man nodded.

"See?" said Tamrin. "See what? What do you want me for?" She raised her voice and confronted Frastfil, determined to show him that she wasn't frightened of him. She'd watched the way the others treated him with respect and obedience, and she wasn't going to do it. He might be the principal, but she wasn't a pupil. There was nothing he could do to her.

"Are you all right, Smedge?" Frastfil asked. "Don't be nervous."

Tamrin felt a moment of fear. Smedge coughed and hesitated. Tamrin waited for something bad to happen.

Smedge spoke quietly at first and Tamrin couldn't believe what he was saying.

"I'm frightened of her," he began, "but not while you're here, sir, and Dr Duddle."

Frastfil tried to look strong and protective. Tamrin thought for a moment he needed to go to the jakes until she realized he was being important, and she laughed.

"You can't laugh," said Duddle. "This is serious."

"Serious?" said Tamrin. "This is stupid. Look at him."

She pointed to Smedge. There was a momentary ripple in the air, just for a second, and then it was gone. For that one moment Smedge appeared to Frastfil and Duddle as he usually did, another pupil at the college, the same age as Tamrin, just a little taller. He was the neatest boy in the place. His uniform always clean and tidy, his hair combed, his shoes shined. His face always wore an expression of eager helpfulness and amiability. Except for that one second. Hidden from the two men, but clear to her, his face took on a look of such empty, stupid hatred that she wanted to run out of the room. And then it was gone, and he was the obedient schoolboy again. She couldn't work out whether she'd imagined it or if it was real, and if it was real had he done it on purpose, to show her what he was like, or had a mask slipped?

By the time she recovered her thoughts a conversation had been going on around her and was coming to a close.

"And I will not tolerate bullying," said Frastfil.

"What?" she said.

"Smedge is frightened of you. You've made this boy's life a misery," he concluded. "You will have to leave."

"He's a liar," she said.

"That will do."

"I've never done anything to him."

"Do you deny that you locked him in a block of ice? For an hour?"

Tamrin's answer was shouted out before she had the time to control herself.

"He was taunting Westrim," she said. "Making him run stupid errands and confusing him. And when Westrim got things wrong Smedge magicked up ants to bite him all over and sting him. Westrim was crying. I only locked Smedge in the ice to stop him and teach him a lesson. Ask Westrim. Ask any of the little boys. Smedge makes their lives a misery."

"We have asked Westrim," Duddle smiled at her. "Smedge said you would make up lies about him. So we've asked the other boys and girls. They like him. They look up to him."

Tamrin saw Smedge's look of triumph and she understood that this was a plan he had set in place for some reason.

"And so we have asked your guardian to take you away from the college," said Frastfil. He stood up, put his hands in his trouser pockets and jingled the coins in there. "You must wait here until he arrives and leave with him immediately. We can't have you upsetting anyone else."

"I'm not going with him," she said. "I can't. I don't know him. I don't remember him. I've always been here."

Tamrin had been left at the college when she was a tiny girl and no one had ever visited her. Her fees were paid in advance, and Frastfil had never said that she wasn't actually in lessons any more.

"I'm sure you'll be well looked after," said Frastfil. "You would never have been happy as a wizard. You don't have the discipline for it."

"You stupid man," she shouted. "You don't even know what a wizard is."

Duddle and Smedge exchanged glances of satisfaction.

A hesitant knock at the door brought silence. The knock was repeated.

"Come in," said Frastfil.

Tim poked his head around the door.

"Person for Tamrin," he said. "Name of Shoddle. He's a tailor. Says he's come to take her away. He's waiting in the porter's lodge."

"You'd better go," said Frastfil. ‖

# Tamrin was out of breath

but she kept running. Her feet slapped against the slabbed surface of the town square. She dodged errand boys pushing handcarts, dogs, an old woman with a heavy shopping basket over her arm, she swerved at the very last moment, only just managing not to knock over a baker with a tray of pies on his head. He staggered. His white apron fluttered and covered her face, blinding her.

"Hey!" he yelled.

He fell back, the tray tilting beyond the point where it must fall. Tamrin dragged the apron away, caught his arm, pulled him upright, waved her other hand at the tray. It grew eagle's wings, flapped, settled itself back on the baker's head and the wings folded away into nothing.

"Sorry. You all right?"

The shoppers cheered. Tamrin grinned. A pie slipped off the tray and flew round into her hand. She sprinted away, snitching an apple from a stall, across the square, round a corner and down a small alley that she knew led to the main gate of Canterstock. The last sight she saw was the baker, small against the huge grey stone of the college, counting his pies and complaining.

It had all happened so fast. And she had caused it.

One moment Tim was at the door telling her that a man had come to take her away, the next moment Frastfil was cowering under his desk, screaming for mercy, Duddle was climbing out of the window and Smedge looked on, fearless because there was nothing to fear and the magic hadn't touched him.

Tamrin acted before she thought. She flicked Tim into silent absence. He stood smiling at whatever peaceful picture had flooded his mind. She conjured up a creature from her nightmares. A mixture of snake and rat, with pointed yellow teeth and foul breath. As big as a horse, yet quick and sly. Both Frastfil and Duddle believed it was looking straight at them, though they stood on opposite sides of the room. So they took cover and tried to escape.

Tamrin looked at Smedge.

"You're not afraid," she said.

"I've eaten worse things than that."

And she believed he had.

"You won't escape," he said.

He sniffed and a smaller creature appeared, crawling out of his nose. A beetle. Black as fear, smooth as lies. It dropped to the floor and headed for her.

So she ran. Out of the room. Out of the building. Round the quadrangle, taking care to skirt the edge to avoid being seen. The tailor was in the porter's lodge. She ducked down, through the wicket gate and out, out into the square.

And now she passed through the other gate, the tall, broad gate of the town.

She didn't stop running until the road met a lane and she turned down that and still ran. Ran until the lane forked and she took a smaller one, to a path across a field, to a break in the hedge, to a dip in the ground, to the slope of a riverbank, to a slow-flowing stream, wider than the passageways in Canterstock College, and there she stopped and panted and drank and cried. ‖

# When Tim came round

from his reverie he couldn't work out what had happened. Smedge was tugging Frastfil's arm and trying to get him out from under the desk. Duddle was half-in half-out of the window, stuck because his backside was bigger than the rest of him and it wouldn't go through. He was flailing his arms and screaming in panic. There was no sign of the nightmare. It had never been there anyway.

"Where's Tam?" asked Tim.

"She's gone," Smedge said.

Frastfil emerged from his hiding place with a jingling of coins and a stupid smile.

"Wasn't frightened," he said. "Dropped something. Just picking it up."

"Gone where?" asked Tim.

"Run away."

"Run away?" said Frastfil. "That's very inconvenient. Oh dear."

Smedge frowned, pursed his lips and blew towards the window. Duddle squeaked and wriggled, the window expanded and he dropped back into the room with a bump and a moan. Tim smiled.

"What shall we do about Tamrin's guardian?" asked Frastfil.

"You'd better send him up," Smedge told Tim.

Duddle heaved himself to his feet, panting.

"I'll just go," he said.

"No, I want you here," said Frastfil.

Tim was interested. They were frightened. Of the tailor?

"Go on," said Frastfil. "Hurry up."

The tailor didn't look that frightening when Tim collected him at the lodge. He was thin and quick, like a needle. His clothes were made of good cloth, but old, worn so that it shone. Tim decided to take no chances, so he didn't tell him that Tamrin had run away.

"What's your name, boy?"

"Tim. I'm a friend of Tam's."

"Who?"

"Tam."

"Oh."

The tailor had a way of walking too close that made Tim nervous. There was something scary about him after all. Not obvious straight away.

"Were you visiting Canterstock on business or have you come specially to see her?" asked Tim.

"I've come," said the tailor, "because she's mine. All right? She's good for business. She can be useful. I'm tired of waiting for her to be trained up by your sort." Tim was glad when they reached Frastfil's office.

"Thank you," said the principal. "You can go now. I'll see Shoddle out when we've finished."

He closed the door in Tim's face, but not before the boy could taste the anxiety there, and not before he wondered why Smedge hadn't left as well. He was torn between listening at the door and going straight to Vengeabil to let him know that Tamrin had run off.

He put his ear to the door.

"You fool," said the tailor. "You've let her go."

"She took us by surprise."

"Call yourself a wizard. And you were supposed to look after her."

"We'll get her back."

"And then what?"

"Then she'll regret it."

"She'll wish she'd never seen me."

Tim moved silently away and sought Vengeabil to tell him the news.

"I'll take Mr Shoddle and get him something to eat before he leaves," said Smedge.

"I don't want anything," said the tailor. "Not here. Not from you lot."

Smedge nodded.

"I'll see you to the gate," he offered.

"I can find it myself."

Smedge noticed that Frastfil couldn't look Shoddle in the eye.

"As you wish," said Frastfil.

Duddle rubbed his back where he had hurt it struggling with the window.

Smedge left them to it and walked behind the tailor.

"I don't need you, boy," he said over his shoulder.

Smedge ignored him and kept following.

The tailor stopped and stared at him.

"I'll show you the back of my hand," he threatened.

Smedge didn't smile or flinch.

"I wouldn't try," he said.

The tailor thought about it. He fumbled in his waist-coat pocket and produced a thimble. It was iron, dull and worn. He put it on his left forefinger and stroked it. Smedge recognized that it was a trick to give the tailor time to think.

"Do you see this?" asked the tailor, showing Smedge the thimble. "I've had this longer than you've been alive."

"I wouldn't be too sure of that," said Smedge.

The tailor tapped the thimble against his thin cheek. He spoke so softly that Smedge could hardly hear him.

"Oh, that's the way of it, is it?" he said. "That's very interesting. Do you think we might be of use to one another?"

"I think we may," said Smedge. "Shall I show you to the gate?"

"You know," said the tailor, "I might be hungry after all. Shall we eat?"

"I can get you some food from the kitchen," said Smedge.

"No. No, I don't think so. Not in here. I don't want to talk in here. Let me buy you something in town? Are you allowed out?"

Smedge leaned forward and whispered, "I can do anything I like here."

"Good boy," said the tailor. "That's what I thought. Come along. We'll have some food and you can tell me all about Tamrin."

"And you can tell me about her, too," said Smedge, under his breath.


You can't cry for ever, and Tamrin wasn't even sure why she was crying.

She scrambled back from the river and lay on the grass, her hands behind her head, face up to the blue sky. The air carried the cool, fresh smell that promised rain soon, and the leaves of the trees blew upwards. A hawk circled.

She was a creature of passageways and corners, small rooms and books. Breeze and sunshine were, if not strangers, then distant acquaintances.

What made her cry like that?

She chewed the question slowly.

Distress. She left without saying goodbye to Vengeabil. She might never see him again. No, she would never see him again.

"I'm not going back," she said out loud.

Her voice sounded odd to her, without a listener. But it was better than not hearing a voice at all.

Distress. She had been called a bully and she wasn't.

"I'm not," she said. With more confidence this time.

She thought of the times she had done things to Smedge. Looking back, there were quite a lot, but never, ever without reason. She'd never picked on him but she had stopped him hurting the littler ones. Thinking about it made her want to cry again. She'd stopped him hurting people and he was calling her a bully.

She actually was crying again now.

"This is stupid," she said.

Distress, then. No. Not distress. Or not just distress. She was angry. The tears came because she was so angry she couldn't stop them.

She jumped up. This was no good. You can't just lie looking up at the sky when you're as angry as this. She jumped up and down, looking around. She had no idea where she was. Her only intention in running away was to go further and further from roads and people, taking ever smaller routes and tracks.

She looked around her, not even sure which direction the college lay in. She didn't want to find herself back there.

"Which way do I go?" she asked.

"Where do you want to get to?" came the answer.

Tamrin clenched her fists and tried to work out where the voice had come from. ‖

# "He said she was a bully?"

"That's right," said Tim.

He had never seen Vengeabil angry before. He had never seen much of him at all, in fact. Until recently Vengeabil had kept himself hidden in the storeroom. A year ago Tim discovered that the man also looked after the library, or seemed to. It didn't make much difference. They were both locked with strong spells that no one could break. Not that anyone would want to go into his kitchen.

Most of the time Vengeabil popped up at the counter in the storeroom as soon as anyone arrived. Some days, if he wasn't around, there was nowhere else to find him. Other days there was a small passageway that led to the kitchen.

"You can only find it by following the smell," everyone said. "Old vegetables."

Tim had found it today. He wrinkled his nose as he brought Vengeabil the news about Tamrin. A stink of stale cooking drifted out to him. The floor was filthy and looked as though your feet would stick to it as you walked across. A scrap of old sack was thrown on the little table, half-covering piles of dirty plates and pots and dishes. Dark, dirty and damp.

"You're making this up," said Vengeabil.

"No. Promise."

"Come in."

"What?"

Vengeabil smiled at Tim's confusion. No one was allowed into his kitchen. No one wanted to, anyway. Very few got as far as Tim and were able to put their head round the door to give a message.

"Come in."

Tim held his breath and stepped through the door.

"Sit down," said Vengeabil.

Tim stopped.

Vengeabil scowled at him.

"Don't stand there gurning like a losel. Sit down."

Tim took a step back, out of the door, stared, stepped forward again and stared harder.

"It's not a dance," said Vengeabil. "This is the last time I'm telling you. Sit down."

"I always felt sorry for Tam, living down here with you," said Tim.

"I know. You were supposed to."

Tim pulled a chair away from the table and sat down. Tamrin's books were in front of him and Vengeabil shuffled them away before Tim could look at them properly.

The kitchen was light, airy, and filled with the scent of freshly baked bread.

"Where does the bad smell come from?" asked Tim.

Vengeabil raised his head and sniffed.

"Smells all right to me," he said.

He took a big knife from a drawer in the table, tipped the loaf of bread on its side and sawed off the crust.

"Do you like crust or inside?" he asked.

"Either. Sorry. Didn't mean it was a bad smell now."

"I know what you meant."

Vengeabil spread a generous layer of butter on to the bread.

"Jam or lemon curd?"

"What sort of jam?"

Vengeabil raised an eyebrow.

"Lemon curd, please."

"I make it myself," said Vengeabil. "Come and look at this."

Tim followed him to a door. Vengeabil let him through and he found himself in a wide, high, stone-flagged glass-house, with plants he had never seen before, including a row of five lemon trees, full of fruit.

"Where are we?" he asked. "I've never seen this place."

"You may never see it again," said Vengeabil. "But now you know the lemons are fresh."

They went back, Tim sat at the table and bit into the thick slice of bread. The crust was crisp. The inside was soft and springy. The butter was yellow, salty and cool. The lemon curd made his mouth water with a sharp, instant bite, then released a wave of sweetness that made him smile.

"Thought you'd like that," said Vengeabil.

"Everyone thinks—" began Tim.

The man waved his hand.

"I know what everyone thinks," he said. "Smelly old Vegetables, the storeman. In his stinky kitchen, with his sad little friend, Tam, the college dunce. Thrown out for being too naughty to learn. I know."

"I wasn't going to say that," said Tim.

"Why not? It's what everyone thinks. You think I don't know what they call me? You think that smell comes from nowhere? Eh? I don't want people knowing how I live here. I don't want scruffy schoolboys pestering me for bread and treats. So I keep them away."

Tim finished his bread with a sense of such loss that he wanted to cry.

"I won't tell," he said.

"I know. That's why you're here. Now, what's happened to Tamrin?"

As he asked the question a small stream of stars fell from his fingertips and bounced on the floor. Tim looked at him, looked down at the stars. Vengeabil was waiting for Tim's answer. He hadn't seen the stars tumble from his hand. Tim was trying to decide whether to tell Vengeabil what had happened when a small, skinny cat, old and slow, only about as big as a mouse, appeared round the table leg and began to lick up the stars.

✠

More voices followed. Louder, harsh and coming closer fast. Tamrin pulled a face. Her lonely place far from the road was quickly becoming as busy as the market square in Canterstock.

"Quick. This way."

A hand seized Tamrin's arm and pulled her into a thicket. Thorns dragged across her skin, cutting into her arms, her cheeks, her legs.

A face stared at her and a hand went to her lips. Tamrin obeyed. Something about the woman who had grabbed her made her pay attention.

The woman inclined her head to the left and Tamrin nodded. The voices approached.

"Gone."

"Not gone."

"Gone."

"Can't have gone."

"Where?"

"Can't see."

"Stop."

Four figures. No, five. Six. At least. Red and booted. Leather-clad. Thick-bodied, with spindly legs. No faces. They had hoods drawn over their heads, masking them. Tamrin looked more closely. No. There were no hoods. They had no faces. Just shiny shells with eyes. And that wasn't leather. It was them.

Tamrin looked to her companion for help, for an explanation. The woman put her finger back to her lips.

She mouthed silently to Tamrin: they're chasing me.

"Look."

"Where?"

"Bushes."

"River."

"Not going on water."

"No. Not water."

"Bushes."

They spread out, scything their long arms, beating down undergrowth. Three were moving away from Tamrin, two were heading straight for her. The woman's face pleaded with her.

Tamrin nodded. She closed her eyes, pursed her lips and blew. When she opened her eyes again she and the woman saw a mist blossom out and cover the whole thicket where they crouched, frozen for silence. Tamrin hoped that the figures would see a tree, old and wide, obstructing their path.

"Not here."

"Here."

"Followed her."

"Run off."

"No."

"Can't."

"Must have."

"Follow?"

"Go back."

"Go back."

"Find later."

"Later."

"Kill."

"I kill."

"Finder kills."

They disappeared, arguing still in brittle voices.

Tamrin couldn't move. The woman took her arm, gently this time, and drew her close.

"It's fine. They've gone."

Tamrin was shaking. The woman put her arm around her and waited.

"What were they?" Tamrin asked when she could breathe normally again.

"Shall we get some sun?" the woman asked with a smile. "I'm getting cold."

Tamrin tried to smile back. She blew hard and the mist in the thicket faded and died. They crawled out and she screwed her eyes up against the suddenness of the sun.

"What were they?" she asked again.

"What are you?" asked the woman. "Making that mist to hide us." She smiled again. "I'm Winny," she said. "You saved my life."

"What were they?"

Tamrin knew that Winny wanted her to say what her name was and she wasn't ready for that.

"I don't know. I don't know if they've got a name. Or where

they come from. I saw them kill a man. Back there."

The world outside the college was becoming as unpleasant as the life inside.

"They weren't men?" she said. "In armour or something?"

"No."

Winny untied her scarf and dabbed Tamrin's cheek.

"That's just making it worse," she said. "Let's get some water."

They found a still section of the river where the water pooled. Winny wetted the scarf and cleaned the blood from Tamrin's face and arms.

"Those were terrible thorns," she said. "I was just on the road over there. Collecting. I heard the noise of the things and I hid in the hedgerow."

"Why?"

"What?"

"Why did you hide?"

"You heard them. You heard their voices. Wouldn't you hide?"

Tamrin took the scarf and started to clean the blood from her legs. The scratches weren't deep. They'd soon heal.

"You're not scratched," she said.

"No?" Winny examined her arms. "Well. Old skin," she smiled. "It's tougher."

Tamrin looked carefully at her.

"You're not old."

Winny's face was smooth enough. Small creases framed

her eyes. She had taken the sun a little. Her arms were browner than her cheeks. Her hair was short enough to be a man's, but cut like a woman's.

"What do you mean, they killed a man?"

"They were carrying him above their heads. They're very strong. They tossed him one to another and swung him round. He was screaming and his legs looked broken. One of them threw him very high and, just as he was about to catch him, stepped aside and let him fall to the ground. His back snapped and his head thudded on the road."

"He was dead?"

Tamrin hated the story. Didn't want to hear it. Needed to know how it finished.

"No. Nearly dead. They just fell on him and started to eat him alive. Then he died. Not soon enough."

Tamrin moved away from Winny. She dipped the scarf in the pool to rinse it out. The blood swirled red around it.

"I must have moved too quickly," said Winny. "Trying to get away. To get further out of danger. They heard me and chased me. You know what happened next."

Tamrin was cold now. Even in the sun. Her face and limbs damp from washing.

Winny stood up.

"Thank you for saving me," she said. "I have to go. You can keep the scarf."

She strode away, sturdy boots beneath a long green skirt, upright and slender.

"I'm Tamrin," she called. "Please don't go."

Winny stopped.

"Are you sure?"

"People call me Tam," she said.

Winny came back and sat down.

"Nice to meet you, Tam. What are you doing out here? And how do you make mists?" ‖

# Smedge looked at the tailor

and the tailor looked at Smedge and they understood something about each other. Dark knows dark when it sees it.

"I want her back," said Shoddle.

"She's trouble," said Smedge. "Always will be. You'll be better off without her."

"She's got magic," said Shoddle. "That's why I sent her to the college. To learn how to use it properly."

Smedge pretended to eat the stew that Shoddle had bought for them.

"Why?"

"Why do you think? Magic's useful."

"For a tailor?" asked Smedge.

Shoddle rapped his thimbled finger on the table.

"For anyone. There's no business won't do better with some magic behind it."

"What if she won't work for you? You can't make her."

The tailor tapped his cheek.

"Yes, I can," he said. "I've got something she wants."

"Have you? What's that?"

"Wouldn't you like to know?"

There was a single red rose in a clay vase on the table. In his annoyance, Smedge touched it and it turned black. The tailor shifted in his seat and eyed Smedge.

"You're a sharp boy," he said.

Smedge looked at the rose.

"Turn it back," said the tailor.

"I don't want to."

The tailor's grin wasn't pleasant and Smedge knew he had discovered a weakness and would prod at it. The tailor feared magic.

"You can't," he said.

"Tamrin's trouble," said Smedge. "She's always in trouble at the college."

"I'll soon sort that out."

"What good is she to you?"

"She can make me money. And there's always other things you can get with magic."

Smedge wanted to hear more so he said nothing.

"Besides," added the tailor, "I found her, so she's mine and no one else can use her."

"You found her?"

The tailor cast a look around the room. Other diners had looked at them when he rapped the table, but only briefly. No one was listening.

"She was extra," he whispered.

Smedge stopped pretending to eat and listened, wanting to hear what the tailor could tell him about where Tamrin was from, who she was.

"I want her back," the tailor said. "And if I can find her, I can make her come back and work for me, can't I?"

"Yes," said Smedge. "I think you can. If you can find her. Perhaps if you told me where she came from?"

The tailor sniggered and shook his head.

"Will you help me?"

"Go home," said Smedge. "I'll look for her."

The tailor shook his hand. He paid the bill and walked off. Smedge watched him flex his fingers and rub his hand on his jacket as he walked away.

"I'll look for her," he said to himself. "But I won't bring her to you."

He ducked round the corner and into an alley. Sidled up along the wall with slow, deliberate steps. The cobbles were slippery where people emptied their chamber pots. He didn't bother stepping aside to avoid anything. Round another corner, into a small courtyard with a pile of bones and meat scraps from a butcher. Three crows were pecking at the offal. Smedge, on silent feet, drew closer. He pounced. The crows cawed and flapped. He seized one by the wing and dragged it back. In a single movement he snapped its neck, pulled off a wing and stuffed it into his mouth. A slow, stupid grin, decorated with black feathers, crept over his face.

✠

When you're running away from one road you're always running towards another. Tamrin was surprised to see how close they were to the road Winny had been travelling when the creatures had appeared.

"This is mine," said Winny.

She dragged a handcart out from behind the hedgerow.

"Those things were so stupid they either didn't see it or didn't bother about it," she said.

Tamrin gave her a hand.

"What is it?"

"What does it look like?"

It looked like a handcart, half-laden with old pans and kettles, iron hinges, a wheel rim, part of a harrow, the door from a kitchen range, and smaller bits of iron and other metals.

"It looks like rubbish," said Tamrin.

"That's what it is. It's rubbish. Unless you've got a use for it. Then it's something."

The cart was back on the road now and Winny grabbed the handles.

"Right," she said. "Your college is that way."

"Is it?"

"It is. I've just come from Canterstock. That's where I got this old oven door. So, you don't want to go back that way?"

"No."

Tamrin made her fight-you face. The one she used a lot at the college.

"Steady on," laughed Winny. "I'm not taking you anywhere you don't want to go. You can just walk off on your own, can't you?"

"Sorry. Yes."

"Right. This tailor of yours, the one who came for you. What do you know about him?"

"Nothing."

"But you want to find him?"

Tamrin had told her story, or part of it. She had not told Winny about the aching need she had to find out who she was and where she had come from. She had not told her how much she missed Vengeabil.

"I'm curious," she said.

"Then let's find him."

"How can we do that?"

"You learn a lot when you're pushing a cart, taking away scrap metal. You see a lot. You hear a lot. You know what I mean?"

Tamrin bit her lip.

"You mean you know him? You know where he lives?"

Winny began to push the cart along the road towards Canterstock. Tamrin didn't follow. An unpleasant, sick sensation in her throat stopped her. She wanted to stay with the woman, but she wouldn't follow her to Canterstock.

"I know the direction he came from," she called. "There's a fork in the road up ahead. One way to Canterstock, the other towards wherever he came from. That's where I'm going. Want to come with me?"

Tamrin sprinted after her and took hold of one of the handles of the cart.

"That's the way," Winny smiled. ||

# A crow circled the high walls

of the Castle of Boolat. It was tired and wanted to land. It was hungry and wanted to eat. It was fearful and wanted to fly off again. Slanting down with the sun at its back it made a last, large circle and found a perch on the rough stone above the main gate. It lowered its glossy black head, listened and watched.

A woman, slim and tall, ghost-grey in a flowing gown, shouted orders.

"Try harder. Get further."

The crow couldn't see clearly. It flapped aching wings and resettled in the courtyard above their heads.

The woman was prodding a stick at an ugly figure. If Tamrin had seen it she would have thought it very like the creatures who had sniffed at her hiding place. This one, though, was bigger, bumpier, smellier, and where they had spoken with short grunts and coughs this one rattled and clattered.

"It hurts," it rattled.

The woman prodded again and a spark arced across the stick.

"Ow. No."

"Move, you lump. Get through there."

The creature, driven by the pain of the prod, tried to get through the great gate. It winced as it passed under the arch, then staggered forward, took a few lame steps across the drawbridge and screamed out in pain. The woman didn't follow.

"Go on," she shouted. "Further."

Her face was lit with smiles. She hugged herself with pleasure. The creature made a final, heaving effort to move ahead and was thrown back with such force that the woman had to step aside to avoid being knocked over. It huddled into a ball and lay shivering and whimpering.

"All right," she said. "That's enough for today. We'll try again tomorrow." She looked at the crow. "What do you think of that, Smedge?"

The crow hopped from its perch, stirred up dust on the courtyard as it landed, spread its wings wide, crouched low and sent a long, croaking caw echoing from the thick stone walls. It shifted shape, taking on the form of a dog for a moment, and Smedge emerged from the process, shaking his shoulders and spitting out a black feather.

"Don't try those tricks with me," said the woman. "Understand? I'll know."

Smedge looked at the lumpish figure on the ground.

"And get out of that stupid uniform," she added.

"Sorry, Ash."

Smedge closed his eyes and the uniform became a grey jerkin and leggings.

"What's happening with Bakkmann?" he asked.

"You saw it yourself," said Ash. "You were watching. She can get through the gate, just a little way. As far as the drawbridge."

"The sealing spell is broken?" asked Smedge.

"Not broken. Melting. Dissolving. Fraying at the edges."

"Bakkmann didn't go far," said Smedge.

"Far enough. It's like a knot. When it's tight there's no shifting it. But once you begin to work it loose then it'll get easier and easier, and then all of a sudden, its strength is gone and it slides undone. You just have to work it."

Bakkmann was scrabbling in the dust, standing up.

"Can you go through?" asked Smedge.

"No. Not at all."

"It hurts," said Smedge, looking at the crouched form of Bakkmann.

"You think the pain stops me?" said Ash.

"No. Of course not."

Ash sneered at him. She stepped away and walked straight towards the gate. As soon as she reached the edge of the courtyard a clap like the slamming of a great door smashed the walls and a line of bright light whipped across her face.

She flinched, stepped once more and was thrown back and sprawled at Smedge's feet. Her face was bleeding from a deep cut. She stood, wiped her sleeve across her face and smiled. She was trembling.

"I don't mind the pain," she said. "It's the indignity. I won't be a prisoner, not any more. I won't."

Smedge was frightened of her ability to bear pain. He waited for her to speak.

"Bakkmann first," she said. "When she's conquered the spell I'll be next. And it's weaker every day. Now, what are you doing here?"

"It's Tamrin," said Smedge. "I got her expelled so the tailor came for her."

"The tailor," she hissed. "So we know where he is now."

"Yes."

"Is he useful to us?"

Smedge smiled.

"He's greedy and dishonest and cruel and sly."

"Good," said Ash. "I like him already. But is he useful?"

"I know more about Tamrin now," said Smedge. "And she is the key to everything. Once we get her back, we'll have won."

Ash stared at him.

"Get her back?" she said. "What do you mean, get her back?"

"She ran away," said Smedge.

"Where is she now?"

"I'm not sure. She can't have got far."

Bakkmann clattered a high, terrified wail and scuttled away on thin sharp legs.

Ash slapped her hand across Smedge's face. The boy felt a lash of flame on his cheek and then he was all fire, blazing like a torch in a dungeon. The pain consumed him. ‖

# Tim was sorry to leave

Vengeabil's kitchen. It was the nearest thing to a real room in a real house that he had known since he was a tiny boy.

"Come back and talk to me," said Vengeabil. "You'll know whether you can or not. Sometimes there'll just be a wall with a curtain over it. Sometimes there'll be a door behind the curtain."

"Thank you," said Tim.

He stopped and sniffed.

"That smell's here again," he said.

"You can smell it, can you?"

"Yes. Are you making it to keep people away?"

"What do you think? Where's it coming from?"

Tim walked up the passageway and back again.

"It's coming from the college," he said. "Not from down here."

"That's right," said Vengeabil. "You've been so used to it that you hardly noticed. When you did, you thought it was from my kitchen. Now you've been away you can smell it."

"What is it?"

"It's rotten. It's decaying. It's like a piece of meat left on the road. It stinks. The college is dying. That's what you can smell. Only you have to step outside to notice it."

"Why? Why's it like that?"

"Ask Frastfil."

Tim watched the kitchen door close. He stood for a while, thinking about all that he had learned in there. He braced himself against the stench and climbed the stairs back into the college.

It took two days. They stopped often on their journey. Winny gave Tamrin a brass bell with a wooden handle.

"Ring this," she told her when they drew near to a group of cottages.

Tamrin swung the bell and enjoyed the sound of the clapper against the metal, liked the feel of the reverberations in her hand.

"Old iron," shouted Winny.

Tamrin laughed at the pleasure of the noise.

"Old iron," she joined in.

People came to their doors and waved. Winny waved back to some of them, stopped at others who beckoned her to them. She sharpened their knives and axes and scythes with a small grindstone on the back of the cart. She let Tamrin turn the handle while she held the blades against the stone. Some paid her in cash, others in kind. She took apples and bread, cheese, cold meat, squares of old linen, a straw hat, anything that might be eaten or traded.

"Got anything for me?" she asked everyone. And she exchanged coins or goods for anything made of iron or copper.

Tamrin kept to the cart and wouldn't go into the houses even when they pressed her to join them for a drink of cordial or a meal. So Winny didn't go in either. She let them bring food out to the cart and she sat there with Tamrin.

A couple of times Winny spoke quietly to a householder and listened.

"He's passed this way," she told Tamrin. "He's on his way home. No one knows who he is but not enough people travel this way to pass without notice."

They rested in the hottest part of the day, under the shade of trees. The cart was heavy to push. Tamrin wished she could magic it along a bit more easily but she held back. Winny was very strong and took most of the strain.

Tamrin took a long time getting her courage up to ask Winny the question.

"Are you a tinker?" she asked.

Winny sucked at a sweet grass stem.

"What do you think?"

"I don't know. Sorry I asked."

Winny patted her arm.

"I don't mind. There's nothing wrong with tinkers. They do a good job and they're not the thieves and liars people say they are. Not most of them, anyway. But they mend pots and pans. I just collect scrap metal."

"So are you?"

Winny squinted at Tamrin. The sun was mid-sky.

"You know I'm not, don't you?"

"Yes."

"So why are you asking me?"

Tamrin shook her head.

"You want me to tell you I'm not a tinker and then tell you what I am, don't you?" she laughed.

"Don't make fun of me," said Tamrin.

"I'm not making fun of you. I like you. I think it's funny that you didn't ask. It's a wizard question."

"What do you mean?"

"I mean that if most people want to know something they ask, straight out. That's not a wizard way. Wizards always come at things sideways."

Tamrin laughed now.

"It's true," she admitted. "I suppose it's the way we're taught."

"Is it just that? There must be a reason."

Tamrin thought about it and decided to tell the woman the truth, and that really isn't the wizard way.

"It's because things look different from the side," she said. "If you always look at something from the front you only know a part of it. It doesn't matter if it's a tree or a person, a building or chair. You only see one side. Wizards are supposed to look at all the different sides. We're supposed to see what other people don't notice."

Winny offered Tamrin an apple. She took it and bit hard.

"Thank you," said Winny. "No, I'm not a tinker. But you knew that. I collect metal and take it back to my father and he melts it down and works it into new things. I don't mend, although I could, because I want to take the metal away."

"Does your father live far from here?"

"A little way."

"That's a sort of wizardy answer," said Tamrin. "It doesn't tell me anything."

Winny stood up and stretched.

"I know," she said. "The sun's getting lower. We can get on our way."

She took hold of the handles of the cart and pushed. Tamrin walked alongside. She looked at the pile of old metal and broken stuff.

"Do people ever give you anything valuable by mistake?" she asked.

Things had changed at Boolat since Smedge had last been there. Ash was stronger. Bakkmann was more sullen. She had always looked at Ash with a mixture of fear and love. Now, Smedge sensed less fear, less love, and a new element of anger. He wondered what Bakkmann would do if she ever managed to break through the sealing spell completely and leave Ash inside. Would she come back? Or would that be the last that

Boolat would see of her?

Smedge let these thoughts drift like dandelion clocks through his head, not trying to catch them and examine them. Leaving them to blow away or take root and grow. The pain of his punishment had almost gone now. The shock of it still remained. The assault still hurt. His flesh had returned to what he had made it. It always did.

He stepped over a filthy, piss-stained corner of the courtyard and slipped into a tight slot that became a passageway deep in the outer wall. He couldn't see where he was going and felt his way along with his hands on the smooth stone. It wasn't long before he reached an obstruction. He couldn't go any further. He put his face to the wall and listened.

Silence.

Sometimes he could hear scratching, like rats. Once or twice, perhaps more, he fancied he heard voices, or just one voice, or the wind through the tunnels like a voice.

More than that, he could smell something in the gap in the walls. Whenever he returned to Boolat his first thought was always to come here and listen. Today there was nothing. Tomorrow was another day.

He emerged from the darkness and looked at the squat creatures entering through the gate.

They were new, too. Bigger than before. Stronger than before. Upright. They almost looked like armoured men. And they could talk now. That was a change. And red. That was new.

But they were still beetles and Smedge hated them.

He had eaten beetles. Back then. Not these beetles. Not Ash's beetles. He remembered eating them and feeling the sick, empty sensation of beetle-life.

Ash's beetles changed all the time. They developed. Smedge didn't know if she was doing it, forming them into an army, or whether it was just the nature of the creatures to change and become ever more skilful, ever more dangerous. Or was it something greater even than Ash that was doing it?

Smedge left them to it and made his way to the dungeon. He needed some fun after his journey.

"Tell me about your father," said Tamrin.

Winny was sweating and her wet hands slipped on the handles of the cart. It was a long hill.

"You'll find out for yourself," she said.

"What?"

"When you meet him."

Tamrin stopped dead.

"Why am I going to meet him?"

Winny carried on pushing the cart so Tamrin had to trot to catch up. She took one of the handles and helped. It was heavy, hard work. She made just a small spell to make the wheels go round on their own.

"Stop that," said Winny. "I'll push on my own if I have to."

Tamrin scowled and took the spell back.

"Is that what they taught you at the college?" said Winny. "To use magic to make your life easier?"

It was what the teachers taught the pupils, but not what Vengeabil told her. He was very strict that she shouldn't do that. She felt ashamed.

"No."

"Why do you do it, then?"

"I've never pushed a heavy cart before."

"Well, that's understandable. But I have. And I'd rather do it properly than have cheap magic."

"Most people want wizards to work magic for them to make things easier," said Tamrin.

"I'm not most people," said Winny. "And I've met wizards who taught me it was wrong."

Tamrin thought about this until they reached the top of the hill. By this time she was hot and sweating, too. They paused, enjoying the breeze.

"Come on," said Winny. "Careful now. This is the hard part."

Tamrin laughed.

"You're joking. We just pushed it up."

"Wait and see."

She was right. The cart moved with a strength of its own. They had to fight to stop it rolling away from them. Tamrin's back hurt and her legs were aching when they reached level ground.

"Going downhill's harder work than going up," said Winny. "Think about it."

Tamrin was still thinking about it and trying to work it out when they saw a house on its own. Not a cottage this time, but a proper house, with windows and many rooms, a garden in front and an orchard to one side with a donkey in it.

Smedge was playing with the prisoners when Ash glided into the cell. She watched him silently and it made him feel uncomfortable.

"Why is this one still alive?" he asked her.

"Khazib?" she said. "He could still be useful. Don't break him."

Khazib listened to them talking about him. He made no sign that he understood or cared what they said. His face, brown as bark, gave no sign of anything.

Smedge laughed.

"He's quite broken already."

Ash poked the man with her toe. He was chained to the wall, his neck fastened with an iron hoop low to the ground so that he couldn't stand.

"Damaged," she said. "But still not destroyed. Yet."

Khazib turned his face away.

Smedge read the disgust in the man's features and he spat at him.

"I'd have killed him," said Smedge. "He's got nothing left to tell us."

Ash steered Smedge away. They left the door open. Khazib could not escape and there were plenty of guards in the corridors. The new, armoured figures as well as the old takkabakks.

"What are these?" asked Smedge. "The new ones?"

Ash smiled.

"Aren't they wonderful?" she said. "They're the best yet." She stopped and touched one. It turned and looked at her from a blank face. "My beetles change and grow all the time. This is a kravvin. In the dark they look like men, but they're all beetle. No fear. No mercy. No desire except to kill and to eat." She stroked its smooth face. "And to serve me," she added.

They climbed the stair to her turret. She looked from the window over the fields and woods, across to the distant hills.

"Why do you keep Khazib?" asked Smedge. "Please don't hurt me."

Ash continued to look out, speaking to him without meeting his eye.

"He was Flaxfield's apprentice," she said. "Years and years ago. There's still something of Flaxfield in him. Something that we may need one day. Something that we may use. Flaxfield's dead. So we need to keep anything we can of his that might help us."

Smedge remembered Flaxfield. The old wizard who had locked Ash and Bakkmann in this castle with magic more years ago than he could recall. Long before Khazib had been born. The takkabakks could come and go. And so could travellers. At least, travellers could come; Ash seldom let them leave.

"Might Khazib be the way to get out?" he asked.

Ash hissed and spun round.

"Do you know how long it is?" she said. "How long it is since I left this place?"

Her anger swept across the room and left a taste in his mouth, like slurry.

"Please don't hurt me," said Smedge again.

Ash crouched with fury, hunched herself small, and for the first time Smedge saw that she was closer to the beetles than he had ever imagined. The tall, slender grey figure was transformed. She stood, and the illusion broke. She put her hand to her mouth and snapped off three teeth, tearing her gums. The taste of blood and the pain restored her calm.

"There's more than one way out of here," she said. She gave Smedge a broad smile, revealing the gap in her teeth, the blood running down her chin. A new corpse, hacked to death in battle. Smedge felt hungry. "There are more doors than the broad gate."

Ash came close to him, gripped his jerkin and put her face right in his. As she spoke, blood spattered from her mouth into his eyes.

"That boy, Sam. And that girl Tamrin. I want them both. You understand? Both of them. He's Flaxfield's, too."

Smedge leaned forward and licked the blood from her chin. Her teeth were already growing back, her gums closing over the wound.

"Go back to the college," she said. "Find out where she's gone. Let me know everything."

"Yes."

"And Frastfil?" she added. "What of him?"

"That fool," said Smedge. "He's ours."

"Good. Use him."

Smedge hesitated.

"He's too stupid," he said. "Duddle is cleverer and he'll enjoy working with us. Can I use him more?"

"If you like," she said.

"And when I've finished with Frastfil," said Smedge, "when he's not any more use, may I eat him?"

Ash patted his cheek.

"Of course you may."

"What's this?" asked Tamrin, pulling a jagged, irregular piece of metal from the cart.

The road was level now, though bumpy. Pushing a hand-cart looked like fun until you tried to do it. Tamrin felt a little guilty that she had not taken as much of her fair share as she could have done.

Winny stopped pushing and looked at Tamrin's find. It was bigger than the woman's palm, with two straight sides and two broken ones. It glinted in the sun and threw their reflections back at them.

"It's nothing. Put it back."

Tamrin pulled a face.

"Can't I have it?"

Winny grabbed the handles and pushed the cart faster than before. The big house was close now.

"Just throw it back," she repeated.

"I'll pay you for it," Tamrin offered.

"It's not for sale."

Tamrin tossed it back, making sure to see where it landed.

"Old iron," Winny shouted out. "Old iron."

It was a big household and they never saw the master or the mistress. The cook gave them some food and a buckled and scarred roasting dish.

"Anything over there?" asked Winny. She pointed to a large barn.

"You can have a look," said the cook, "but Barbaron had better take you."

Barbaron, a sort of groom-handyman, wasn't pleased to leave his comfortable seat in the kitchen. He led them across to the barn in surly silence and as soon as they were through the door he left them and sat in the sun, throwing small pebbles at the geese to make them honk.

"If you see anything metal and old, let me know," said Winny.

"What are we looking for?" asked Tamrin.

"The usual stuff. Anything. As long as it's metal. As long as it's old. Nothing new."

Tamrin wandered off and didn't look very hard. She liked the barn and decided to measure it. The walls were high, rough stone, and crumbly. She paced the width. Thirty-seven. Then the length. Seventy-four. The roof was pointed against wet weather, with oak beams like laced fingers.

"Found anything?" called Winny.

Tamrin couldn't see her. There were piles of old sacks, some hay bales, a farm cart with only one wheel, a harrow and a plough. One corner had a stack of wooden furniture that had been tipped out to make way for better stuff. Tamrin found an elbow chair, set it up on its legs and sat on it, looking up and round.

The barn smelled sweet and dry. Sun sliced in through slit windows and picked out the motes and dust like stars. She could hear Winny rummaging through the stuff at the other end.

Sitting in a chair for the first time since she ran away made her sad. She missed Vengeabil. She missed the silences of the hidden corners of the college, the nooks in the library where she was shielded by walls of books, the winding stair to the turret, the empty studies where teachers used to sit and mark books before the numbers in the college dwindled.

"Anything?" shouted Winny.

Tamrin stood up and moved quickly, trying to look as though she had been searching.

She didn't fool Winny, who gave her a reproachful look. They left Barbaron sitting in the sun and made their way in silence to the cart. Winny threw her finds on and lifted the handles. Tamrin snitched her scrap of metal from where she had tossed it and hid it in her cloak. Folding her thoughts on themselves she trudged alongside, away from the setting sun. ‖

# Tim was in the college garden

practising a shape-shift spell when he saw the crow. The bird circled the college, black against blue, soared to the left, and dipped out of sight behind the wall. Minutes later Smedge walked round the side of the wall and into the garden. He shrugged his shoulders as though getting used to his arms again.

"Hello," said Tim. "Where've you been?"

Smedge smiled. Tim wished he wouldn't do that. It made him nervous.

"What are you supposed to be?" asked Smedge.

Tim had hands like a dog's paws. He looked down at them. Cat's whiskers either side of his nose made him look startled.

"I'm not sure," he said. "Dog?"

"What's it like?"

"It hurts, you know," said Tim.

He clapped his paws together and screwed up his eyes. The paws were still there.

"It took me ages to get them," he explained, "and now I can't get rid of them."

"Why are you doing it?"

"Homework."

Tim kicked a stone in an embarrassed way. "I'm falling behind a bit, you know?"

Smedge listened and made Tim carry on by his silence.

"I really need to do well," said Tim. "I can't end up as some sort of village trickster, making charms to stop the cow's milk drying up or keeping the hay dry in the barn. I can't. I'd hate that. I'd rather be a farmer or a grocer."

He looked helplessly at Smedge.

"Dr Duddle says he'll put me on a special report if I don't get shape-shifting right by tomorrow. And then I'll be in real trouble."

Tim hated himself for talking to Smedge like this. If only Tam had been around he would have gone to her. She'd helped him before. But she'd gone now. He missed her.

Smedge smiled. Again.

"You have to work hard," he said.

Tim clapped his paws together again.

"See? Can't change back."

"Were you completely a dog?" asked Smedge.

Tim blushed.

"Not completely," he admitted.

"How much?"

"Oh, you know. Not all."

"Just the paws?"

"Yes."

"Oh dear."

Tim wanted to leave Smedge now. He was nervous.

"Do you think I could help?"

"No, thanks. It's all right."

Tim edged away. He felt Smedge's hand on his shoulder.

"Try this," said Smedge.

Tim crouched. He fell forward. His arms were covered in fur. He turned his head. His feet were brindle, bent. He sniffed the grass. It was clean, sweet. He rolled on his back.

"How's that?" asked Smedge.

It was uncomfortable. Sort of. Tim thought he might get used to it. He might grow to like it.

"Is that better?" asked Smedge.

What Tim tried to say was, "How do you do it?" What he actually said was, "Woof!"

"Ah," said Smedge. "It's not too difficult when you've got the trick of it. It's like spinning a top. It's a knack."

"Can you teach me?" woofed Tim.

"I can help. If you want."

Tim wriggled round and found his feet. He ran in a circle, chasing his tail.

"You remember," said Smedge, "when Tamrin used to bully me?"

Tim stopped and cocked his head to one side.

He woofed a hesitant, "I don't think so."

"No?" smiled Smedge. "That's a shame. Oh well. I'd better be off now."

"Stop," woofed Tim. "You can't leave me like this. I can't change back."

"It's odd, isn't it, memory?" said Smedge. "You can't remember how Tamrin bullied me. I can't remember how to change you back. Never mind."

He walked away. Tim bounded alongside him.

"I might," he woofed. "I mean... You know?"

"You do remember?"

Tim sat down and looked up at Smedge. Smedge stroked his head.

"Good boy," he said. "There's a good boy."

He picked up a stick and threw it. Without even thinking, Tim raced across the grass and brought it back. He dropped it at Smedge's feet. He even enjoyed doing it at the same time as he hated Smedge. It was strange, being a dog.

"What do you remember?" asked Smedge.

"She locked you in a block of ice," Tim woofed. "And left you there."

"Do you remember other things?"

Tim remembered. He told Smedge.

"Good boy. Now, will you come with me to Professor Frastfil and tell him?"

Tim woofed a sad yes.

Smedge put his hand into Tim's armpit, lifted him up and he was a boy again.

"Come with me," he said.

Tim followed him from the sunlit garden through the door into the shade. ‖

# Tamrin got ready

to swing the brass bell when she saw the small group of houses ahead on the road.

They'd been, if not silent, then guarded in their speech since leaving the barn. Tamrin knew she had been lazy and she was uncomfortable. Perhaps there had been things in the barn they'd missed because she hadn't bothered to look? Perhaps she could have taken more of a turn with the cart?

"I'm sorry," she said.

Winny didn't answer her.

"I don't do much with other people," said Tamrin. "I'm not used to it. To helping. To doing what I'm told."

Winny nodded. The cart was heavy. She kept her breath for pushing.

"Are we collecting?" asked Tamrin. "I'll look properly this time."

They had passed several houses and reached one with a path up to the door. Winny turned in and put down the cart handles. The house was long and low. Two storeys, with old red tiles. Small windows and a wide door. Tamrin could smell smoke; a brick chimney, twice the height of the house, stood back and to the right.

"Not here," said Winny. "We're delivering. Come on."

She took the handles again and pushed the cart round the side of the house. Set back a little, and joined to the chimney, was a second building, bigger than the first. Dusk had edged in, and the glow of a fire within the second building looked both inviting and dangerous.

"Old iron," shouted Winny. "Get your old iron."

A man appeared in the doorway, blocking the view of the fire. He was big, wide-shouldered, his face back-lit, obscured. He held out his arms. Winny ran to him and hugged him.

"What have you brought me?" he asked.

"Come and see."

They walked towards Tamrin, his arm over her shoulders.

"This is strange old iron," he said, looking at her.

"This is Tam," said Winny.

"Hello, Tam."

He held out his hand for her to shake. She ignored it.

"I'm Smith," he said.

"That's not a name, it's a job."

"So it is," he agreed. "But it's what you can call me. Are you hungry?"

She was. She was also afraid now. It was too soon. Winny hadn't told her they were there. And what about the tailor?

"No, thanks," she said. "I'm not staying. I've got to find someone. Thank you for the company," she said to Winny. "I've got to go now."

Winny stepped forward, put her hand on Tamrin's shoulder.

"Please stay and eat. Stay for the night. We'll pick up the trail tomorrow. I haven't forgotten your tailor. I promise."

"Tailors, is it?" said Smith. "I can tell you a thing or two about tailors. Come on."

He seized Tamrin's hand and led her inside the house.

There were three places set at a table in the kitchen and the appetizing aroma of something roasting. Tamrin discovered she was very hungry and her legs ached. Even the little she had pushed the cart was more than she was used to.

The only two kitchens she had ever known were Vengeabil's lair and the high, arched space of the college kitchen. This was like neither. It was smaller than Vengeabil's. And where his was kitchen, study, dining room and workshop all in one, this was just a place to cook and eat.

None the worse for that, though. Tamrin looked at it and approved. There was no nonsense here. Everything was useful. She didn't have to steer her way past an experiment or a pile of books. She could sit down at the table without having to check that the chair was clear first. So she did.

"You must be starving," said Winny. She poured Tamrin a beaker of cordial and put it in front of her.

"Elderflower and rosehip," she said.

Smith dipped a ladle into a bowl of hot fat and meat juices and poured it over the chicken that was roasting on a spit over the fire.

Fresh bread, crusty and brown, a dish of butter, peas and sliced runner beans, a jug of gravy, and finally the chicken, glistening and golden, were set in front of Tamrin. Winny re-filled her glass, Smith carved the bird and they fell to eating and talking as though they had known each other for years.

Tamrin didn't forget the tailor, but her first mouthful of the soft, moist chicken persuaded her that she could afford to wait until tomorrow to follow him. His trail would still be clear. And that reminded her.

"What were you going to tell me about tailors?" she asked Smith.

"Nothing."

He forked another piece of chicken on to his plate.

"You said you were."

"I said I could. I'm not going to."

"Why not?"

"Not yet, anyway. I might one day."

Winny frowned at her father.

"He's like this," she said. "Pay no attention to him."

"What sort of wizard are you?" he asked Tamrin.

"Who says I'm a wizard?"

"You think I don't know a wizard when I see one?"

He gave her a challenging look.

"How do you know?"

"Because," he said, lowering his voice so that she had to strain to hear him, "because you haven't done any magic."

"If I wasn't a wizard I couldn't do any magic, so that doesn't make sense," she argued.

"Ah, but you could if you wanted. You chose not to. That's the difference."

Tamrin knew what was wrong with this argument. She just didn't know where to begin to show it was wrong.

"Tell me," said Smith. "Where did magic come from? At the beginning."

Tamrin was becoming full. The chicken was so good that she didn't want to stop eating it. She took a small slice, and a little more bread and some beans. It gave her time to think. She dipped the bread into the gravy and ate it.

"There are different stories," she said, when she had swallowed the bread. "About where magic comes from."

"Which one is best?"

"The mirror," said Tamrin.

"How does that story go?" He sat back, comfortable from his meal, folded his arms and waited.

"I'm not allowed to tell you," said Tamrin.

Winny started to clear the plates. Tamrin began to help her but Winny touched her hand and stopped her.

"You two need to talk," she said.

"So you won't tell?" asked Smith.

She shook her head.

"Why?"

"If I know it, then it's wizard stuff and not for the likes of you," said Tamrin.

She thought that Smith was going to hit her. His face twisted and he clenched his huge fist. She flinched back.

"The likes of me!" he shouted. And he erupted into the longest, loudest, most violent laugh Tamrin had ever heard. By the time he was finished his cheeks were wet with tears. "Oh, Winny. Thank you for bringing Tam. I haven't had so much fun in years. The likes of me?"

Tamrin felt very foolish and she didn't know why.

"Because I'm just a man who makes horseshoes?" he said.

Tamrin looked away.

"Because I'm a man who stands at an anvil all day with a hammer in his hand? Is that it? The likes of me? Not like a clever college-educated wizard?"

"They're not clever," she said quickly.

He puffed out his cheeks.

"No, they're not," he said. "You got that right at least. Now, are you going to tell me the mirror story?"

"No."

"Is it the one where the king gets someone to make him a mirror of polished steel? The first real mirror ever made? Is that it? Where the king's wife is expecting a baby and she's the first person ever to see herself in a mirror? She stands in front of it and there are two of her. A queen and a reflected queen. She sees herself and faints. When the baby is born the next day, it's laid in its cot. And the next time they look at it, there are two of them. Is that the story? What happened to the second baby?"

"It was taken to the forest and killed," said Tamrin.

"Was it? Is that what the story said?"

"Yes."

"And what happened to the mirror?"

"It was covered over so no one else could look at it. It was put away and never seen again. No one knows where it is."

"But the magic had already spilled out," said Smith.

"Yes."

"Fancy," he said. "The likes of me knowing a story like that. A working man with hard hands and strong arms."

Tamrin didn't like this. One moment Smith was a welcoming, friendly person, the next he was challenging her, laughing at her. And why had there been three places already set at the table when she arrived? She changed her mind about staying for the night.

"I think I'll be going now," she said. "Thank you for the food."

She pushed her chair back and went to the door. It wouldn't open. There was no bolt, no lock, just a light catch. She rattled it and tugged. The door wouldn't move.

"Stay the night," said Winny. "We'll talk more tomorrow."

"No. I want to go."

"It's dark out," said Smith. "You'll get lost. It's dangerous at night."

Tamrin tested for a sealing spell on the door. She couldn't

find one. She made a spell of her own to spring it open. It stayed firmly shut.

"I can't open the door," she said.

Smith stood up and came towards her.

"Smiths make good locks," he said. ||

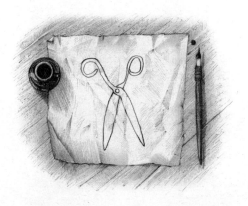

---

*Part Two*

---

# DOUBLEDRAGON

# It was a Friday, one year save a day

since Flaxfield had died. They should have eaten trout but Sam couldn't face it. He went down to the river to look at the fish, brown swirls in the water, heads to the current, tails rippling.

Starback nuzzled against his legs.

Sam let his fingers play with a thin leather cord round his neck, an odd-shaped weight hanging from it.

"I'll make an omelette," said Sam. "Let the trout swim in peace."

He looked downriver, in the direction that Flaxfield's body had floated off. Sam had cut the willow wands to plait the basket they had laid him in. His memory could smell the sweet herbs around the old wizard's face.

"He shouldn't have left us," he said. "Not like that. Not yet. We weren't ready."

He climbed the path back to the house and found the kitchen empty. He poured water into a basin, washed his hands carefully and then his face. He was scrupulous in his determination to keep clean. He remembered last year, when he had discovered that other people found him dirty. Smelly.

Starback chased a bee around the kitchen. His claws clattered and scratched on the floor. The bee drifted higher, bumped on the ceiling. Starback sprang up, spread his wings and chased it round. Sam frowned and Starback swooped back to earth.

"Are you hungry?" asked Sam. "Of course I am," he answered.

He fetched eggs from the pantry, and butter and cheese.

"No trout?"

Sam had not heard Flaxfold come in. She moved quietly.

"Do you mind?" he asked. "We can eat omelettes."

Flaxfold pushed a strand of grey hair back from her face and tucked it into her scarf.

"Cheese in mine, please," she said. "And I'll cut some ham to go with it. Would you like some?"

"No thanks."

"I'll give it to Starback."

She was old and stout, yet Sam had never heard her short of breath and she moved swiftly and lightly on small feet. The ham was a joint she had cured herself, hanging from a hook in the ceiling of the pantry. Her knife was sharp enough to cut thin slices like pages of a book.

Sam beat the eggs and dropped butter into the pan. It sizzled against the hot iron. He poured the beaten eggs in before the butter could burn and he moved it around with the back of a fork.

"There's a Finishing tomorrow," said Flaxfold. "Will you come with me?"

"Is it far?"

"We'll need to set off before it's light. But we'll be home the same day."

"I'll come with you," he said.

He slid her omelette on to her plate and scooped another gout of butter into the pan.

Flaxfold dropped some ham without looking. Starback swept past her and snapped at it, catching it before it hit the floor. She smiled and tossed him another piece. The rest she put on her plate.

"It's a year today since Flaxfield died," he said.

"Tomorrow," she said. "Though Friday seems the better day to remember."

She touched his cheek.

"Did you think I'd forgotten?" she asked.


Sam was up before dawn, though the sun had begun to interrupt the darkness and the stars had gone.

He stood in the garden by the ash tree under the study window. He looked up at the slate-grey sky.

Another part of him soared overhead. Starback and Sam were one. Dragon and boy at one time. He was still not really used to it. No one had warned him that it would happen.

He had thought he was ill. He was ill. He had thought he was dying. He was close to dying. He had looked through the door into the Finished World and had nearly stepped through it.

He hadn't died. He had changed. Starback had changed. He was Sam and he was Starback. He could stand on the earth and he could fly overhead, both at the same time. He didn't know how he did it. He didn't know sometimes whether he was boy or dragon or both or neither.

He talked to Flaxfold about it. No one else. He tried to explain it to her. She never asked questions. She just listened.

"Breakfast?" she asked.

Sam turned and smiled.

"I never hear you coming," he said.

"You're always somewhere else. Are you hungry?"

The dragon landed close to her with a flourish and folded dry wings.

"You're always hungry," said Flaxfold. Starback nuzzled against her.

They ate in silence and Flaxfold packed more food for the journey.

"There'll be food after the Finishing," she said. "But it's always sensible to take something just in case. It's a long journey."

It was a dead girl. She had drowned. Twelve years old. Short hair and strong face. When Sam saw her he thought it was Tamrin and he stepped back and looked away.

A second look told him that he'd been tricked by the size and likeness of the girl. And the suddenness. He hadn't been expecting a young person. Most Finishings are for the old, though accidents and violence are everywhere and the young die, too.

He took control of himself and made preparations. While Flaxfold made ready to carry out the Finishing he assembled the herbs and flowers they had gathered on the journey. He examined the instruments the family had laid out ready for the ritual. They'd chosen a book, scuffed and worn, one that had been read by others before it came to her, and a bracelet made of small, square stones, multi-coloured and linked with silver, a cup, perhaps the special one that only she used. Sam picked it up and turned it over in his hands. Rough clay, with a band of glaze about the rim to please the lips, a simple line-drawn pattern round the side, impressed before firing.

"Are you ready?" asked Flaxfold.

It was a gentle rebuke to tell him to hurry up. She wouldn't embarrass him in front of these strangers by telling him to get a move on.

He looked at them. Her family and neighbours, gathered to Finish her. He nodded.

Flaxfold began the words. Sam handed her the herbs and instruments at the proper time. He ignored the tears, the silent grief, the set faces, the averted eyes. This would be done well and then they would go.

At the right moment he nodded to the group. It was not for him to choose. That was their part.

"Are you ready?" he asked. "It's time."

The girl's father stepped from the others, holding the hand of a smaller girl, the little sister.

The father carried the book and the bracelet, the little girl brought the cup. They laid them by the body and the little girl said the words.

Sam felt proud of her. She kept her back straight, her voice steady, her eyes on her sister. She was nervous, of course, but she did it well, as well as anyone could. She would be a comfort to her family when they had gone.

As soon as the last words were said the door to the Finished World opened for the dead girl to go through. Only Sam and Flaxfold saw it. To the others it was like a slant of sunlight or the dazzle of glare from water. Flaxfold let go of the girl's hand. She brushed away the lock of hair from her face, tucking it in. Sam felt the different air brush his cheek, saw the shimmer of light by the girl, heard the slightest murmur from the place beyond.

He stood between Flaxfold and the door. As the girl slipped through and disappeared the door shifted. The room tilted. People staggered and grabbed for something to hold on to. Like the deck of a ship in high seas the floor lifted to one side. Sam slipped and put his hands out for support, skittering towards the door.

"Sam," Flaxfold called.

He turned his head and saw confusion on her face and something that in a less reliable person he would have thought was panic.

"Come back," she shouted.

He leaned away from the door, knees bent. His flailing arms tried to restore his balance. One of them plunged into the space where the door still stood open. The others in the room saw only his right arm disappear as far as the elbow.

A hand seized his arm and drew him in. He pulled back. By pulling he helped the one the other side to step through.

A woman appeared in the doorway, slender and tall, face half-hidden, more than half, by the folds of a grey hooded gown.

The tugging had stopped. Sam wasn't being dragged into the Finished World, he was helping one out of it.

No one should ever come from the Finished World. No one ever tried. No one ever could. This woman was crossing that barrier. And Sam recognized her. The cord round his neck tightened and hurt. The metal weight grew hot, burning his throat.

He tried to free his arm. The harder he pulled the more she emerged through the door. She was stuck, struggling. The Finished World didn't want to let her go.

Sam tugged to free himself. She pulled back. Each time she came a little further out, freed herself a little more. Sam knew he couldn't let her. Couldn't allow her to come through. If she did, he would have brought a plague into the world, a bringer of death.

"You'll stay there," he said. "I'll come to you."

He stopped struggling and relaxed. The Finished World

breathed in and the woman was sucked back, Sam drawn in with her. His head approached the door. He gave up the fight.

"No you don't."

Flaxfold's voice pierced his submission. His arm froze and the woman released it with a shriek of pain. Flaxfold seized his other hand and jerked him to her. The door slammed, with the woman still the other side. Sam gasped. He looked at Flaxfold. By a trick of the light she was taller, no longer stout but upright and angry. No, not angry. Prepared for any fight. Fierce. His arm was dead with cold.

She stepped between him and the shocked assembly.

The room was level now, restored. The faces of the family were clothed with anger and disappointment.

Flaxfold, small and stout again, smiled at them.

"You're very lucky," she said.

The girl's father began to protest and complain that the Finishing had been badly done, spoiled. Sam flexed his fingers to bring life and warmth back to them.

"Hush," said Flaxfold, taking the father's arm and sitting him down. "Hush. It's all right. It's good. Sometimes, with a young one, with a special child, the Finished World is as glad to receive her as we are sad to lose her. The depth of your sorrow is balanced by the surplus of their joy. When that happens..." She shrugged. "Well, you saw how it was."

Sam knew they had seen nothing, of course. People never did. Just shadows and flashes.

Flaxfold stayed longer than she would have done, creating

confidence, rebuilding the family for each other. She heard their memories, encouraged plans, shared their food and helped them to be ready for the next day, and the next.

Sam was impatient to leave, to talk, to explain and to ask questions. He had to wait. He ate a little and went outdoors and looked up at Starback, circling the sky. The dragon had been unsettled by the event. Sam closed his eyes and circled with him, looking down at the house until Flaxfold waved goodbye.

Rejoining her he waited until they were on the road.

"I thought it was Tamrin," he said. "Dead, I mean."

"Yes. I saw that. You were upset."

"And then the woman. What happened?"

"Something," said Flaxfold, "that changes everything. There's dangerous work ahead. Now. For all of us. But mostly for you."

"Tell me," said Sam.

"It's like this," she began. "Your old master, Flaxfield, died because he was wounded. Long ago. His magic was tested and torn."

Sam trudged along next to her. The day was closing and they still had a long way to go.

"A weak, greedy wizard tried to steal magic from a young girl, his apprentice," she said. "It went wrong and magic was distorted, infected. The wizard changed, grew younger and stronger, and new magic ripped through into the world. Flaxfield was the only one who could tame it."

She looked at the darkening sky. Starback flew overhead,

leading the way, effortlessly riding the air. Sam waited for her to continue. He knew stories took their own time. They're not dogs to call to heel.

Flaxfold's face was sad. She was living the events again in her mind.

"It damaged him very much," she said. "It never showed. He had many apprentices afterwards, and only one of them knew what he had endured. But it changed him. And, in the end, weakened him to his early death last year. He wasn't supposed to die. He was supposed to stay until your apprenticeship was complete."

"I still don't know why he had to die," Sam complained.

Twilight contracted the world. Trees were closer, the road more narrow. The moon rode low in the sky.

"Tell me about the woman," said Flaxfold. "The one who tried to come from the Finished World."

"You haven't finished your story yet," said Sam. "Let's hear the end of that first."

"It's the same story," said Flaxfold. "Tell me about her."

Sam had known this all along. He had known without knowing that these two tales would cross.

"Last year," he said, "at a different Finishing, in the mines, she was the one who appeared then, and tried to pull me into the Finished World."

"And this time," said Flaxfold, "she tried to use you to get out. That's bad."

"Who is she?" asked Sam.

Flaxfold stopped and looked at him.

"She's the wizard that Flaxfield fought and defeated," she said. "He put her in prison. He had her sealed tight, together with her assistant. And now she's found you, and she thinks she can break out through the Finished World."

"That's impossible," said Sam. The thought of travelling through that place filled him with panic. "You can't move through the Finished World."

"That's what we've always thought," said Flaxfold. "Enough. It's dark now. We need daylight to talk of these things. We'll be later home than I thought."

She touched the burned skin on his throat. He winced at the initial pain, then her fingers took the heat away and soothed it.

"I'll give you a salve for that when we get home," she said.

They walked in silence, the folded night around them, until the house was in sight.

"What happened to the girl?" asked Sam. "The one he stole the magic from?"

# The next morning Sam found a roffle

at the breakfast table, waiting to be fed.

"How did you get in?" he asked.

"How does a snail sing a sausage?" asked the roffle.

Sam sighed. He found the roffles' way of talking very irritating. You never got a straight answer to anything.

"You're Megatorine," he said. "Right?"

"Does a cat know its own bread knife?" said the roffle. "Clever boy. You remember me?"

"I remember you cheated me last year," said Sam. "You lied to me. You led me to the college and left me there."

Flaxfold bustled in and put a frying pan on the range.

"You two have met before," she said. "You'll want bacon, I suppose? And eggs?"

"A few sausages would be nice as well, missus," said the roffle. "And some fried bread."

Sam made a private note that a roffle could speak straight enough when he was hungry. Sam had grown since last year and was now taller than the roffle, who was the usual height for someone from the Deep World. He noticed that the roffle sat at the table on the upturned, small, hard-leather pack they all carried, shaped like a squashed barrel. He waited for his food with his knife and fork in his hands, ready to fall on it as soon as it was placed in front of him.

This roffle had betrayed Sam, led him into danger, watched him as he nearly died, and he did nothing to help him. And somehow Sam still found it hard to dislike him. There was something about roffles.

"What have you come for?" he asked. "What do you want?"

Flaxfold gave him a friendly clip round the ear, so light he scarcely felt it.

"How long since you started being my apprentice?" she asked.

"Nearly a year," said Sam.

"Oh," said the roffle, "that's the way of it, is it? He's your boy?"

"As if you didn't know," said Flaxfold. She pointed her fork at Sam before turning the bacon in the pan. "Nearly a year. And you've met him before, besides, and you still think you can ask a roffle a direct question and get a direct answer. I'm ashamed of you." She laughed.

They got no more from the roffle for the rest of the meal. He ate his breakfast as though he'd been starved for a month, interrupting his work only to ask if there would be toast and marmalade next, and to wonder if there was a sausage left in the pan. Sam couldn't help smiling.

When he was sure that no more food would be coming he sat back, undid the bottom two buttons of his waistcoat and folded his arms.

"Don't settle yourself," said Flaxfold. "You can either wash up or wait outside while Sam does. Do you want to wash up?"

"Does a fiddle need a fox when it can have a sideboard?" said the roffle, and he hoisted his barrel on to his back and left.

"Hey," Sam called. "Don't go. I want to talk."

He started to follow him.

"Leave him alone," said Flaxfold, "and get these plates washed. He's not going anywhere."

"What?"

"He's come here to talk to you. And he won't go until he has."

"How do you know that?"

Flaxfold raised her eyebrows.

"Because he's a roffle," she said.

Sam poured water from a bucket into the basin and added boiling water from the kettle. He washed the mugs first, then the greasy plates and left the pan for later. The bacon fat was tasty and he wouldn't waste it.

"That girl," he said.

Flaxfold carried on tidying up.

"The dead one. The one who looked like Tamrin," he continued.

"Yes?"

"It started me thinking."

Flaxfold looked through the window. The roffle was half-way down the small decline that led from the house to the river. He couldn't hear them.

"What about it?"

"You remember when I met Tamrin last year at the college? Well, she seemed to know me. She knew I was going to be there. She even knew my name."

"Perhaps someone told her you were on the way? Perhaps that roffle did?"

Sam shook his head.

"It was more than that. And I've thought about her a lot since. I dream about her sometimes."

Flaxfold kept one eye on the roffle. He was nearer the river now.

"And when I saw the girl, dead, and thought it was Tamrin, I was frightened. Really frightened."

"What do you want to do about it?" she asked.

"I want to see her again. I don't know why. I want to talk to her. Ask her what she knew about me. How she seemed to know me."

He finished drying the plate and his hands, folded the towel and hung it on the rail of the range to dry.

"You'd better have a word with the roffle, then," said Flaxfold. "That's why he's here."

The roffle sat on his barrel-pack by the side of the river. He had a rod and line and was casting in.

"Caught anything?" asked Sam.

"I think so," said Megatorine.

Sam couldn't see any fish on the grass.

"Where are they?"

The roffle pulled the hook from the water, flicked the rod and sent it back with a small splash. It landed near the opposite bank, under an overhanging tree, the water freckled with light and shade.

"Where does a bumblebee go for the best shoes?"

"Can we talk properly, please?" said Sam. "I know you can."

Megatorine winked.

"Can a memmont paint a parsnip?"

"What have you come here for?" asked Sam.

"That was a good breakfast. A roffle would go a long way to eat like that."

It wasn't an answer, but at least it wasn't a riddle. Sam was making progress.

"Catch me a trout, wizard," said the roffle.

"No. That's not what magic's for."

He sighed, reeled in his line, wrapped it around the rod and hopped on to the grass. He opened the pack and dropped the fishing gear in, so swiftly that even though Sam tried to look he didn't see what else was in there.

"Ha!" said the roffle. "Caught you. Wouldn't you like to see? I want a trout."

He hopped back on and sat with his legs swinging.

Sam raised his head and looked up to the sky, morning-pale with slow clouds. He waited. Without warning, a shape crashed through the trees, sending leaves and twigs spinning. It plunged into the water, through and out in a shower of shining drops. It rose, swung round and dived again, coming to rest on the bank in front of them. Sam grinned.

Starback held a fish tenderly in his jaws. It flapped and twisted.

Megatorine jumped off the barrel and clapped his hands. Starback laid the fish at his feet. The roffle lifted it up, hands clutching at the wriggling, slippery trout. He tossed it back into the river and watched it speed away.

"That wasn't magic," said Sam. "It's what dragons do."

The roffle hoisted his barrel on to his back and walked alongside the riverbank.

"You've come to tell me about Tamrin," said Sam.

"Have I?"

"Yes."

"Yes, I have, then."

He kicked at reeds, scattering their feathery tops into the breeze.

"What are you going to tell me?"

Sam gritted his teeth as he asked the question. Roffles were so difficult. They were so used to hiding information about the Deep World that they found it hard to tell you anything.

"She's left the college."

"Where's she gone?"

"Couple of days ago."

"How do you know?"

"Oh, you know roffles. We pop up here and there. We notice things. We see what's happening."

"Why did she leave?"

They reached a stile. Megatorine leaned on it and rested his pack on the crossbar.

"She met someone," he said. "With a cart."

"A cart? What do you mean, a cart? Where's she gone?"

Megatorine clambered over the stile, dropped down on the other side and disappeared. Sam hurried after him. There was nowhere for the roffle to hide. The plaited hedge-row ran in both directions. He climbed back, looked over his shoulder and the roffle was leaning on the stile.

"How do you do that?" asked Sam.

"Come back over."

Sam climbed up and when he was over, the roffle had gone again.

"Where are you?" shouted Sam.

Megatorine appeared. He took Sam's hand and led him to the side of the stile and vanished. Sam could just make out a slit of darkness. He reached his hand into it, but Megatorine pushed him back and appeared again. It was a roffle hole, a doorway to the Deep World.

"We come and go," said the roffle. "We see a lot that people don't think we see. Tamrin's gone to find the tailor who left her at the college. But she's been detained."

"I want to see her," said Sam.

"I know you do."

"Where is she? Can you take me to her?"

"Find the tailor and you'll find Tamrin," he said.

He stepped backwards and vanished into the roffle hole, down, back to the Deep World.

Sam tried to follow him but he couldn't find the way. The roffle hole was there still, but he needed a roffle to show him just exactly where.

He looked up at Starback and shook his head. ‖

# Sam stood in the kitchen doorway

looking in.

"What am I supposed to do?" he asked.

Starback crouched next to him, close against his legs for comfort. Sam fingered the metal weight that hung at his throat.

"No one knows," said Flaxfold. "That's the truth of it. No one ever knows."

"Am I supposed to run off and look for Tamrin?"

"You could," she said.

She sat at the table that Flaxfield had used. Her hair refused to stay tucked in her headband. Her fingers were stained with ink and dyes and burnt skin from experiments with spells.

"What about the wizard who Flaxfield locked up?" he asked. "Am I supposed to go and kill her?"

"Sealed," said Flaxfold.

"What?"

"Sealed up. He didn't lock her up, he sealed her up. It's different. And he could only make the magic work for the two of them. She's got armies of takkabakks that can come and go as they please."

Sam shuddered. Takkabakks were things of nightmare and story. He hardly dared to think that these winter-tale horrors were real.

"They've always kept close to the Castle of Boolat, where she's prisoner," said Flaxfold. "But stories now are that they're roaming further, attacking farms and villages."

"How can they do that? Doesn't the magic stop them?"

"It's getting weaker," she said. "Wearing thin. And there are new beetles. They change and grow over the years, you know. These are more like men. More dangerous. They plan and organize."

"And she's trying to escape as well," he said. "Through the Finished World."

Flaxfold scratched the side of her head with the end of her pen.

"Remember last year?" she said. "When you were very ill?"

Sam shook his head.

"I don't want to talk about it," he said.

"It's time. You have to."

His fingers found the leather cord round his neck. He tugged at it and enjoyed the tight pressure. It made him slow down.

Flaxfold waited for him to look at her.

"Last year, when you were ill almost to death, it was the one who was attacking you, attacking us all."

"She's locked in. She can't."

Flaxfold didn't bother to correct him. She just waited. An embarrassed smile stole over his face.

"That was stupid," he said. "I know you attack even when you're locked up."

"We made a contract," said Flaxfold. "Not to talk about this until you were ready. Until you were better."

"I'm not ready."

"You're my apprentice. I'll decide when you're ready. The great enemy who was brought under control by Flaxfield is breaking free. If we allow it to happen she'll escape and ruin us all. The wild magic will slip loose. It will be worse than ever this time. Houses will just explode in flames. People will burn up in the streets. Cattle in the fields will be blazing torches. Nothing will stop it. We can't allow it to happen."

"She's not free yet."

"It's only a matter of time," she said.

"It's not my fault," said Sam. "Why am I supposed to do something? And what am I supposed to do?"

"Why you? Because she only comes through the Finished World when you're there. She's drawn to you."

Sam came in and sat opposite her. The rushes and herbs on the floor bunched up where he dragged his chair.

"Were you there," he asked, "when Flaxfield sealed her up in the castle?"

"No. Not there. But not far away. It wasn't just Flaxfield who did it. There were others."

Sam held his breath. This was one of those moments when Flaxfold was ready to tell him something. That's the way of wizards. They wait for the right time. A weaver's apprentice might learn to thread the shuttle, to comb the wool, to fangle the loom, all in the same order. Always the same. With a wizard's apprentice, the knowledge comes differently, at the apprentice's time, not the teacher's. Sam sensed that Flaxfold thought it was time.

"There was Waterburn," she said. "Only no one called him that. We called him Cabbage. And there was the girl. The one the magic was stolen from."

"What was her name?"

"Ah, now there's a question. He stole her magic by stealing her name. She's got a new name now."

"What's her new name?" asked Sam.

Flaxfold thought about this for a long time.

"People have to tell you their names themselves," she said at last. "I expect you'll find out if it's ever the right time."

"How can I do anything if you don't tell me things?" he objected.

"There's nothing like finding things out for yourself," she said. "And there was Perry, the roffle."

"Roffles don't have magic," said Sam.

"No. They don't. But they're roffles. And there was a

woman, Dorwin. Between them they sealed the castle. They all played their part."

"Where are they now?"

Flaxfold put down her pen and rested her arms on the table.

"It was years ago," she said. "Houses have been built and fallen since then."

"You remember it, though."

"I'm a very old wizard. Remember?"

Sam's hand slid round the leather cord and found the weight at his throat. He stroked it to help him think.

"I want to find Tamrin," he said. "I want to ask her what she knows about me. I want to know who she is."

"Then perhaps you should."

"I don't know where to look."

"Didn't the roffle help?"

Sam kicked the leg of the table.

"He told me to look for the tailor."

Flaxfold picked up the pen and doodled a pair of scissors. Sam watched. She put the pen down and smiled. He waited. Wizards don't doodle aimlessly.

"How many things is that?" she asked Sam.

"One."

"Name it."

"Scissors."

"Scissor?"

"Scissors."

"Two scissors."

"A pair of scissors."

"So," she said. "It's two things."

"It's one thing. It's scissors."

"One thing is two things. You can't have a scissor."

"Two things are one thing," he corrected her.

"Where do you find scissors?" she asked.

"In a tailor's shop."

"Yes," said Flaxfold. "Tailors use scissors. They know the difference between one thing and two things."

Sam stood up.

"Where are you going?" she asked.

"To look for the tailor."

"Did the roffle tell you where he is?"

Sam scowled.

"No. He vanished down his filthy roffle hole and I couldn't find him."

She laughed.

"Take some food," she said. "I'll pack some for you."

Sam shrugged.

"I'll find food," he said. "I'll go through the inn."

"Are you sure?"

"Where is it now?" he asked.

"Where it needs to be. Same as ever."

Sam nodded.

Flaxfold stood and gave him a hug. She had to reach up to hold him. He had outgrown her.

"Be careful," she said. "Look for the scissors and you'll find the tailor."

Starback ran out of the kitchen across the grass, spread his wings and leaped into the air. Sam watched him until he was only a speck, glinting in the light. He climbed the stairs and opened the heavy oak door of the study, locking it behind him.

Of all the rooms in the house it was the place Sam loved best. Oak and leather and rows of books, a fireplace and a small window. Sam picked up a piece of blue and white pottery and remembered times in there with Flaxfield.

He loosened his hold and allowed the plate to slip from his fingers and watched it as it hit the hearth, shattered and scattered.

"You shouldn't have left me," he said. "Not like that. Not then. Not yet."

He sat at the table, put his head on his arms and found it hard to breathe. When he lifted his head again his arms were wet. He wiped his eyes with his sleeve.

"Look what you made me do," he said.

He leaned down and picked up a large fragment of the shattered plate. It was bright against the dark wood. He picked up others, got on his knees and found them. He ordered them on the table, bringing the shape back, frowning at the gaps. Pieces were still missing. Ducking below the table, Sam found smaller pieces, tiny fragments. When they were added there were still gaps.

"It has to be all here," he said.

Back below the table he whistled softly and held out his hand. Like a cloud of stars, a host of tiny points of light glowed in the shadow. He changed the whistle tone as a shepherd directs his dog. The motes of broken plate drifted up and settled in his hand.

Sam sprinkled the shards over the broken pieces, letting them find their own places. Looking at the crooked assembly of broken bits he nudged them into the best shape he could. He held his hands over them, palms down, raised his eyes and sighed.

When he looked down, the plate was restored. Not a crack, not a chip, not a blemish in the pattern. His hands were shaking. A small line of white foam gathered at the corners of his lips. He let his hands rest on the table on either side of the plate and looked at it. They were still trembling and he was short of breath.

"My own fault," he said.

He remembered another lesson he had learned from Flaxfield, never to do what you can't undo. Undoing was always much more effort than doing.

Sam waited until his hands were steady and his breathing easy. He put the plate back above the fireplace.

"Time to go."

The door he had come in through had two handles, one on the left, one on the right. He took the handle on the left and opened it.

When he stepped through he was no longer in Flaxfield's house.

"Let's see," he said. "What gossip is there about a tailor?"

He walked along the corridor, down the stairs and into the parlour of an inn, bright with custom, open to travellers.

"Hello," he said.

The customers turned their heads and nodded. ‖

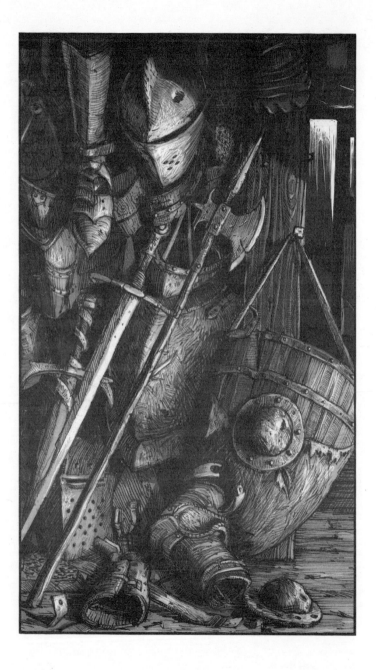

## Part Three

# DOUBLEDISCOVERY

# Tamrin didn't let herself look

at Smith in the morning.

"Who are you?" he asked.

Tamrin ignored him and crossed the room to the door. She was angry and ready to start to fight to get out. Trying the handle first, before she launched into her attack, she was surprised to find that it turned and the door opened.

"And where are you going?" he added.

Now that the door was open Tamrin didn't know what to do. She had slept well, against her expectations, and had woken feeling better than she had for a long time. But angry at being locked in. And hungry.

"Just who do you think you are?" she demanded. "Locking me in."

He leaned back in his chair and put his hands behind his head.

"You're not locked in."

"Not now."

"So go if you want to."

He lowered his hands, picked up a book and started to read.

Tamrin was angrier than ever. She had come downstairs ready for a fight and he had denied it her.

"I wanted to go last night," she said.

"No, you didn't."

"Don't tell me what I want and what I don't."

"Don't tell lies, then. It was late. It was dark. It was dangerous out. You wanted to flounce out, but you didn't want to leave."

He didn't look up from his book.

Tamrin felt herself shaking with anger. She darted a quick toothache spell across the room to him.

"Ouch," she said. Her tooth jabbed a needle of pain into her.

Smith smiled and continued reading.

Tamrin quickly removed the spell and rubbed her cheek.

"Shut the door after you," he said.

She shut the door, still inside.

"How did that happen?" she asked.

"If you're staying you can help yourself to some breakfast."

"Am I really free to leave?"

"Any time you want."

He put the book down. Tamrin could see that it was well-used, old, and the pages were covered with diagrams and measurements.

She dragged a toe across the floor.

"If I can go," she said, "I may as well eat first."

He nodded and carried on reading. No matter how much she clattered a plate and cup, sawed furiously at a loaf of bread and slapped butter and marmalade on it, he made no response. He read steadily as though she was not there. She dragged the chair with as much noise as she could make and sat down with a thud.

After her first mouthful of food she stared at him. He didn't look up.

"How did that toothache thing happen?" she asked.

"I really don't know what you mean."

"You do. You know you do. I sent a toothache spell to you and it came to me. How did that happen?"

He put down his book and took a drink from the mug next to him.

"It was toothache, was it?"

He laughed.

The tooth was still a little sore so Tamrin didn't join in and laugh with him.

"Can you do magic?" she asked.

"No."

She bit into the bread again and chewed while she thought.

"What happened, then?" she asked.

"Have you ever seen a blacksmith work?"

"No."

"I'll show you, if you like."

"I haven't got time. I'm leaving when I've finished this."

"As you like," he said, and picked up his book again.

Tamrin came close to throwing her breakfast at him.

"I said I was leaving," she said, "not that I didn't want you to explain."

"It's easier if I show you."

"Tell me. I'm quick. I'll understand."

"There's a hammer," he said. "And an anvil. An anvil is a big—"

"I know what an anvil is. Tell me."

"Did your teachers like you at the college?" he asked.

"Just tell me."

"You put the hot iron on the anvil and strike it with the hammer. To shape it. No matter how hard you hold the hammer, no matter how much you try to control it, as soon as it strikes the anvil it bounces off. There's no stopping it."

Tamrin chewed the last of her bread and considered cutting more.

"You're not an anvil," she said.

"No. But I'm a smith. And smiths are not like anyone else. You'll see that when you've had a look around."

"I'm not going to have a look around. I'm leaving."

"Winny will pack you some food."

"Where is she?"

"Oh, not here just now."

He went back to his book.

"Come back any time you want," he said. "We'll talk some more about tailors."

Tamrin felt that the room was tilting or that the sunlight

through the window was affecting her eyes. He was so frustrating that she was unbalanced.

"We didn't talk about tailors," she said. "You know we didn't."

He seemed to think about this, but Tamrin knew he remembered perfectly well.

"We didn't," he admitted. "Well, it's too late now if you're off. I'll say goodbye to Winny for you."

"I want to say goodbye to her myself. Where is she?"

"I'll take you to her," he offered. "She's in the storeroom, unloading the cart."

They crossed the yard together. He was taller than she remembered from the night before, broader at the shoulder, and with strong arms.

He pointed out the arrangement of buildings to her.

"The house runs along the side of the road," he said. "And the forge is set at the back, separate and on the square from the house. The storeroom is an extension of the forge."

Together the forge and the storeroom were more than half as big again as the house.

"Forge is a strange word," he said. "It means the furnace where you heat the metal, and it means the building you work in as well."

"It means to make a false copy," said Tamrin. "To try to cheat."

"Clever girl," he said. "It means exactly that. You would forge a signature on a contract, or forge a painting."

"Or a coin," said Tamrin.

Smith pulled open a heavy door, twice as high as himself and broad enough for a pair of horses pulling a wagon to pass through.

"This way," he said. "Mind your step. Winny," he called out. "Are you there? Tam wants to talk to you. She wants to say goodbye."

His voice echoed round the room and back to them. No reply joined in.

"She's not here," said Tam.

"Oh, she's in here," he said. "She's wandered off and she's busy. We'll look for her."

He walked away from her and was gone, leaving his first question of the day rolling around in her head.

"Who are you?" he had asked. Reflecting on it, she thought it had been a strange question to ask.

It was her own question.

"Winny."

He was still calling for her. Tamrin had the idea that it was just a game to him. He was teasing. He knew where Winny was.

She looked up and around. It wasn't a storeroom at all. It was very like the other big barn they had been in on the way. Stone walls, high oak roof. And it was full of stuff. Piled up, heaped high, taller than she was. With paths between the stacks. It was a library of junk.

Tamrin walked in and turned left. A passageway unfolded

ahead of her, with side alleys branching off. She walked a few paces, turned right and found the same. This was no good. She decided to go back to the door, readjust her directions and start again. She retraced her steps but didn't find the door. It was a maze. She had made one false turn and now had no idea at all which way was out.

"Winny."

Smith's voice sounded impossibly far away and there was still no answer.

Tamrin made a tracker spell. She took off her shoe, tapped it on the ground six times, tossed it into the air. It span and tumbled, taking longer to fall than was quite normal. As it hit the floor a line of footprints glowed against the stone slabs. Tamrin smiled and put her shoe back on. Every step she had taken since entering the barn was illuminated and all she had to do was follow them and she would be back at the door.

She felt better now. She was in control again. She stuck her tongue out at Smith, wherever he was, and set off.

Now that she wasn't worried about getting lost she took the time to look at the piles of junk as she passed.

Much of it was the sort of thing she had thrown on the cart with Winny. Household objects that had broken or worn out or were no longer loved. Some of it was not like that at all. Her eyes found a handle, not quite neatly tucked in. She stopped, grabbed it and pulled out a sword.

"You don't want to mess with that."

Tamrin dropped the sword and wheeled around. No one.

"Are you going to pick it up?"

She worked out where the voice was from and looked up.

Someone was lying on top of the pile of junk, looking down at her.

"You should put that back," he said. ‖

# Tamrin picked up the sword

but she didn't put it back.

She held it for protection.

The face disappeared. A leather object landed on the floor next to her with a thud. She stepped back. A pair of feet dangled over the edge and then, in a second, he dropped down and fell over, rolled into a ball like a woodlouse, came to a halt, unrolled and stood up, dusting himself down. He set the leather object on its end and sat on it.

"You should put that back," he said.

Tamrin didn't like roffles. The first one she had ever come across was Megatorine, who had betrayed Sam, and she didn't trust them.

"I'll keep it if I want to," she said.

"Do you want to?"

Tamrin slid the sword back into the pile of junk. The handle still didn't go right in so she left it.

"I don't want to talk to you," she said. "I'm leaving."

The roffle nodded and she left, following her footprints.

After three turns she was back where she had left him. He was still sitting on his barrel.

"That was quick," he said.

Tamrin walked away again. She must have made a mistake. She tried to remember something from each pile, to keep her sense of direction. A broken wheel from a mangle, a large kettle, a twisted gate. It was no use. The same sorts of things kept reappearing. Common items discarded. She turned the corner and the roffle was there again.

"You keep following me," she said.

He pointed to the sword handle.

"I haven't moved."

It was time to try something different.

"Do you know where the door is?" she asked.

"Oh, yes. Of course."

"Show me."

"Please."

Tamrin wanted to slap him.

"Please," she said.

He didn't move from his barrel.

"You're not saying it as though you mean it," he said. "But I suppose it'll do."

Tamrin waited for him to move.

"What's your name?" he asked.

"I don't want to tell you."

"I can't show a stranger the door, can I?"

"Tamrin."

"Hello, Tamrin. I'm Solder."

She nodded.

"You mean Megasolder," she said. "All roffle names begin with Mega."

She smiled to show she had won a point from him.

"Well," he said, "my real name, in the Deep World, is Megapolitifricabilitihitti. You can call me that if you like. But most people call me Solder."

Tamrin scowled at him.

"You have to say, "Hello, Solder," he said. "It's polite."

He was cheerful. And that made him even more irritating. Tamrin forced herself.

"Hello, Solder."

He hopped off his barrel and hauled it on to his back.

"This way."

Tamrin didn't follow him.

"Are you coming with me?"

"That's not the way."

He sighed.

"How do you know?"

Tamrin pointed to her glowing footprints.

"Oh, that," he said. "You shouldn't have followed those."

"They're the way I came in," she said.

"If you follow me, I'll tell you what's wrong," he offered, and set off.

Tamrin watched him disappear round the corner. She

hesitated. There was no other way she could think of, so she ran after him.

"Wait."

She caught him up.

"What's wrong with the footprints?" she asked.

"You think they're showing you the way you've walked, don't you?"

"Yes."

"They're really showing you the way you will walk in the future."

"That's not the spell I made."

"No, it's the reflection of the spell you made. It bounced back at you, like a hammer—"

"Like a hammer from an anvil," she finished his sentence.

He grinned at her.

"You've been talking to Smith," he said.

"Yes. Yes, I have."

"What do you think of him?"

The piles of scrap metal were different here. Household junk — the mangles, the oven doors, the lamp brackets, pots, pans and hinges — were less frequent. Broken swords, dented helmets, shields, breastplates, twisted armour took their place.

Tamrin stopped and ran her finger over the articulated iron of a knee-protector.

Solder waited.

"Is this stuff older?" she asked.

"Some of it."

He found a spearhead and prodded the pile.

"We've been walking a long time."

"It's a big storeroom."

She looked up at the roof, cruck-beamed, oak. The piles were so high she couldn't see far enough along the gable to the end walls.

Solder pushed the spearhead back into the stack and trotted on.

"Are you sure you're taking me to the door?" she asked.

"Look at this," he called. "You'll like it."

He led her into a side room with high windows far above her head. A waterfall of light splashed down and bounced from a hundred mirrors leaning and hanging all around the walls.

Tamrin looked at herself looking at herself. She saw herself disappearing, endlessly repeated into the distance. She saw the top of her head, the side of her face, her back, her front. She raised her arm and a thousand Tamrins raised their arm. She stepped back and out of the room.

"Come on," he said. He stood on his barrel and waved his arms, watching himself wave back.

Tamrin hesitated, stepped back in.

It was like being confronted by a poisonous snake or a wolf. She was fascinated and fearful.

"Never seen yourself before?" he asked.

Tamrin shook her head.

"What?"

"No. Not really."

"Never?"

"In a window," she said. "Reflected in water. In the bowl of a shiny spoon. There's a small mirror, a glass one, in my friend's kitchen. But you can only see your face, and not really all of it at once."

She moved slowly as she spoke, watching herself bounce back, reflected into infinity. The question elbowed its way back into her mind.

"Who are you?" it whispered.

She looked at the endless Tamrins.

"Who are you?"

"Some of these are glass," said Solder.

He jumped from his barrel and found a round looking glass, just within his reach if he stood on tiptoe and touched it with his fingertips. "Most of them are polished metal."

"How do you get them so bright?"

"You'll have to ask Smith about that."

"Did he make them all?"

"You'll have to ask him. I think he did. But there are other people who used to make them, before there was good glass and they learned how to silver the back of it."

Tamrin stood in front of one that showed the whole of her from tip to toe. It was buckled about a third of the way down so that her face seemed to be disfigured. She reached out her hand and touched it.

"He collects them," said Solder. "Or Winny does. With her cart."

"Why?"

The light in the room was greater than the amount the windows let in. It was as though the mirrors caught it, kept it and threw it back to be caught and kept and thrown out again, over and over, getting brighter all the time. Like lighting a thousand candles from a single taper.

Tamrin stood quite still and waited and watched. She wanted one of the other Tamrins to move on her own, independently of the others. They all stood and waited with her.

"Yes, but why does he collect them?"

"You'll have to ask Smith that."

Tamrin was getting tired of this answer. Especially as Smith wasn't there to ask.

She wondered what magic would be like here. She raised her arm and pointed straight up. She took a deep breath and her lips parted.

"Don't say a word!"

Smith pushed into the room and nearly knocked her over.

"Don't. Not a word." ||

# Tamrin stepped aside

to avoid Smith's rush at her.

"Why did you bring her in here?" he demanded.

"I thought you wanted her to see it."

Solder didn't seem to mind that he was being told off. He was as cheerful as ever.

"I'll decide when she sees this," said Smith.

"Too late, Smith. I've shown her."

"Has she done any magic yet?"

"I think she was just about to."

"And do you think you could have stopped her? And what would have happened then?"

"We'd have found out if you hadn't come in," said Solder. "Wouldn't we?"

Smith glared at him.

"Roffles," he said. "You're all the same. You've no sense of danger. She could have killed herself. And you. You know that?"

Solder began to answer but Tamrin interrupted.

"Hey," she said. "I am in here, you know. You're talking about me as though I can't hear you."

Smith turned the full gaze of his anger on her. Tamrin glared back, not to be intimidated. He held her stare and she found herself growing afraid. He had more authority in his look, more danger, than any of the teachers in the college who had tried to overcome her with a stare. She turned away. He still stared at her, a thousand times reflected in the shining metal. She looked back at him, looked again at the reflections.

Face to face, Smith looked old enough to be Winny's father. In the middle of life. In reflected light he was old. Older than it was possible to live. Not old as a person grows old, weak and enfeebled, prey to death. Old as a tree is old, worn, weathered and strong. Old as stone is old, shaped by the weather, moulded by time.

She looked from reality to reflection and lost track of which was which.

Smith spoke softly now.

"You see me?" he asked.

"Yes. Yes, I do."

"He doesn't," said Smith, pointing to Solder.

Winny arrived and hesitated at the door. Tamrin caught just a glimpse of her in the mirror before she stepped back. Enough to see that she had been Smith's daughter for longer than a lifetime.

"We should not stay in here," Winny called in.

"No," agreed Smith.

Tamrin was glad to be led out and back among the stacks of scrap.

"Will you come to look at the forge?" asked Smith. "Or do you have to be running after your tailor straight away?"

"I'd like to see the forge," she said. "Please."

He nodded.

"I'll show you the way," said Solder. He pushed in front of them, lifting his pack and trotting ahead. "Follow me."

Smith went next, Tamrin following, and Winny last.

"You weren't taking me to the door, were you?" asked Tamrin.

Solder turned left and stopped. He gestured with his left arm. It was a door. Low, narrow and closed. Not the wide door into the barn.

"Here it is," he announced.

"I mean the door out," said Tamrin.

"You didn't say that. You said the door."

Winny laid her hand on Tamrin's shoulder, her delicate fingers cool on the girl's neck.

"You can never trust a roffle," she said.

Tamrin looked straight into her eyes.

"I don't think I can trust anyone," she said.

"Perhaps not. Perhaps it's best you don't, just now."

This wasn't the answer Tamrin had expected and she turned away. Smith took out a key and unlocked the door. He stepped through; Solder followed. Tamrin stayed where she was.

"Are you going in?" asked Winny.

"If I don't?"

"I can show you the other door. It's quite close. You can leave if you like. But you said you wanted to see the forge."

Tamrin stepped through.

Tim wished he was somewhere else, anywhere else. Smedge lined up the children outside Frastfil's office, Tim at the front.

"Remember," said Smedge. "Tell him."

They nodded.

He knocked and waited. Tim noted this. He had expected him to go straight in.

"Come in."

Frastfil sat behind his desk, failing to look important. Dr Duddle stood as far away from the window as he could. Five other teachers looked uncomfortable in the centre of the room. There was Miss Plang, who taught the little ones when they first came to the college; Dr Frescing, the art teacher, who taught picture magic and making clay pots for spells; Mr Fouller, who was a specialist in writing out spells in exactly the correct way so that they meant what they were supposed to mean and nothing else; Miss Makawley, the old-spells teacher and the expert on wizards from the past; and there was Mr Faraway. Mr Faraway had a white coat and he had lost all of the hair on the right side of his head just that morning when a new spell had exploded. He was in charge of the laboratory for dangerous new spells and one had gone wrong. Again.

Smedge closed the door.

"Thank you for coming to the meeting," said Frastfil. "As heads of departments in the college you need to know about a very serious development."

They all listened carefully except for Faraway, who was rubbing the bald side of his head and looking at the bookshelves.

"There has been a serious case of bullying," said Frastfil, "and you need to be aware of it."

Smedge took over and instructed the other boys and girls to say that they had all seen Tamrin bullying him at different times. Tim tried to keep quiet, but Smedge made him add his account of the block of ice.

"So," concluded Frastfil, "I tried to expel Tamrin and send her home with her guardian, Shoddle, the tailor, but she ran away from the college and has disappeared."

"Eh?" said Faraway, as though he had just started listening.

Frastfil frowned.

"So," he continued, "it is most important that if she returns you make sure I am informed as soon as you see her."

"She wouldn't do that," said Faraway.

"I beg your pardon?" Frastfil glared at him.

"Tamrin. She wouldn't bully anyone."

Frastfil pointed at the line of witnesses.

"Did you listen to any of these children? Did you hear what they had to say? They all saw her do it."

Faraway tapped his finger against his teeth.

"Any of you been bullied by her?" he asked.

They shook their heads.

"Just him?"

He indicated Smedge.

They nodded.

"And you all saw it?"

There was the smallest pause before they nodded again.

Faraway spoke to Tim. Tim had been trying to avoid his eye but it was no good.

"Tim Masrani, you saw her bullying Smedge?"

Tim nodded.

"You sure?"

Tim hesitated. He wanted to explain properly. He felt ashamed at what was happening. He didn't want to be part of it. Making sure he didn't look at Smedge, in case he lost his courage, he started to explain that Tamrin was only sticking up for the little ones, helping them against Smedge's spite and cruelty.

"Woof," he said.

They stared at him.

Tim felt fur growing on his arms and on his back, under his shirt. He felt his toenails turning to claws. It was hopeless.

"Sorry," he said. "Just clearing my throat. Yes. I did."

He saw the look of disgust on Faraway's face and knew that the man knew he was lying. He hung his head. The fur disappeared, and the claws retracted.

Frastfil finished the meeting quickly.

"Tell all your colleagues," he said. "We won't have bullies here. No bullying at Canterstock."

Tim hated him. Hated the lying. Hated the stupidity. Hated the way Frastfil gave in to Smedge.

Frastfil couldn't wait to get rid of them.

"Goodbye. Thank you." He jumped to his feet, coins jangling in his pockets, clapping his hands, grinning and bouncing. "Well done. Goodbye. Yes."

Tim slipped out first and ran down the corridor. He felt as though he had vomited black sick on the carpet and left it there, stinking and steaming.

Smedge was turning the whole college against Tamrin. She wouldn't be the strange girl who hung around the place any more. She would be seen as a nasty bully, someone to fear, someone to hate. And Tim was helping. Because he was afraid not to.

He found his way down the steps to the store areas. He needed to tell Vengeabil what had happened. He pushed aside the curtain and saw that the door was there. He could go through to the passageway that led to the kitchen. He put his hand to the door and drew away again.

The thought of telling the man what he had done was too much for him. He climbed the stairs slowly, back to the damp corridors and stinking staircases of the college. Back to lessons. ‖

# Smith tossed lumps of charcoal

on to the fire. Solder ran round the back of the furnace and pumped the bellows, shooting jets of air into the embers. They glowed with new life. More charcoal. More air. More heat. Tamrin was attracted to the fire and repelled by it at the same time. It fascinated her and filled her with dread.

"Why is it so hot?"

She felt it was a stupid question and wished she could take it back. Smith smiled.

"You're right," he agreed. "It's not like a normal fire, is it? The forge concentrates heat, builds it up so that the iron melts."

He thrust an iron bar into the depth of the fire to demonstrate.

Tamrin had never felt so useless. She had always learned everything so easily that it was not like learning at all, more like remembering. She couldn't learn how to use the forge, how to strike the metal, how to twist the hot iron.

Smith stood back and folded his arms.

"I've never seen anyone so bad at it," he said.

Tamrin clamped her teeth tight shut to stop herself from saying something angry.

"No magic," he had said. "Not in here. If you try, it will hurt you. Badly. Understand?"

"Of course I understand what you're saying. I just don't understand why you're saying it."

And now they looked down at the things she had fashioned without the aid of magic. They were hopeless. Poor, twisted and uneven things. However hard she tried the hot metal would not move the way she wanted it to. It seemed to twist away from her like a snake. The hammer was heavy in her hand. The heat from the furnace made her brow sweat and turned her face red. Her hair grew wet and stuck down to her head. She looked and felt wretched.

Smith leaned his backside against a workbench and tapped a file against the top.

"You're like a cat in a river," he said.

Tamrin had had enough of failure and was in the mood for an argument.

"What's that supposed to mean?"

He didn't laugh at her.

"Don't worry," he said. "I'm not judging you. Cats are good creatures, but they can't swim. They can run and hunt. They can fall from a tree and land on their feet and be all right. They can climb where dogs can't. But, put one in the river and it'll be dead in no time. Cats and water. That's you and fire. It's not a good thing or a bad thing."

"I tried."

"You did. You tried hard. But it's never going to work."

Tamrin searched for a reason that would be to her credit.

"It's because of the magic," she said. "If I hadn't got such strong magic I could do it."

This time he did smile.

"I don't think so."

He moved to a row of shelves.

"Come and look at these," he said.

He handed her a small iron bird, perfect in simple design and the very barest of detail, yet Tamrin had never seen anything that so perfectly captured what it was to be a bird. He gave her a frog, in one way just a casual sweep of curves and lines, yet the most exact impression of what it is to be a frog. A snail. A flat, curved object that was handle and dull blade of a letter opener all in one unbroken line. A spoon, the bowl perfectly rounded. Tamrin held them one by one, loving the perfection of what they were, their simplicity, grace and accuracy.

"So?" she demanded. "You've been making things like this for years. It's your job. And anyway, you haven't got any magic."

She reluctantly allowed him to take them from her and replace them on the shelf. She longed to keep one, to own it. The frog, perhaps. No, the bird, wings folded, head down, like an egg in her hand.

"I didn't make them," he said. "A girl did. A girl your age, on her first day at the forge."

Tamrin shrugged.

"I'm not just a girl. I'm a wizard. It's the magic that stops me."

Smith looked for something else on the shelf. Tamrin kept her eyes on the bird, wondering if she couldn't just borrow it for a while. He need never know.

"So was she," he said. "She was full of magic. It poured out of her, into the fire and back again into the iron, hot as hate, soft as love. Everything she touched she formed into something wonderful. She made things on her first day at the forge that I've never been able to make in a long lifetime."

"You said I couldn't use magic in here."

"Nor you can. Nor did she. Her magic was fire. Yours isn't. That's all there is to it. She wasn't using magic, it was using her. Ah, here we are."

He handed her a pair of scissors. She slipped her fingers into the handle and flexed them.

"Careful. They're sharp."

"Did she make these?"

"Mostly. She didn't have time to finish them. She made the two halves. I sharpened the blade and I riveted them in the centre. You can have them."

"I'd rather have the bird."

"I know you would, but you can't. You'll have these or nothing."

Tamrin handed them back.

"No, thanks."

Winny laid her hand on Tamrin's shoulder.

"Take them," she said. "You're on a journey and they're a gift. Take them."

Tamrin reached out her hand, took them without thanks and pushed them into her pocket. Smith edged the bird to the back of the shelf and led her away.

They stepped from the forge into the yard. It was growing dark. Tamrin shut her eyes in disbelief and opened them again.

"What's happened?" she asked.

"You must be hungry," said Winny. "Let's go and eat."

"But it's nearly night," said Tamrin. "We were only in there about an hour."

Solder came out of the forge last and closed the door behind him, checking it was locked. Smith took Tamrin's elbow and escorted her back to the house. There were four places laid at the table.

"You can stay for dinner," he said. "It's too late to set off now."

"You're keeping me prisoner," said Tamrin. "You'll lock me in again."

"Not tonight," said Smith.

He stirred the fire.

"How could we have been in there so long?" she asked.

"You're a wizard and you don't know that time goes

differently in different places? I don't believe it."

Tamrin didn't know that and thought some very bad thoughts about Vengeabil for not teaching her.

"There's one time for the outside," said Smith. "And another time for the storeroom, and another time for the forge," he explained, without explaining anything.

"And the room of mirrors?" she said. "What's the time for there?"

Smith gave Solder a stern look and the roffle grinned back, unconcerned.

"You weren't supposed to go in there," said Smith. "Not today."

"Why not? What's so secret about there?"

"Let's eat," he said.

"It strikes me," said Solder, when he had eaten more beef stew than Tamrin thought anyone could manage, "that you'd want to run away from this tailor, rather than run after him."

"Roffles like their food," said Winny, noticing Tamrin's amazement at the way he'd cleared his dish. Tamrin blushed.

"I wouldn't want to get closer to someone who seemed to want to harm me," the roffle continued.

"If there was a wolf circling the village," said Smith, "attacking at night, picking out small children in their beds, killing for sport as well as hunger, what would you do? You wouldn't run away, would you?"

"I would," he said.

"No, you wouldn't. You'd arm yourself, go out and hunt

the wolf. You'd take the battle to the enemy, not just bar the doors and hope you'd be safe. Not just run away. Wolves run fast and they can scent their prey."

Tamrin laid down her spoon and listened. Nothing seemed to upset Solder. No rebuke or scorn or teasing. He took it all in his stride, grinning back.

"You do right," said Smith to Tamrin. "You need to hunt the tailor down. Or he'll be more dangerous when you do meet."

Solder wasn't easily put off.

"But why do they need to meet at all?" he said. "She could just stay away from him."

"He came to the college to find her and she ran away," said Smith. "He won't give up. He may have gone home now, but he's still looking."

"He's got something I want," said Tamrin.

She had held on to this secret for so long that it was difficult to let it go. But once she loosened her grip on it, talking made it easier.

"I'm a twin," she said. "At least, I think I am. As long as I can remember I've known that I am. And I feel it. Sometimes I feel that there's a person out there that I'm part of, that I was born with."

She stopped and let the kitchen absorb this fact. It had grown full dark while they ate. The lights of candles were reflected in the windows.

"I met him once," she continued. "He came to the college, just for a few days, and then he left."

"Was he glad to see you?" asked Solder.

"He didn't know."

The roffle stared at her.

"What do you mean, he didn't know?"

Tamrin tried to smile. She failed.

"No one had ever told him that he was a twin as well. He just didn't know."

"Didn't he feel it, the way you feel it?"

"That's enough, Solder," said Winny. "Give me your dish."

"But didn't he?"

"He didn't seem to," said Tamrin.

"Perhaps you don't really feel it, then," he said. "Perhaps you only imagine you do because you've been told you've got a twin."

He smiled, expecting them to congratulate him on having solved the problem.

"No. I do feel it. I do know I'm a twin. I've read about it. Twins, even when they've never met, know they are. One twin falls and the other one feels pain. One twin eats something bad and the other one gets sick. It's happened to me. I know I'm a twin. And the tailor knows who I am and how we were separated. He's got the answers. And he's going to have to tell me."

She wanted to keep her voice down and was annoyed with the way it kept getting louder.

"You shall," said Smith. "You must. Go in the morning."

Tamrin stood up without speaking. She crossed the room and tried the door. It opened.

"But not tonight, eh?" said Smith. "Get some sleep. You'll be stronger for the journey."

"I'll go with you," said Solder.

"No," said Tamrin and Smith simultaneously.

"Oh."

They laughed.

"I'm better on my own," said Tamrin.

"And you've got work to do here," said Smith.

Tamrin was eager to turn the conversation away from telling Solder she didn't want him with her. She didn't want to hurt his feelings. Not that he seemed capable of having them hurt.

"What do you do here?" she asked.

"I'm learning to be a smith."

"Don't they have smiths in the Deep World?"

"Of course, or why would I want to learn how to be one?"

Tamrin worked out the fault in this argument.

"Then why don't you learn from a Deep World smith? Why come Up Top?"

Solder looked at Smith for help in answering the question.

"Because I'm the best," said Smith. "And young Solder here only wants to learn from the best."

"What do you mean, 'young Solder'?"

"How old do you think he is?" asked Smith.

This unsettled Tamrin. Roffles were all so short that she imagined Solder was grown up.

"I don't like guessing," she said.

"Have a try."

Solder jumped off his barrel, stood away from the table so she could get a clear look at him and turned around for the full effect.

"Thirty," she said.

Solder laughed. Winny shushed him.

"Don't make fun," she warned. "It's not polite."

"Tell her," said Smith.

"I'm sort of twelve," he said. "Or fourteen."

"I'm really sorry," said Tamrin. "It's hard to tell, because—"

"I wouldn't say anything else if I were you," warned Smith. "You'll only make it worse."

They sat and talked some more before it was time to go to bed. Tamrin couldn't stop herself from trying the door before she went upstairs. Just in case.

"It will always be open to you," Smith assured her. "Now that you know you're with friends."

"And you won't trick me again in the morning?" she asked. "Show me another room or a stable or somewhere where time runs at a different pace?"

"Trick you?"

Smith spread his huge hands and painted a picture of pained innocence on his face.

"You know," she said.

"Goodnight."

As she lay in bed, reflecting on the day just past and

pondering the day to come, she kept returning in her mind to Solder. It was strange how her feelings about him were different now that she knew he was more or less the same age as she was. When she had thought he was a grown-up, his behaviour had been annoying and a little frightening. Now, she was amused by him, found herself starting to like him.

She fell into a deep sleep, where she dreamed of tailors and scissors and a twin's face reflected in the kitchen window against the dark outside. ||

# In the end, Tamrin didn't say goodbye

to anyone. She woke before it was light, dressed quietly, ate standing up, and was on the road before the sun lifted its eyes above the hedgerow.

"It's better this way," she said out loud to no one.

It made her feel better about leaving Canterstock without saying goodbye to Vengeabil. But not much better.

The way was plain going for miles. She took the road she and Winny had been following. It twisted and it rose and fell. It passed under arches of trees and it took her across open fields divided into strips for the plough, but it didn't fork and it didn't have lanes off to the right or to the left.

She lingered on a small stone bridge over a river. The water looked cool and inviting so she slid down the side of the bridge and cupped her hands in the stream to drink. Her face was still wet when she travelled on.

She enjoyed the inevitability of the unbroken road. She liked the limits it placed on her direction.

And then she reached the point where the road split into two. It was at its high point. She had been aware of the gentle rise for the last mile or two, the landscape falling away on either side, the opening vista. She saw the fork in the road long before she reached it. She prepared herself for a decision. And when she arrived she had no more idea which way to take than when she had first spotted it.

There was no signpost. Not that it would have made any difference, as she had no idea where she was going anyway.

It was a time for magic. It was a time for caution.

She sat on the grass and thought about it.

A small spell wouldn't do any harm.

Would it?

No.

Probably not.

She thought again.

If she closed her eyes she could see the tailor. She had enough of a glimpse of him in the porter's lodge to recall him. She could use that to send a tracking spell. It was dangerous. It would leave a trail back to her. If the tailor had any magic at his disposal he could use it against her. If he was even employing a humble town wizard then he would know she had sent the spell out to find him. Instead of hunting him, she would be hunted.

She opened her eyes and looked along both roads from the fork.

They looked as good as each other.

A small spell.

She lay back on the grass and felt something hard against her back. She sat up. The scissors. She took them from the fold in her cloak and examined them.

Scissors.

Tailors.

She could cast a spell on the scissors and send them to find a tailor. Not her tailor. Any tailor. That would not alert him. Would it? It might.

It was worth a try.

She held the scissors in both hands, closed her eyes and started the spell. As soon as she began, the face of her tailor filled her thoughts. She snapped her eyes open. That wouldn't do.

She started the spell again, this time with her eyes open.

That was no good.

She couldn't focus her thoughts.

Magic wouldn't do it.

She jumped to her feet, grabbed a stone from the road, turned her back to the fork, tossed the stone over her shoulder.

When she turned back it had landed on the left-hand road.

One's as good as another.

She set off down that way.

"Come back."

Tamrin stopped and turned.

Solder waved to her.

"It's the other way," he said.

"Where did you come from?"

Solder showed her the roffle hole three times. He went into it and out of it, and she saw it clearly each time. As soon as he stepped away and told her to find it she couldn't. It wasn't there. All she could see was a stone land marker between two fields.

"And you can see it clearly?" she asked.

"Of course."

"Are they everywhere?"

He laughed.

"Nothing's everywhere."

"Some things are."

"What things?"

She thought about it.

"The breeze. The sunlight."

"There's no sunlight in shade. And if I lock you in a cave the breeze will go and you'll die."

She changed the subject.

"You shouldn't be here," she said.

"It's my day off."

Tamrin didn't think he had days off.

"Smith will be angry," she predicted. "You'd better go back before he misses you."

"Smith doesn't miss anything," said Solder. "Anyway, you're on the wrong road."

"How do you know?"

"That doesn't go anywhere."

"Everything goes somewhere."

"That's true. But that's not going where you want to go."

"Where does it go?"

Solder whispered. "Boolat."

He took her arm and led her down the other road.

"This one goes to a town. It might not be the right town, but it's a town. And there'll be a tailor. It might not be the right tailor, but it's a tailor."

"What if it's the wrong town, the wrong tailor?"

Solder was very cheerful now that they were on the road he had chosen and on the move.

"Then we'll go to the next town, and the next. Till we find the right one."

"I want to go on my own," she said.

"No, you don't."

"I don't want you with me."

"Yes, you do."

He tripped along next to her, moving his legs more than she did to keep up.

"You didn't walk this fast when you were on your own," he said.

"How would you know?"

"Oh, I just guessed."

Tamrin gave him a withering look and he grinned back.

"It's a good job you didn't make a spell back there," he said.

"Let's just walk. Keep quiet. I'm thinking."

Solder didn't talk again for nearly a whole minute. ‖

# The town took them by surprise

when it finally appeared. They had been walking through woods and downhill. The path turned, the tree cover broke and the town was in a dip ahead of them, its shops and houses gripping a river that ran through the centre.

"Good," said Solder. "I'm hungry."

They followed the road in, turned down a street, into another and saw the sign.

It was a tailor's shop.

Too simple for Tamrin. Too easy to find. She wanted it not to be his as much as she wanted to have arrived.

"But is it his shop?" asked Tamrin.

"We could go in and ask," suggested Solder.

Tamrin shuddered.

"I never want to talk to him, never meet him."

Solder sat on his barrel. Roffles never stand up for long if they can avoid it.

The shop was down a side street, away from the main

road through the town. There was a goldsmiths', a small tavern that was just one room with barrels in it, a junk shop piled high with old furniture and lamps and books and rugs and kettles and glass dishes and all sorts; there was a tiny shop that sold cheese and a big shop that seemed to sell nothing at all and only had a vase on a round table in the window. And there was the tailor's shop, with a small window of leaded squares and a giant pair of scissors hanging on the wall outside.

"Do you think that tavern sells food?" asked Solder.

"If it does I'm not buying any."

"All right."

Tamrin stepped back and leaned against the wall. Someone had come out of the tailor's shop. A tall man with a wide black hat and pointy shoes.

"Is that him?" asked Solder.

"No."

"Perhaps it's not the right shop."

"Perhaps he was a customer."

"He wasn't carrying any shopping."

"That doesn't mean anything, with a tailor. He might have been ordering something."

"I could go in and order something," said Solder, "and then I could come and tell you if it's the right shop."

He hopped off his barrel, ready to go.

"You've never seen him," said Tamrin. "How would you know?"

He climbed back on to his barrel and kicked his heels against it.

"We could walk past," he said, "and you could look in through the window."

"It's a small window. Brighter outside than inside. He'd see us and we wouldn't see him."

"We could think about it and make a plan while we're eating."

"We're not eating."

Solder jumped off the barrel again.

"Good idea," he said. "Let's eat."

"We'll go round the back of the shops," said Tamrin, "and see if we can see anything from there."

"Are you all right?" asked Solder.

"Yes. Why not?"

Tamrin strode ahead of him. She strode out as though she wasn't frightened of what she might find. Taking care not to pass in front of the shop window, she doubled back, left at the corner, left again and into an alleyway that ran down the back of the shops.

"You don't seem all right," said Solder. "You seem angry."

"I am angry."

Being angry sounded better than being frightened.

"With me? What have I done?"

Tamrin stopped and let him catch her up.

"Not with you," she said. "With the tailor."

"All right."

"Good."

"Yes."

"Ready now?" she asked.

"Yes. But can we go and eat next, whether it's his shop or not?"

"All right."

"It stinks down here."

Tamrin looked around.

"Who'd have thought it?" she said.

"What?"

"Those shops. At the front they're all clean and careful. It looks as though it would cost a lot to buy something."

"Except the junk shop," said Solder.

"Except the junk shop. But that was clean even if it wasn't smart. And look at this. This ... this..."

She struggled not to say a word. Solder giggled and pointed to a small shack, leaning to one side, the roof full of holes, the door hanging open to show a board with a hole cut into the top for someone to sit on with their trousers round their ankles.

"That's right," said Tamrin. "The whole place stinks like that."

They passed the tavern yard, tumbled with barrels and jars, the junk shop yard with even more useless-looking stuff than they had seen in the window. The shop that sold nothing had nothing in the yard either except for a tall, iron post that might have had a lamp on it once. They were all open to anyone who passed by, the gates ajar, to allow quick access from the shop and the yard to the privies. All except the tailor's yard, which was quite secure, the wall high, the gate locked.

"He doesn't like people looking in," said Tamrin.

"Cloth's expensive," said Solder. "People would steal it."

"People would steal beer," said Tamrin, "but the tavern yard's open. He doesn't want people looking in."

"We'd better go and eat, then, and think it through."

The gate was painted dark blue, with a black iron handle. Tamrin put her hand to the handle and turned it slowly, softly. It turned, but the gate did not give way.

"Locked. Bolted," she said. "Made very safe. No sealing spell, though."

"Can you open it?"

"Of course I can. If I want to. But can I open it without him knowing?"

"Can you?"

"I don't know. I think so. I can't feel an alarm spell."

Solder stood on his barrel and tried to peer over the wall. Tamrin grabbed his hand and pulled him so he was crouching above her.

"What are you doing?"

"Looking to see if he's there."

She tugged and he dropped to the ground, very lightly for someone who didn't seem very keen on walking or standing.

"And what if he sees you?"

"I'll wave."

Tamrin gaped.

"You'll what?"

"I'll wave," he said. "And smile."

"What are you thinking of?"

He hoisted his barrel and trotted off. Tamrin hadn't finished telling him off and she felt put out at having to do it while she was keeping up with him.

"It's a roffle thing," said Solder.

He led her from the alley into the street, along, left and right and into a busier road.

"Normally, if someone's spying on someone else and they get caught, they duck and hide or look away and it's easy to see if they've been spying. Understand?"

"Yes."

"What you should do, if you're caught spying, is wave and smile. Sometimes I put my thumbs up."

"Why do you do that?"

"No sensible spy is going to draw attention to himself, is he? Think about it. So, if I do that, I'm not a spy, I'm just nosy, and a bit stupid. See?"

Tamrin did see, and she felt a new admiration for Solder at the same time as she began to feel a little nervous of him. All this time she had thought he was a cheerful but rather silly boy. Now she began to wonder what he thought of her and what he was doing following her so obviously.

"Here's a place," he said, and he darted into an open

doorway, found a table by the wall and sat down ready to order something to eat.

Solder had lots of ideas for how they could spy on the tailor.

"Will you just shut up," said Tamrin. "I'm trying to think."

She pulled a "sorry" face straight away because she thought she'd hurt his feelings. Solder grinned at her, ate a piece of cheese and said, "Or we could climb on the roof and I could lower you down on a piece of rope and you could look through his window."

"No. Really. Please just shut up."

"Are you going to pay for this?" he asked.

They had eaten a big meal. Or he had. Tamrin only had a bowl of soup and some bread and a mug of water.

"I haven't got any money," she said. "You'll have to pay."

Solder finished his cheese quickly.

"We'll have to make a run for it," he said.

"We can't do that."

Tamrin was shocked at his easy acceptance that they could steal their food and run away.

"Magic some money," he suggested.

The woman who had served them was watching their whispered conference. She moved slowly and not completely unobtrusively towards the door. They couldn't get out without pushing her out of the way. She was short, fairly slim and with close-cut black hair, but she looked as though she could put up a fight if they tried to dodge past her.

"I can't," said Tamrin.

"You're a wizard. You can."

"Yes, I can," she agreed, "but I can't."

He shook his head.

"That's wizards for you," he said. "And they say that roffles talk in riddles."

"I can," she said. "But I'm not going to. It's not what magic's for. It would cost more than the meal's worth."

"All right. We're in trouble, then."

He grinned at her and waited for her to sort it out.

The woman came over to their table.

"That's ten shillings and fourpence," she said. "Please."

Solder gave her his friendliest smile.

"My friend will settle the bill," he said.

Tamrin glared at him.

"I'll pay for my own," she said. "He can pay for his."

For the first time, she saw Solder become alarmed.

"That isn't right," he said. "And anyway, you haven't got any money either."

The woman crossed her arms, stood with her feet slightly apart and stared at them.

"You're thieves," she said.

"No," Tamrin protested.

"What else are you? You've stolen food from me. I call that thieving."

Tamrin found herself close to tears. She couldn't believe how suddenly she had changed from being a girl who hid in passageways, and learned her lessons, and kept away from people as much as she could, into a bully and now a thief.

She jumped to her feet and shouted at the woman.

"I'm not a thief! I'm not! It was a mistake."

The woman backed away.

"I'm not a thief. I'm not a bully. I'm not a liar."

She was really crying now. The tears poured down her face and her nose was running.

She clenched her fist and shook it. She stamped her foot.

The window shimmered and clouded over, grey and heavy. The light in the shop faded. The table they had been sitting at buckled, its legs bent and it collapsed to one side, all the plates falling off and shattering on the floor. The door slammed and was covered in an instant with old ivy. The woman lurched to one side and fell to the floor. Solder grabbed his barrel and stood on it. Tamrin gasped and stopped shaking her fist.

She dragged her sleeve across her face, wet with tears and snot.

"I'm not," she whispered. "I'm not a thief."

Her side hurt. Her fist hurt. She tried to unclench it and found she couldn't move her fingers. They were locked with rage. She looked down at the woman.

"I'm not," she said. "I'm not a thief."

The woman nodded and put her hand out. Tamrin took it and helped her to her feet. She leaned in towards Tamrin.

"It's all right," she said.

"I'm not," said Tamrin.

"I'm Jaimar," she said. "What's your name?"

"Say it," said Tamrin. "Say I'm not a thief."

Jaimar took Tamrin's hand in hers. She gently unfolded the fingers, disarming the fist.

"No, you're not," she said. "You're not a thief. It was all a mistake."

Tamrin nodded.

"Say you mean it."

"I do. I really do mean it. You're not a thief."

Tamrin couldn't stop herself from asking the next question. She knew it was stupid. She knew it was a waste of time, it was just the question she asked herself every day, many times a day. It was the only question she cared about. She asked it without thinking. She asked it from habit, not from the expectation of an answer.

"Who am I?" she asked.

"You're Shoddle's girl," said Jaimar.

"What?"

"Shoddle. The tailor. You're his girl. You've come back."

Tamrin allowed Jaimar to put her arm around her and lead her out of the shop, through a door at the back and into her own living quarters. Solder trotted after them, his barrel on his back.

Jaimar guided Tamrin, making soft noises of comfort. Tamrin had stopped shouting and sobbing but the tears kept running down her face. She couldn't stop them. It was still hard to breathe as well.

Tamrin sat when Jaimar led her to a chair. She shrugged her shoulders to indicate that the woman could take her arm away. Jaimar left it there. She sat on the arm of the chair and waited for Tamrin to be ready to speak.

Solder hopped on to his barrel, sat with his legs swinging and surveyed the room.

"This is nice," he said.

Jaimar put her finger to her lips to tell him to be silent while Tamrin was distressed.

"It's cosy," he said.

Jaimar frowned and shook her head. She exaggerated lifting her finger to her lips again, to make sure he understood.

"It's not cosy like a roffle house," he said. "But it's comfortable, and it's nice and light with that big window. What's out at the back of the shop? Have you got a garden?"

Jaimar whispered, "Shh. Let's just think for a moment."

Tamrin laughed. Dragged her sleeve across her face again. Jaimar produced a big clean handkerchief and gave it to her. Tamrin blew her nose very loud and cleaned herself up.

"You can't shut roffles up," said Tamrin. "Not this one, anyway."

Jaimar smiled.

Solder crossed the room and looked out of the window.

"It's a lovely garden," he said. "Is that a medlar tree?"

"Yes."

"And figs, and a quince. And the orchard is bigger than you'd think."

The more she got used to Solder the more Tamrin liked him. She appreciated that he had broken the painful mood she had fallen into.

Jaimar took her arm away and moved off the arm of the chair, allowing Tamrin more room.

"What do you know about me?" asked Tamrin. "What did you mean about being Shoddle's girl?"

"Is he the tailor with the big scissors hanging outside the shop?" asked Solder.

"Yes," said Jaimar.

"Good." Solder pointed to Tamrin. "I won't have to hang you by a rope from the roof now."

"What's that?" asked Jaimar.

Tamrin smiled.

"We weren't going to do that," she assured her.

Jaimar took another chair and picked up a square of linen she had been embroidering. She found a needle and silk thread and started to sew. Tamrin found it reassuring, and it meant that the woman's eyes were fixed on something else. They didn't have to look at one another much now.

"Is Shoddle a friend of yours?" asked Tamrin.

"I sell food in the town," said Jaimar. "I try to keep on good terms with everyone."

"So he is a friend?"

"Not everyone is as easy to get on with as everyone else."

It sounded like a no to Tamrin and she decided not to ask again.

"Do you think I should go and see him?" she asked.

"Well, that would depend on whether you like him a lot."

"Would you go?"

"If I were you?"

"Yes."

"That's a difficult question."

Tamrin took her time and thought about this.

"Are you frightened of him?" she asked at last.

Jaimar concentrated on her sewing.

There was a question that Tamrin was frightened to ask. She had hidden it from herself for a long time. She saw that Jaimar might be able to answer it. And it had all come too soon, too quickly. She thought only the tailor could tell her and now she thought differently. She started to cry silent tears again.

Solder looked out of the window. Jaimar started to stand up and go to her. Tamrin held up a hand to stop her. Jaimar sat back down and concentrated on her sewing. The needle glinted in the sunlight.

Tamrin asked the question. Jaimar heard something and looked up. It was so soft, so hesitant she had not caught it.

"Sorry?"

"Is he my father? The tailor. Is he?"

Each word was stronger than the one before it.

"Oh, no," said Jaimar. "No. He can't be."

"Don't you know?"

"He's not. I'm sure of it."

This was too difficult for Tamrin. Either he was or he wasn't.

"But do you know?"

Jaimar looked up and they held each other's gaze.

"I'll tell you what I know, shall I?"

"Yes."

Jaimar put her sewing down, started to speak, then picked it up and started again, her eyes occupied.

"It was about twelve, thirteen years ago. Shoddle was making a living. His shop sold clothes enough to keep him, and his work was good enough for most people around here. There were better tailors in bigger towns and richer people went to them.

"He came in here one day for his dinner. He didn't often do that then. He couldn't afford to. But this day he was happy as a haystack in the sunshine. He bought the best food I had and he even had a small flask of wine with it. He wouldn't say much except that he was going off to make some clothes for a rich man a day's journey away.

"I congratulated him, of course. I was glad to see him go. He wasn't easy to get on with when he was miserable. Being happy made him even more difficult.

"He was away for weeks. The shop was locked up and I thought that it had better be a good job he'd been offered because he was losing a lot of trade while he was away.

"He came back late at night. The streets are narrow here, as you've seen, and we know mostly who comes and goes.

"Anyway, it was late at night. He locked himself in the shop and didn't appear for days. People knocked on the door and called in to him. At first he didn't answer. Then, when they started to say they'd better knock the door down to see if he was all right, he called out through the window that he was fine. He was busy. He'd come out in a few days.

"When he finally appeared he carried you in a basket. He came here first and asked for some food."

Tamrin held up her hand again to stop her.

"What do you mean, he was carrying me in a basket?"

"Just that. We asked him who you were and why he had you. He just wouldn't answer at first. When we pressed him, and believe me it isn't easy to press Shoddle for an answer, but when we pressed him he said you were a foundling."

"What's a foundling?" asked Solder.

Jaimar hesitated and looked to Tamrin for permission to interrupt her story.

"You'd better tell him or he'll never stop asking."

"Sometimes, when people don't want their babies they leave them on doorsteps or in the town square or somewhere where they know someone will find them and look after them."

"Why wouldn't they want them?"

"There are all sorts of reasons," said Jaimar. "That's not the important thing. What matters is that they're found. Foundlings."

"Why they don't want them sounds important to me," he said.

"It really isn't," she insisted. "Not in this story."

Solder shrugged and carried on looking out of the window.

"Where did I come from?" asked Tamrin. "And why had he got me? And what did he do with me? And how did he find me?"

She spoke very fast and was looking for more questions when Jaimar replied.

"We asked him all those things and more," she said. "Over and over. We even tried to take you away from him, because we said he couldn't look after you. He wouldn't tell us any more. He just said he found you on his travels. He kept calling you a foundling, as though that explained everything."

"It doesn't explain anything," said Tamrin, growing distressed again.

"I know. I know it doesn't. It was all he would say, though. And he wouldn't give you up."

Jaimar stopped sewing.

"I offered to look after you," she said.

Her voice was low and sweet. Tamrin had a sudden picture of a different life that might have been hers. A life where she had been born without magic. Living in this place, in this room, with this woman. A home. A proper business. A sort of family. Not dodging into dark corners, an outsider in a big, impersonal college. She saw herself making food and serving it to the customers, laughing and being busy in an ordinary way.

She tried to answer Jaimar. Tried to thank her for trying, and there were no words in her mouth so she just nodded.

"Nothing would shift Shoddle. He had found you. He would raise you. You would help in the shop when you were old enough."

"Why did he send her away, then?" asked Solder.

"Because of the magic," said Tamrin.

"Of course," said Jaimar.

"What happened?"

"You were such a funny little thing," said Jaimar, "in the basket. It wasn't even a proper baby basket, just a shopping one. Big enough for the first few weeks, and nicely dressed and cushioned with good linen, I'll say that for him. He made you comfortable.

"He had hoped to keep the magic a secret. That's why he kept you hidden at first. You can't hide magic, though. Not when it's strong. Lots of babies have the little magic, when they're first born. It wears off very quickly. Only a few, like you, have the real magic that never goes. Yours was real from the start."

"What was it like?" asked Solder.

"Colours at first," said Jaimar. "She'd lie in the basket and there were colours all around her. Better than rainbows. And she could reach her little hands out and gather them up into ribbons. And scents. Better than any flower."

Tamrin was trying to remember and there was nothing there. No memory at all.

"It was always beautiful," said Jaimar. "Some baby magic is cross or frightened or angry. It's not nice to see. Yours was always so lovely. People wanted you to be around so they could see it. It made us happy."

Tamrin really had no memory of it. No memory of ever being happy like that.

"When you got older, a toddler, and you learned about the things around you, the magic was more playful. Flowers and leaves, and lights and small animals, the sort you can cuddle."

"It doesn't sound like me."

"It was. It is."

"What went wrong?"

Jaimar made her lips straight.

"It did," she said. "Of course it went wrong. I don't know why. I don't know what the tailor was doing. I think he was trying to use you to make his business better. Trying to exploit the magic."

"What happened?" asked Tamrin.

"It was the clothes he was selling. He tried to charge more for them at first, and people wouldn't pay. Then he charged the same but he said they were special. And they were. He offered to sell a coat that would keep the wearer warm in the coldest weather. He sold a lot and they were very good. Lighter to wear than ordinary winter coats, and you never felt the cold. Then one person found he was so hot that he couldn't bear it. He tried to take it off and he couldn't. It was in the high street. He was screaming for help. People tried cutting it off him and the material wouldn't yield. He died in front of them, writing and screaming in terrible pain. It was as though he was being boiled alive."

Tamrin could see it in her mind. She put her hands over her face.

"I did that," she said.

"No."

Jaimar sprang up and put her arms round her. "It wasn't you."

"It was my magic, wasn't it?"

"There were other accidents. People were angry and nearly attacked his shop. Soon after that he took you away. We never knew where. He said you were safe and that he'd taken you where you'd be looked after. Some of us thought he'd had you killed but what could we do? You came by night and disappeared by night. Others said he'd sold you to a wizard. There were stories that you'd gone back to your real parents. No one knew."

"What about my twin?" said Tamrin. "What happened to him? Did Shoddle have him as well?"

Jaimar looked blank.

"What twin?" she asked.

They tidied the shop together. Tamrin started by taking away the ivy from the door. Jaimar gathered up the broken plates and beakers. Solder sat on his barrel and chattered to them, telling them the best order to do jobs in and pointing out things they'd missed.

Jaimar had asked Tamrin what she meant about being

a twin. Tamrin called a halt to the story there and refused to say any more. They went back into the shop to get over the awkward silence.

Tamrin began by stroking her hands over the ivy leaves, enjoying their waxy surface, the green bright smoothness shot through with prominent veins. It made her sad to get rid of it. She put her face to the foliage, letting it cool her. Her hands found the thick, rough roundness of the main stem. It felt older than she was. It was strong magic.

She couldn't just let it wither and die and be gathered up and burned.

The problem of what to do with it brought Vengeabil to her mind. He had been so frugal with his magic, so sparing. She had learned from him to be frugal, too. This overabundance of growth showed her how right he had been. It's one thing to make something with a spell; much more difficult to unmake it.

She knew Solder was watching her.

"What are you going to do with it?" he asked.

"I'm not sure."

"Doesn't it just disappear when you take the magic away? Is it real?"

"Come and try it."

He hopped off the barrel. His hands were busy in the leaves and tendrils.

"It's stuck fast to the door," he said. "As though it's been growing against it for a hundred years."

Jaimar left her broom and joined them. She added her hands to the others.

"I've seen other magic," she said. "Wizards pass through sometimes and they always need to eat. Most of their magic feels cheap, like something you buy at a fair, tawdry. It doesn't last. It was never meant to." She tugged at the ivy. "This feels more real than real ivy. That's silly, I know. But you know what I mean."

"College wizards," said Tamrin. "Town wizards who sell their charms. Not proper ones. Not wizards who've been apprenticed to masters."

"Can you get rid of it?" asked Solder.

Tamrin crossed to the table. She righted it on its legs, moved her hands over the bent and buckled parts, restoring them to rights. She struggled with her breathing. It was like running uphill. She picked up the chairs and pushed them back into place. She took the broom and swept the shards of pot.

"I'll do that," said Jaimar, taking it from her. "Sit down."

"You could magic them into a pile," said Solder, going back to his barrel.

Tamrin sat and recovered her breath. Jaimar swept and scooped up the broken fragments.

"No one ever told me," said Tamrin. "But I always knew. I always knew I had a twin."

Jaimar listened. Solder interrupted.

"How could you know if no one ever told you?"

"Close your eyes," said Tamrin. "Now, don't move. How many hands have you got?"

"Two?"

"How many feet?"

"Two."

"How many toes?"

"Twelve."

"What?"

Tamrin stared at Solder's shoes.

"Just joking," said Solder.

Tamrin didn't smile.

"Eight," said Solder.

Tamrin wanted to ask but decided it wasn't the time.

"How do you know you've got two hands if you can't see them and you're not moving them?"

"I just know," he said.

"There you are. I've always just known that there are two of me. I don't know how I know."

"Perhaps it's just an idea," said Jaimar. "There was never any talk here of you being a twin. And Shoddle never said you were."

"I've met him," said Tamrin. "He came to the college last year. Just for about a week. He's called Sam."

"Did you ask him about where you came from?" asked Solder.

"He doesn't even know we're twins."

"Didn't you tell him?"

"I couldn't. Not then. It didn't seem the right time. And then he went away."

The room was back to normal, except for the ivy over the door, and the darkened window. Jaimar sat down next to Tamrin and took her hand in hers. Tamrin let it stay.

"There's no need to take the ivy away," said Jaimar.

Tamrin laughed.

"And close the shop? And lose your business? The door will never open if I don't take it away."

"There's more to life than selling food," said Jaimar. "I'm so glad you're back and you're safe. We'll find a way."

"I'll find a way," said Tamrin.

She saw Jaimar's look of pain.

"I'm sorry," she said. "Sorry. I didn't mean it like that. Thank you. Thank you for helping me."

She squeezed the woman's hand.

"I made it," she said. "I'll have to find a way. There is a way. There has to be."

She moved across to the door and, putting out her arms, she pressed against the ivy. For a moment her face shimmered and seemed to become made up of leaves. Her finger ends sprouted green shoots. She felt herself to be lost in the foliage. A green dream in a green shade.

She stepped back and broke a branch away. She stepped back again, stretched out her hand and ran it over the leaves.

The ivy unfolded itself from the door. The main stem immersed itself into the left side of the door frame. The branches and shoots and leaves followed the line of the wood, up, and across the top of the frame, and down the other side.

Tamrin sang a short, soft chant. The green faded. The movement ceased. The gentle rustling subsided. Where before the simple, straight lines of carpentered oak had framed the door, now it was an intricate design of leaves and tendrils. A visitor would see a carved masterpiece.

"May I take this to the garden?" Tamrin asked, holding out the broken branch.

"Of course."

Jaimar led her through.

The air was cooler, the evening releasing its scents. Tamrin found a stretch of wall. She pushed the branch into the damp earth. It embraced the brickwork, spread to double its first size and settled in the slanting light of the dying sun.

"Will it grow?" asked Solder.

"It will," said Tamrin. "Nothing's lost."

She trailed her fingers on the shining leaves.

"You're tired," said Jaimar. "Come back inside."

They sat, three now, where two had eaten. Tamrin restored the window and was grateful when Jaimar gave her a glass of fresh cordial.

"From our own fruit in the orchard," she said.

"I still can't pay," said Tamrin.

Jaimar put her hand on Tamrin's head.

"You've never needed to pay here," she said. "You never will."

"I've still got lots to do," said Tamrin. "Shoddle. I still need to know."

"All in good time. Rest first. Restore yourself now."

Tamrin drank and her hands stopped shaking, her head began to lose its aching beat. Only her thoughts retained the pain of the question that drove her on. ‖

Part Four

# DOUBLEDANGER

# It was so simple

that Tamrin couldn't think why they hadn't thought of it before. During the day Shoddle could look out of the shop and see them in the sunlight. At night, they were outside in the dark and could look in on him as he worked by lamplight.

So they did.

Jaimar didn't try to stop them, which surprised Tamrin and gave her a pang of worry that the woman was only pretending to be on their side.

"Adults always try to stop you doing things," she said to Solder.

"Not in the Deep World."

"Really?"

"Yes. Really."

Tamrin slowed down as they approached the tailor's shop and she looked carefully at the sides of the street.

"Are there any roffle holes here?" she asked. "Straight down to the Deep World?"

"I'm not allowed to tell you that," he said, and he slipped to one side of a large door frame and disappeared. Tamrin darted after him but it was no good. He was too fast for her. She felt at the edges of the door frame for gaps to slip through. As far as she could work out it was tight to the wall.

"Come on," said Solder.

She looked up and he was standing three doors along, grinning and tapping his fingers on his leather barrel.

Tamrin flapped a "shh" hand at him and caught him up.

"Are they everywhere?" she whispered.

"Not everywhere. Some places there are hardly any. It's useful to have a lot in towns, just in case you need to slip away in a hurry. We try not to go in and out when anyone's watching, so they don't know how many there are or where they are."

"I can't find them, even when I know where to look," she complained.

"You'll learn."

"Will I?"

"If I teach you."

"Will you teach me?" Tamrin hesitated. "I was in the Deep World," she said. "Once."

Solder shook his head.

"I was."

"Up Toppers don't go there any more," he said.

Tamrin was beginning to feel that everything she had known about herself was slipping away.

"I'm not a liar," she said. "I've been down there."

Solder looked steadily at her.

"What's it like?" he asked. "In the Deep World. Tell me three things."

"That's just the thing. I was there for a long time, and I can't remember."

Solder whistled softly.

"So you have been," he said.

"Don't make fun of me."

"I'm not. People who tell you about the Deep World have never seen it. A few people have, and they can't remember. Most of them don't even remember that they've even been there."

"I was ill," she said. "Before I went there. When I was there."

"How did you get in?"

Tamrin shrugged. She remembered that part, but she wasn't ready to tell him yet.

Solder put his hand on her arm and pointed to the shop. They had left Jaimar's at dusk. Now the street was in full darkness. All the shops were closed, most of them shuttered. Some of the shopkeepers lived over the shop and there were lights on in the upper windows. Others were dark from top to earth.

The upper windows of Shoddle's were lit. And the lower window, the shop front itself. They could see the rolls of cloth propped up, and his shadow on the wall.

"Why is it only his shop with lights burning?" asked Solder.

"He needs his bench," said Tamrin. "A tailor can't work anywhere. You need a long, clean surface to spread the cloth out, to measure it, cut it, keep it smooth."

"That's all right, then. I thought it might be a trap. He's just working late."

Tamrin bit her lip.

"I don't know," she said.

"What?"

"Well, a tailor needs lots of light. Small stitches, careful cutting, neat edges. You can't do those by lamplight."

"We should go back," said Solder. "It's not such a good idea to look in. We'll come back tomorrow."

"And dangle by a rope from the roof?" said Tamrin. "I don't think so. Come on."

"This doesn't make sense," he objected. "You said we could watch him by night, when he works by lamplight. Now you say tailors don't work at night. So it can't be right. That's just what he's doing."

"It means he's not just a tailor, doesn't it?" she said. "And he's not just making ordinary clothes.

She looked up, startled at a movement in the corner of her eye. Bats flapped overhead, diving for food, swerving to miss the overhanging upper chambers.

"I knew it. I knew there would be something wrong with him."

She moved carefully towards the tailor's, her shoulder against the wall. His lamp threw a yellow square of light on the shutters opposite.

"If he's doing something wrong," said Solder, "why isn't he doing it with his shutters closed? Why would he want people to be able to see in?"

"He might be expecting someone."

Solder clicked his tongue at her.

"They could knock! He's waiting for us. Of course he is."

Tamrin edged closer.

"He doesn't even know you," she said.

"He's waiting for you. And I'm with you. So if it's a trap for you it's a trap for me, too."

Tamrin stopped.

"You're right," she said.

"I am?"

"Yes. It's a trap. It's obvious. He may not know we're in town. He may not know how near or far we are." She corrected herself. "How near I am. But he's waiting for me. He knows I'll come looking for him."

Solder relaxed and smiled.

"Good. We can go back and think it through."

He started to walk towards the end of the street.

"No."

He stopped.

"No?"

"No. I'm going into the shop."

"You can't."

"Watch me."

Before Solder could call out to stop her Tamrin ran across the street, knocked on the door and, without waiting for an answer, threw it open and walked in.

A bell jangled above her head. She didn't give Solder time to follow. She shut the door and looked at the tailor sitting cross-legged on his bench.

"You've taken your time," he said. ‖

# Shoddle was holding the cloth

close up to his face, stitching with fast strokes of the needle. He took his eyes from his work, stared for a moment at Tamrin as if to make sure it was her, then looked down and continued.

"You knew I was coming?" asked Tamrin.

"Where else could you go?"

Tamrin stepped closer to see what he was sewing. He didn't look up.

It was a sack.

She looked at the rolls of cloth against the walls.

Except there weren't any.

They were just piles of sacks.

"What are you doing?"

He stopped sewing and held up his work. It was a jacket, ragged and rough, not fit for a labourer in the field.

"Nice, isn't it?" he said.

He lowered it to his lap and continued sewing. The needle

was thick and long to get through the harsh cloth.

"It's rubbish. It's a sack."

Shoddle's needle jabbed and stitched. He tugged the coarse thread through the sacking.

"So you can see it? You see all the sacks?"

"Of course."

"They can't. The man who chose this thinks it's the softest worsted, green flecked with red threads. He rubbed it against his face and said it was the finest cloth he'd ever seen."

Tamrin walked round the shop, touching the sacks. They were clean and new, but rough, hard, loose-woven.

"How did I get here?" she asked, her back to Shoddle.

"Can't you remember?"

"No."

"Did you walk? All the way from the college?" he asked.

He was playing games.

"Not just now," she said. "At first. How did I get here at first?"

"Oh, back then. Why didn't you say?"

Tamrin spun round and pointed at him. He pushed the needle through the sacking and it carried on straight through the palm of his hand. He held his hand up and looked at it, the thread still connected to the sack, the point sticking through the back. Blood dripped on to the cloth and ran down and along his wrist. Tamrin could see he was in pain. He didn't show it except for the tightness in his jaw and the set of his shoulders.

"You always were a spiteful little thing," he said.

"I wasn't," she said. "I'm not."

He held his hand out to her.

"No?" he asked.

Tamrin hesitated, caught between the need to show him that she wasn't spiteful and the desire to hurt him more.

She reached forward, tugged the needle and drew it right through his hand, pulling the thread after it so that his hand was stitched to the sack. He grimaced as the coarse fibre passed through his flesh.

"Perhaps I am," she said.

She held the needle at arm's length and watched the thread pull further through his hand.

"How did I get here?" she asked.

"I stole you."

He watched her reaction.

"You didn't expect that, did you?"

She let go of the needle.

"Where from?"

"Oh, that's not so easy to answer."

Tamrin reached her hand for the needle again. Stopped. Left it alone.

"Are you going to leave me like this?" he asked.

"Where did you steal me from? Who from? Why?"

"All in good time. You're hurting me."

Tamrin picked up Shoddle's scissors and snipped the thread. She pulled it from his hand. Blood gushed from the wound. He looked at her, waiting.

"You'll need to put something round that," she said. "Sacking won't be much good. It'll go bad."

She admired the way he ignored the pain. She wouldn't have been able to. She almost admired the way he kept staring at her, challenging. He was not going to be an easy enemy to defeat. He put his hand on the bench, the blood pooling around it.

"You did it," he said.

"I know. I'm not going to say sorry."

"Not my hand. The sacks. You did that."

Tamrin slid the half-sewn coat towards his hand, letting it soak up the blood.

"You made the magic that makes people think that sacks are fine clothes. Don't you remember?"

He uncrossed his legs and re-crossed them the other way round.

"I didn't. I wouldn't."

"You were little. I told you to do it."

The jacket was heavy with blood. Shoddle's face was becoming pale. He spoke more quickly. Tamrin took his hand and lifted it. She wound the thread loosely around his wrist and tied it. The bleeding stopped. He nodded.

"It's worked well enough these years," he said. "Until recently. Two months ago a lawyer came in with a gown I'd made for him." Shoddle flapped his hand. "Pins and needles," he said. He took the sack off and waggled his fingers.

"There was a patch on the shoulder. Not a patch, really. A

ragged piece of sacking, inset, part of the fabric. The rest of it looked like silk."

He opened and closed his fist. The wound had disappeared.

"That's a neat job," he said. "Anyway, the lawyer's cloak."

Tamrin concentrated hard and listened to him. His voice reached her through a long pipe, distant and with an echo. His face was blurred.

"This lawyer, he said that the patch of sacking had begun as big as a thumbnail. Every day it grew bigger. Now it was the size of a law book. He wanted his money back and a new gown."

Tamrin leaned against the bench. It felt unstable, flexible. She could hear Shoddle but it was difficult to follow what he was saying. He was jumping from subject to subject.

"That's it," he said. "You lean against the bench. You're tired. I remember that. Mending magic is always harder work you always said." He held up his hand. "You mended this all right. No pain. Feels better than ever. You should do the other one. It aches in the cold weather."

"Can I have a drink?"

"What's that? Speak up."

"Can I have a drink? Some water?"

"I'll get you some in a minute. Don't you remember? You made the bench turn any material I had into whatever I wanted it to be. Magic, you see. But it's wearing off. There have been others bring their clothes back. And last week a man came in and he saw one of the sacks. Only one. But it was enough."

"Magic always wears off, in time," Tamrin whispered. It hurt her throat to talk.

"Well, you're back now. You can top up the magic. Make it strong again. Before I lose all my customers."

He jumped down from the bench. Tamrin stepped back. Turning her head she saw Solder's face pressed against the glass.

"And more," said Shoddle. "Much more magic. I've got plans for you."

Tamrin steadied herself with her hand.

"I must have a drink."

"Later. Plenty of time."

He took her arm and led her through the shop. She staggered and he steadied her. There was a curtain. There was a stair. There was a door at the top of the stair. There was a room beyond the door. The room was small and low. A thick beam supported the ceiling. Black beams against bare, knapped flint crossed the walls. Sconces on the walls held lighted candles. The room had been prepared. He had known that she was coming. He had made it ready for her.

Tamrin looked for somewhere to sit. Shoddle let go of her arm and she stumbled. There was a window seat and Tamrin managed to get there without falling over. Her throat hurt right into her ears. Shoddle was grinning, running his hands through his hair, hopping, unable to keep still for excitement.

"Please let me have a drink."

"Later. Later. Look here."

The room was empty, save for something the size of a door standing near to the wall adjacent to the window. Shoddle stood next to it. His fingers twitched against a length of green dark damask that hung over it.

Tamrin struggled to sit up. Her back pressed against the window. She turned her face to put her cheek against the glass. It cooled her a little. Her sight cleared and came into sharp distinction. All at once she knew what the object was. It had wooden feet and an oak frame. Bigger than a door now that she looked properly. It was a mirror. Much like several she had seen in Smith's room. The damask hid the reflecting surface, but she knew that was what it was.

Shoddle stood to one side. If he lifted the cloth she would see herself reflected in it.

She knew then, knew beyond doubt, that this was the mirror that Smith was looking for, the one that the handcart went round the lanes and roads searching out. And she knew which mirror it was.

"Don't uncover it," she said. It tore her throat to speak.

He grinned and made a theatrical gesture as if to lift the cloth.

"You wanted to know," he said.

"What?"

"Where you come from. Don't you want to know, after all?"

He couldn't keep still. His glee spilled out into little dance steps and twitches.

Tamrin tried to stand and fell back. Something sharp dug into her back. She reached round to remove it. Her hand closed on the scissors that Smith had given her.

"Look," said Shoddle. He lifted the corner of the damask. The glint of polished steel. A bright triangle.

"Don't."

The scissors were cool, heavy in her hand. She shifted round and switched them over to her other hand. Her head began to clear. The pain lifted from her throat. Her voice strengthened.

"Don't you want to see yourself? You're not a pretty girl, I know, but, all the same, you must be curious."

Tamrin stood.

"Get away from there," she said.

He raised his hand and gripped the cloth firmly.

"Move away."

He tugged. It started to slide down.

Tamrin stepped forward, the scissors high in front of her. Shoddle saw them for the first time.

"Well," he said. "That's nice. I call that handsome. You've come with scissors ready for the tailor's trade. You're going to help me, after all."

"I'm warning you."

Another tug. The damask slid further down. The end of the cloth was now just visible at the top of the frame. Soon, its own weight would send it folding down and the mirror would stand exposed. Poised in front of it, brandishing her scissors, point first, Tamrin would see herself, from head to toe.

She jumped aside to get out of the way. She tripped and fell towards Shoddle.

The cloth slid down. The polished surface appeared. Tamrin reached out to steady herself.

"Careful," shouted Shoddle.

Tamrin tried not to look at the mirror, tried not to see herself reflected back. Her arms flailed. She fell into him.

"You're going to—" Shoddle started to call.

Tamrin never heard whatever he was going to say next. It stopped and changed into a wet, gurgling cough.

"No," said Tamrin. "No."

The scissors stuck into his throat, cutting off his objection. She pulled them out, her mouth open in shock. Blood spouted from the open wound, splashing into her face and down her front. She wiped her sleeve against her eyes to clear them. Shoddle's eyes were wide open, staring at her. He mouthed words that never came, blood trickling from his lips.

Tamrin stepped back, away from the horror she had created.

Stepped into the sight of the mirror.

She stood and looked at herself. Red and wet. Hand still raised. Scissors open, jagged and sharp. Behind her in the room, the flint and beamed walls, the candles in their sconces, the window into the black night. Behind her in the mirror, none of these. A stone wall. A slit window. Light reflected endlessly. A high ceiling. And the dark, hunched forms of the creatures with no faces. And a figure, moving towards her, deliberately, with the light of recognition in its eyes.

Tamrin screamed and the figure stepped through the mirror into the room and seized her.

"Stop. Who are you?" she shouted.


The talk was all of kravvins.

Sam listened, sitting near enough to be part of the company, far enough not to have to join in unless he wanted to.

He had a plate of crusty bread, yellow butter and sharp cheese for company, and a tankard of cordial.

"How near are they?" he asked, and immediately put a large chunk of bread into his mouth so that he wouldn't have to say any more for a while.

"Too near."

The men nodded and looked determined.

"It's magic that's made them."

"Wizards."

A man hawked phlegm into his throat and looked round for somewhere to spit.

"Don't you dare, Danwick Plunt!"

Sam chewed more slowly to keep himself from the conversation. The woman behind the serving counter folded her arms and stared at the man. He looked at the empty fireplace, where he liked to spit in the winter, watching the green snot sizzle on the hot coals. She glowered. He looked down at the shining tiled floor. She leaned on the counter. He looked to his friends for support. They looked away. He moved his tongue and swallowed the slimy gob.

"There should be sawdust on the floor," he said.

"There should be manners," she answered. "So don't bring your filthy tricks in here. Understand?"

Danwick took a deep drink of his beer and let the conversation continue without him. Sam felt the man's distrust of him over his silence.

"Wizards made them," said another. "That's the truth of it."

"Why would they do that?"

"Because they're wizards. Because they can."

"Because they can't leave alone."

"So they're magic, are they? The kravvins? They can do magic like wizards?"

"Made of magic, I said. Not working magic themselves."

Danwick couldn't keep out of the talk for long. He was one of those who liked to be heard. Liked hearing himself more than he liked hearing others.

"They don't need no magic," he said. "Not they. Look at 'em."

"Have you seen them?"

Danwick paused and looked directly at Sam.

"You're very quiet," he said.

"I'm hungry." Sam took a bite of cheese, tore off a hunk of bread and chewed them both together.

"Where are you from?"

Sam pointed to his mouth and smiled.

"Have you? Have you seen one?"

Danwick turned back to his questioner.

"Yes," he said. "Haven't we all?"

There were seven of them. Only Danwick and another, the youngest of them, about twenty years old, admitted that they had actually seen a kravvin. The others knew of them only by accounts from others who had escaped their raids.

"Tell us, Remmble. And Danwick, you tell us. We'll see if you agree."

Remmble, the younger man, had been away visiting relatives. He returned late in the evening and saw the kravvins attacking his parents' home.

"I wanted to help them," he said. He looked round for support. "I wanted to fight the kravvins, drive them away. I couldn't. I hid. At first I watched. In case anyone escaped. Then I didn't watch any more. I ran away."

They said nothing.

"I was frightened," he said. "See? I don't mind telling you. I was."

No one offered him support.

"You think I'm a coward. What could I have done?"

Sam saw the helpless need in the young man's face, the shame. No one spoke.

"At least they killed them all," said Remmble. "At least they're dead. They didn't take any of them away with them."

He was pleading now for approval. The men looked down

at the table. Remmble stood up, spilling his beer, rattling his chair on the tiles.

Danwick put his hand on the young man's sleeve, tugged at it, brought him back to the table.

"They're the cowards," he said.

"What?" Remmble looked alarmed. "Speak up."

Danwick kept his voice low so that they had to lean forward to hear him. Sam chewed as quietly as he could.

"These," said Danwick, pointing to their companions. "They're judging you, and they've never even seen a kravvin. Well, I have. Just like you did. Only you never see one. They're like ants. You see one and you see ten, fifty."

Remmble looked at him with gratitude.

"They're brave enough sitting round this table," said Danwick. "They'll go home and they'll say to their wives that you ran away and didn't fight. But give them one look at a kravvin themselves and they'll run all right."

He stared at them.

"They'll run, all right. You've never seen anything like it. Smooth faces. No faces, really. Red as rage. And they talk. Yes, you can look up and stare if you like. I know you think that part's all been tales and fancy, but it's not. I've seen them. I've heard them. They talk, right. And all they talk is death and killing. That's all they know."

He leaned back and reached for his tankard. More questions followed his outburst.

"And you think they're made of magic, do you? Not some

army come from far off?"

"That's what they say," said one of the others. His voice was hesitant now, after Danwick's attack on them.

"Well I say you're right," said Danwick. "I say they're made from magic. And I say we can find out. Do you know how?"

"I'm not going near them," said the oldest.

"No need," said Danwick. "You want to know about magic, who do you ask?"

He waited for an answer.

"Eh?" he said. "Who do you ask? I'll tell you who you ask. You ask a wizard."

He swung round and looked at Sam.

"Isn't that right, boy? You want to know about magic, you ask a wizard?"

"Sounds about right," said Sam.

"So, tell us, wizard, are the kravvins made from magic?"

"What makes you think I'm a wizard?"

Danwick laughed.

"Look at you," he said. "You're sitting alone, but not alone. You can hear us if you like and ask a question, but you don't like giving an answer. Look at you. You're with us at this table, but sitting along the settle, just a bit far off from us. You don't join in. You don't stay out. You're a wizard. Now, are the kravvins made of magic or not?"

"No," said Sam, and he ran the last of his bread over the plate, catching up the last of the butter, the scraps of cheese and the crumbs, and he put it into his mouth.

"We'll wait," said Danwick. "Chew away as long as you like. We'll wait."

"Why would someone magic them up?" one of the others asked.

Danwick signalled for him to be quiet.

"We'll wait for the wizard," he said. "He's nearly finished."

Sam couldn't chew any longer. He swallowed, drank some cordial and sighed.

"And come closer," Danwick ordered him. "We don't want to have to shout, do we?"

Sam slid along and joined them at their table.

"No," he said. "They weren't made by magic."

Danwick leaned forward, too close, his beery breath in Sam's face.

"So," he said. "You know about them?"

"No."

There was a clatter of excited talk at table. Danwick raised his hand for silence.

"You know magic didn't make them and you don't know anything about them?"

"That's right."

Sam watched the serving woman position herself to intervene if things became too heated. He gave her a slight shake of his head.

"Tell us about the kravvins," said Remmble. "Where did they come from?"

"Have you seen one?"

"What do they want?"

"How many are there?"

Danwick couldn't slow the stream of questions. He sat back, annoyed at losing control. Sam waited for them to be quiet.

"I know nothing about them," he said. "Except that they're new and dangerous and you should stay away from them."

A cloud of complaint rolled over him.

"We stay away."

"It's them that attacks."

"They're getting closer."

Danwick forced his voice above theirs.

"I say," he said, staring at Sam, "that they're made of magic, and that we've got a wizard to blame for it. That's what I say. And I say that you're a wizard, so why should we believe you?"

Sam felt he was losing control of things. He had come here to learn about what was happening, and now he was the one being called to account. He needed to get back in charge. He leaned over the table to take Danwick's tankard. It was nearly empty.

"What are you doing?"

Danwick tried to grab it.

Sam raised the pewter tankard, tipped it up and poured the beer out. It splashed on the table top, poured off and soaked into Danwick's clothes. The man sprang back. The others scattered to avoid the spill.

"I just need this," said Sam, holding the tankard aloft.

They were still protesting when he tossed the tankard into the air. It span round, more droplets of beer scattering out, splashing their faces.

He clapped his hands and whistled.

Each droplet became a slender silk ribbon, blue and green and yellow and red, shot through with silver threads that mimicked the sunlight. Where the beer had spilled on their clothes the material was threaded through with the coloured strips.

They laughed and caught at them, pulling them from their hair and faces, holding them up to see the light glance from them.

Sam watched, relieved to have averted attention from the questions. Danwick watched, grim-faced, ignoring the ribbons that dangled over his face. The men came back to their seats, safe from a soaking.

Sam held out the tankard for them and started to gather up the ribbons into it. He reached over and pulled one free from the shoulder of Remmble's jerkin.

"Put them all back," he said.

The men amused themselves recovering the ribbons from their clothing. Sam watched them, making sure all were replaced into the tankard. He took it by the handle, rapped it on the table top and the ribbons disappeared.

"Here's your beer," he said.

Danwick pushed it aside.

"I won't drink now it's been tricked."

"It's just the same as before," said Sam.

Danwick pushed it further away.

"Magic doesn't make anything," said Sam. "It can change things, but it can't make them. The kravvins weren't made by magic."

"What's the difference?" Danwick demanded. "Whether a wizard made them or changed them from something else? It's all the same in the end."

"It's not. Of course it's not."

"The kravvins are kravvins whether they're made or changed."

Sam stood up.

"I'm leaving now," he said.

No one offered him a goodbye.

They watched in silence as he paid for his meal. He ignored their stares. His hand was on the door when Danwick said, louder than he needed to for his companions to hear, "They say Flaxfield made the kravvins. That's why he disappeared."

Sam stood with his hand still on the door, ready to open it.

"Don't be stupid," he said.

His back was to the men.

Danwick grinned at his friends.

"That's what they say," he said. "Flaxfield's at Boolat, making the kravvins."

Sam's fingers hurt from gripping the door so tightly.

"I was with Flaxfield the day he died," he said.

"Speak up."

"You heard me."

"Flaxfield disappeared. Then the next thing you know, villages are in flames. People killed and eaten, taken away. Never seen again."

Sam listened, his back to Danwick. He could see through the window to his left the shape of a dragon in the sky. He changed the focus of his mind, as you change the focus of your eyes to see through a window or on to the glass. With Danwick's voice still in his ears he looked down through dragon's eyes to the inn beneath. He circled and keeled to the right, circled again.

"And it's all close to Boolat," said Danwick. "All the attacks have been close to the castle. What do you make of that?"

Sam's voice answered though his eyes were elsewhere.

"What do I make of it? I make out that you're a fool."

In a single movement Danwick seized his tankard and sent it spinning through the air, aimed at Sam's head.

"Fool, am I?"

Starback swooped, bearing down on the inn.

The tankard bounced off nothing, an inch from Sam's head, and fell clattering to the floor. The beer spilled out. Sam moved back from the door slowly, turned, as though walking in his sleep, touched the tankard with the toe of his shoe. Stepped aside from the door.

The door slammed open and the air was sucked out of the room. Sam saw the men put their hands to their chests and open their mouths. They were drowning.

Starback flew through the door, circled the room once, as

agile as a bat, missing all objects. His claws scraped the floor and he settled next to Sam.

The air rushed back in. The men gasped at it, sucking it into their lungs.

Sam shuddered, blinked, looked at them.

"Tell me. Make no mistake. Who says Flaxfield's the cause of this trouble?" he said.

Danwick stood.

"We'd better talk while we're walking," he said. "Come on, Remmble."

"This isn't getting me to a tailor," said Sam.

They kept on walking.

The road was strewn with broken glass and smashed furniture, scored with the deep tracks of heavy objects dragged along it, pitted with the marks of sharp feet.

Behind him, far behind him, the inn.

Beside him, Danwick and Remmble. Danwick, surly and set. Remmble, nervous, talkative.

Overhead, the circling shape of Starback.

Ahead of him, in clear sight now, the village, sacked, razed, ravished.

"What's that?" asked Remmble.

"Nothing," said Sam. "I was just thinking out loud."

"Tailors, you say?" said Danwick. "There's no trusting tailors."

"That's what they say," said Sam.

They stopped and surveyed the village.

"Are you sure there's nothing there?" asked Remmble.

"No," said Danwick. "But it's your village?"

"Yes. That's my house."

He pointed to a smouldering black heap.

"I was there," he said, pointing back to a copse on an eminence.

"In the trees?"

"Yes. People were running away. Covered in ash and dust. Screaming. Arms like wings. Why did they do that? It's harder to run that way?" He did not stay for an answer. "I didn't see any of my family. But I saw people I knew. I knew everyone, really. The kravvins were too quick for them. They ran them down, snapped them up, threw them in the air, caught them, killed them. Ate them. Dragged them back. Tossed them like puppets to one another."

Sam couldn't look at him. He wanted him to be quiet. He needed Remmble to tell them everything. He needed to know all he could about the kravvins.

"They ran through the houses, setting them on fire as they left. Sometimes they didn't find everyone in a house and when the flames bit, the people ran out and the kravvins were waiting for them. I couldn't watch. I couldn't stop looking. I wanted to run away. I wanted to see it all. I wanted to save them. I wanted to save myself. I hid. And I ran."

"There's still smoke," said Danwick.

"Fires take weeks to die," said Sam. "Longer."

"Sometimes, never," said Danwick.

"What do you mean?" asked Remmble.

"He knows." Danwick indicated Sam.

"Yes. Sometimes, never. Or as good as never."

"Come on," said Danwick.

The man took Remmble's arm with a protective kindness that surprised Sam. None the less, it was firm and brooked no resistance. Remmble allowed himself to be led to the smoking village, though he trembled and stumbled and his breathing grew short and swift.

"They've all gone," said Danwick. "Be sure of that."

Sam allowed himself to see the village from overhead. Used the sharp dragon sight to make sure there were no traps, no hidden enemies. It was clear. As far as he could tell.

The road was sharp on his feet and he stepped carefully to avoid the broken debris. The closer they drew to the houses the more the road was covered in black ash, fine and clinging. It stained their ankles as their feet brushed them. Some was dry as dust and swirled in the breeze; the ash of the wooden frames of the buildings. Some was greasy and stank; the ash of other things. Sam hoped that Remmble was not noticing the difference.

"There's not a single dead kravvin," said Danwick. "Not a broken leg. Not a trace of any of them. All this death and killing and not one of them damaged."

"Unless they took the wounded away," said Remmble.

"There were none wounded," said Danwick. "None."

Danwick put his hand on Sam's shoulder.

"This is what magic does," he said.

"What do you mean?"

"Men don't do this. Ordinary men. This is magic damage."

Remmble was regaining his nerve. He had stopped trembling. Sam saw that he was growing angry now.

"Why are we here?" he shouted. "I don't want to see this again."

He advanced on Sam.

"You made me come here. With your magic and your questions and your threats."

"Steady on," Danwick restrained him. "It was my idea. Remember? I said we should come. I said we should show him what the kravvins had done."

Remmble shook his head.

"It was him," he said. "The wizard. You said he made the kravvins."

"No. Not him. Sam didn't make this happen."

Remmble pointed to his left.

"That's my house," he said.

It had gone, entirely. All that remained was a heap of smouldering ash.

"You already showed us," said Danwick.

"My parents are in there. And my sister. I'm going to look for them."

"They're not there. Come on. We've seen enough."

Danwick's voice was gentle and reassuring. Sam couldn't understand the change in him.

Remmble walked over to where his house had stood. He stooped down, scooped a handful of ash and rubbed it over his face, his neck, his head.

"Come on," said Danwick. "We'll go back."

Remmble turned his back and walked away, his feet scraping against the burned village, the ash rising around him.

"Come on," called Danwick.

"Stay away," Remmble called over his shoulder.

"I can stop him," said Sam.

"No. You know you can't."

They watched him clear the boundary of the houses and gain the fields.

"Where will he go?" asked Sam.

"If he keeps on that way? Boolat."

"We have to stop him."

Danwick began to leave the village, taking the road they had entered by. Sam hesitated, then caught up with him.

"This is nothing to do with Flaxfield," he said.

They stopped.

Sam couldn't make out what he thought of Danwick. The man had been so aggressive, so harsh in the inn, then so gentle, so fatherly to Remmble.

"So you say," said Danwick. "All I know is, the kravvins are new. It's only about a year since the first reports of them. And that's when Flaxfield disappeared."

"He died. I helped at his Finishing. I saw him leave."

"You saw him? You watched him through the doorway?"

"What do you know of that?"

Danwick sneered.

"We know more of things than wizards think we know."

"I was upset. It was a good Finishing. We stood on the riverbank and watched the basket bear him downstream. He died while I was catching trout."

Sam stopped talking while he still could.

Danwick pointed to the smouldering village.

"No one sent these to the Finished World. What happens to them? Where do they go?"

Sam shook his head.

"I don't want to talk about these things."

Danwick walked away.

Sam lingered, then wandered back to the smoky heaps of ash, drawn there against his will. The air was harsh and scratched the back of his throat. The smell of fear was stronger than the smell of death and that was fierce enough. Remmble trudged towards the sky line, feet stained with grey dust. Sam wanted him to turn and wave, to come back. Remmble did not. Danwick was out of sight already. His road turned and disappeared, consumed by trees.

Not a day went by but Sam missed Flaxfield. As an apprentice Sam had spent all his time with the old wizard. If he saw a tree he didn't know the name of he wanted to ask Flaxfield. If he worked a new spell for the first time and it was perfect he wanted Flaxfield to congratulate him. If he fell he wanted Flaxfield to tell him he was all right. If he saw a kingfisher disappear beneath the water and come back with a fish he felt a surge of joy and wanted to turn to Flaxfield and share the beauty of it. If he found a stone shaped like a mouse or an arrowhead Sam wanted to show it to Flaxfield and ask if it meant something. Once, when they were fishing, Flaxfield had stooped and picked up a smooth stone, green with the river and ridged beyond what the current could do.

"See this?" he asked.

Sam cupped it in his hands, wet and cold, slippery.

"It looks like a frog," he said.

"Do you think it is?"

"It's a stone."

"But was it a frog, once? And can it be a frog again?"

Sam raised it to his face and sniffed it.

"Well?"

Sam weighed it in his hands.

"It's lighter than a stone."

"It is."

"I think it's a frog."

"How did it become a stone?"

This was how Flaxfield taught.

"Magic?" Sam guessed.

"I think you're right."

Flaxfield held out his hand for it. Sam didn't want to give it back. There was something about it. There was a life in it, a presence, a possibility, a past.

"Can you turn it back into a frog?" asked Flaxfield.

Sam held the stone in his left hand, ran his right hand over it, testing it.

"I think so," he offered.

"Are you going to?"

"Shall I try?"

"What do you think?"

That all seemed a long time ago now. Sam looked at the heaps of ash around him. He could feel the heat from the fires that still cringed deep inside them. He recalled the green shade of the riverbank, the soft speech of the water, the damp stone.

Flaxfield had led him through all the challenges of his life, had taught him how to go carefully. Sam wanted Flaxfield there now, to ask him what to do as he had asked him then.

"What do you need to know?" said Flaxfield.

Sam moved the stone from hand to hand.

"Can I really do it?" he said. "Will the frog live if I do? Will it be in pain? Can I put it right if the spell goes wrong?" He paused, waiting for the bigger questions to form in his head. "Who did this to the frog? Why did he do it?"

"Good," said Flaxfield. "Very good. Whether you can turn this stone back into the frog isn't the best question. The others are better. But there's still another question."

Sam cupped the stone in both hands and looked at it. Now it looked more like a frog than like a stone. He had already begun to think of it as a frog. He had already begun to turn it back in his own mind. He could almost feel the pulse of it in his hand, the kicking of the feet, the squirm to escape, to leap into the water.

"I can't think of any more real questions," he said.

Flaxfield held out his hand again. Sam returned the stone. Flaxfield held it as he would a living creature.

"No?" said Flaxfield.

"No."

"Perhaps it never was a frog?"

Sam shook his head.

"I can feel it," he said. "I can feel the life inside the stone. I can taste the magic, smell the spell. That's no ordinary stone."

"No," said Flaxfield. "No ordinary stone. But what if it wasn't a frog? You asked a question and didn't stay to answer it. Why would anyone turn a frog into a stone?"

"For fun?"

"What fun is there in that?"

"No fun. I know," said Sam.

"There's no good reason," said Flaxfield. "But I might want to turn something dangerous into a stone shaped like a frog."

"So if I undid the changing spell..." said Sam.

"Then you just might find yourself holding something much more dangerous," said Flaxfield.

He held up the stone.

"What shall we do?" he asked.

"It could be a good man, tricked, and hurt," said Sam. "We could do good by undoing the spell."

"It may. We might."

Sam pondered the puzzle.

"You tell me," he said to Flaxfield. "What shall we do?"

"That's the right answer," said the wizard. "If in doubt, ask, don't act."

He slipped the stone back into the water.

"Another day," he said. "When we know more."

Sam still remembered the pain he felt as the stone disappeared into the water. A good man, condemned to more imprisonment, or a danger avoided? He didn't know. But he knew he didn't want to walk away from it. He wasn't one to walk away. Not from a strange stone. Not from a challenge, a puzzle, a question.

"What am I supposed to do here?" he asked.

No voices answered him. Flaxfield was dead and gone. The villagers were ash around him. Remmble and Danwick had left him there.

But Flaxfield was dead and Finished. The villagers were dead and ignored. Sam looked at the furrows of ash where Remmble had scooped it into his hand. Something glinted in the tracks. Sam prodded it with his boot. It lifted. He stooped, pulled it from the grey ash.

It was a locket. Silver, slender, a loop of metal held by a delicate chain.

It dangled from his fingers, staining them with ash.

The light caught it and was reflected out, making a pattern on the scorched ground.

Sam wasn't allowed to perform Finishings on his own. Not yet. Not without Flaxfold. And here was a whole village, dead and not Finished. And here was Sam, alone, with nothing else to offer.

"I'm sorry," he said, to the absent Flaxfold. "I have to do something. It won't be a Finishing. Not properly. Just a chance for them. Just a small gift. A hope. Probably nothing will happen."

The ash muffled his words, low-spoken and hesitant.

He held the locket aloft, allowing the light to catch it as it twisted on its chain. He raised his eyes. Starback keeled in the blue air, dipped and swerved, seemed to falter. Sam's head reeled with the movement. He steered Starback to the treetops and settled there for stability.

He spoke the opening words of the Finishing. A gust of wind stirred the ashes. He stopped, looked around. No sign of Remmble. No sign of Danwick. The tree line that had enfolded Danwick stood close by, beyond the turn. Starback looked on.

The silence was more uncomfortable than speech so he continued, louder now, more confident.

The ashes whipped against his legs, swirled round him.

Sam altered the words as he had been taught, tailoring them to the village. Eddies of wind fumbled at the houses. Little wraiths of ash formed in the current. They grew and shaped themselves. Like crows returning to the roost at evening they advanced on Sam.

The air blurred and broke. The wraith at Sam's ankles darted up and slid through the cleft. The others rushed forward and pressed after it.

Sam found himself buffeted by them, as by a gale. He staggered. The locket grew hot in his hand. The chain writhed. He held it towards the opening to drop it in.

And a hand took it from him. ||

# Starback rode the air currents,

hardly moving his wings. He let himself glide softly to the treetop, settled on a sturdy branch, turned his head to left and right and breathed out, small tufts of smoke from each nostril.

He watched Sam raise his arm. Saw the glint of sunlight on the silver. Heard the words of the Finishing. Watched the wind whip up the ash. Grew fearful as he saw the dark eddies rise up, spinning. Hopped from one clawed foot to the other as he saw the air shudder and split.

He arched his wings and lifted into the lifting air.

A red stain spilled across the landscape beyond the village. Starback saw it as he dived towards the ash-peopled village.

Sam's hand was in the grip of one who seemed to be another creature of the ash. Sam's wrist hurt and Starback felt the pain. When Sam pulled away Starback's wing was wrenched. The dragon staggered, righted himself and soared down, fire foaming from his mouth. He flew straight at Sam. The impact jarred them both, knocking Sam to his knees and sending Starback spinning out of control until he flicked his tail, flew up, veered and righted, and swooped again to land next to Sam, sending puffs of ash into their faces.

The jolt had freed Sam. The cleft in the air snapped shut. The chain, half-in, half-out, hung as though suspended by an invisible thread. A dozen or so dust eddies hovered where the opening had been, trying to get through. They disturbed the chain. They moaned, as the wind complains in autumn branches.

Starback nuzzled against Sam, making him get up.

The stain was spreading. It had reached the field's edge, drawing nearer.

Sam stood, then toppled over, his ankle twisted and useless from the force of Starback's assault. He couldn't walk.

"I can see them," he said. "They're fast. Too fast for me."

Starback crouched. Sam put his arms around him. Together they rose up and left the world of ash for the world of air.

It was an unsteady flight, and Sam was glad when they landed on Starback's perch, high atop the trees.

The red stain spilled over the hedgerow into the village. The dust eddies fled shrieking from it. As it grew closer it revealed the shapes that made it. Hard and smooth, shine and shout, red and roaring, hot from hate.

"Kravvins," whispered Sam.

And he knew that Remmble had been right to run, and he knew why Danwick would not let the others call the young man a coward.

These creatures were monstrous. Not just their appearance, but their movements, their strength. There was something about them like a force of nature. Sam wanted to forget that he had ever seen them, but he knew they would stay in his memory for ever. This moment, this first sight of them, would never leave him.

Sam couldn't hear the words the kravvins mouthed. With his dragon's ears Starback could.

"No kill."

"Kill."

"Dead before."

"She here?"

"Not she?"

"All kill."

Their voices carried no emotion, no thought. Only the words told their confusion and alarm.

"Stay kill."

"She come?"

They swarmed over the ash, looking for prey, jabbing the grey ground with sharp legs, pushing smooth faces deep into the debris, bumping into each other in their haste and urgency to kill.

Sam thought of the frog stone and wondered what he had worked.

"Well," he said to Starback. "It's done now. Whether it should be or not."

He rubbed his ankle. The pain was wearing off.

The kravvins had finished at the village. Outriders darted in all directions. Some came halfway to the trees, listened, waited, darted nearer, then fell back and rejoined the main group.

Noon gave way to a softer time and they moved off, away from Sam, back where they had come from.

"Back to Boolat," said Sam.

Starback stepped off the branch and flew round, high above easy sight, until they were far off.

"I ought to get down," said Sam.

Starback was losing height, dropping towards the ash heaps. Sam let his mind shift to one side and he saw as Starback saw. He saw the silver chain with its locket. Saw the small groove in the air where the door to the Finished World had been. Saw a woman, alone, tall and graceful, approach the village. She was a tiny figure to Sam, indistinguishable. Starback saw her grey eyes, her straight hair beneath the scarf, her set mouth a determined line. Sam saw her look up and see the dragon, wheeling above and ahead of her.

She stopped, put her hand to her head to adjust the scarf, drawing it over her mouth and nose. Looking away from Starback she continued towards the smouldering ash, heading straight for the locket. When she reached it she put out her hand and grasped the chain, letting the locket settle against the back of her hand.

Starback flapped soft wings and drifted down to land just out of her reach, close enough to threaten.

"What brings you here, dragon?" she asked.

Sam caught his breath. People were usually more wary of dragons, more ill at ease.

"Lost your tongue?" she said, smiling.

Starback flicked his tail, sending a fine spray of dust into the air. She tightened her scarf around her mouth. Sam wanted her to take it away so he could see her face clearly.

"I'm just going to take this," she said, indicating the locket. "It shouldn't be left like this, should it?"

Sam wanted to laugh at the idea of a woman being able to draw something out from the Finished World. Perhaps she was half-witted? Not apprehensive about a dragon and now expecting to reclaim the locket.

"And then you can come home with me, if you'd like," she said. "There's food there, and lodging for the night."

For a moment Sam had an impulse of fear, that she was not talking to Starback at all, but to him. Dragons don't need lodgings, and though Starback liked a slice of ham or a hunk of cheese from Flaxfold, dragons need no feeding. They find their own food when they need to.

"I'll just…" she said, and, to Sam's astonishment, she drew the chain out from the cleft and held the locket in her hand, free from the grip of the tense air. The cleft snapped shut with a click and the scar disappeared.

"Shall I wear it?" she asked.

She unclasped it and held her hands to her neck.

"No. I don't think so, do you?"

Starback flexed his claws in the ash.

"It's not mine to wear. And it's not mine to give or take. I'll look after it until I can find a proper home for it."

Sam half-closed his eyes. Starback half-closed his eyes. He looked at her from far off and from up close at the same time. And she knew he did.

"Who are you?" said Sam.

But Starback said nothing so she didn't hear.

"If I go now I'll be home soon after dark," she said. She pointed to the road beneath the trees that Sam had settled on.

"It's that way. I'll be beneath the trees. Don't lose sight of me, will you?"

She pocketed the chain and locket and walked away.

Starback launched into the air with a single flap of wings, a flick of tail, a spurt of fire and a flurry of ash.

Sam clambered down the tree, ripping his clothes on the branches, testing his weight on his bad ankle, which only throbbed a little now and ached even less.

He sat on a low branch and watched for her approach. She passed beneath him, face still covered. He let her walk a little along the forest path and dropped down, as silently as he could.

"There you are," she said, not turning. "Are you going to walk with me?" ||

# They walked together in silence

in a creased green light.

Sam had first met Megatorine, the roffle, in a forest such as this and he looked out for one now, even though he was no more likely to see one there than anywhere else.

He hugged his cloak tight to himself, not for warmth. He fingered the hem and could feel the image of a memmont that was woven into it.

The woman walked with easy strides, her face still covered. The path was narrow at first, and grew wider as they approached the end of the forest. Sam lagged behind, partly from the sense that she was leading him along a way that she knew and he didn't, partly to keep her in sight.

She stepped to one side to allow him to draw alongside her.

"How did you do that?" he asked. "With the chain."

She loosened her scarf and let it fall away from her face. She was younger than Sam had thought.

"I'm Winny," she said.

"You can't do that," said Sam. "No one can mess with the Finished World. That chain was stuck."

She smiled and walked on for a moment.

"You're supposed to tell me your name now," she said. "I tell you mine and you say you're pleased to meet me and you tell me your name."

Sam fell back and walked behind her again, though the path was still wide enough for two. He was pleased when the tree cover unfolded and he could see Starback overhead. It still took a great effort for him to reconnect the boy and the dragon. It made his head ache. He fuzzed his eyes and saw himself and Winny walk from the trees into the open. He saw, a few miles ahead, a house, with outbuildings, a high chimney that smoked in the summer.

"We're nearly there," said Winny.

"Wait," said Sam.

Winny stopped.

They cast long shadows on the yellow stubble.

"Where are we going?" he asked.

She pointed to the ribbon of grey smoke.

"It's not far," she said.

Sam held out his hand.

"Give me the locket."

"Didn't anyone teach you to say please?"

"Give it to me now."

Starback circled higher and higher, almost out of sight.

Sam shrugged back his cloak to free both his arms. He

leaned to one side on his staff and Winny smiled.

"I'm not joking," said Sam. "Give it to me."

"I'm sorry. I wasn't laughing at you. It's just that you remind me of someone. He used to lean on his staff in just that way."

Starback wheeled and dipped, flew low over the field and circled just above their heads.

"You're leading me into a trap," said Sam.

"No. Why would I do that?"

"I don't know. Why would you?"

"I want to help," she said. "I didn't know you'd be at the village."

"Why are you leading me to the kravvins?"

"I don't understand. I'm not."

"Give me the locket."

She frowned.

"Please."

She handed it over.

Sam opened it. On one side was a tiny glass mirror, the size of his thumbnail. The other, a delicate picture of a girl, about thirteen. Sam guessed it was Remmble's sister and he felt sad. He hoped that she had been one of the ash eddies that had slipped through into the Finished World.

"What is it?" asked Winny.

Sam moved closer so that she could see inside the locket. The sun reflected a circle of light on her tunic.

Sam cupped it in his hands and gasped on it. The mirror

misted over. When it cleared they saw, not themselves, but a house, a chimney, grey smoke.

"Is that where we're going?" asked Sam.

She nodded.

"Look closely," he said.

She leaned in.

"See them?"

She drew in a startled breath, nodded again.

"Kravvins," she said.

"All around the house," said Sam. "You're leading me into a trap."

"No. I'm not. But we have to go there. Now."

He caught her arm.

All at once she looked older, stronger. She pulled her arm away with a force that unsettled him. He steadied himself with his staff. Starback pounced forward, mouth gaping and fire dribbling out.

"Don't stop me, Sam," she said. "Don't try."

Sam rapped his staff on the hard earth. The field made a responsive, low booming. Winny tripped and fell sprawling on her face.

"Oomph," she gasped.

She tried to stand. Roots grasped her wrists, her ankles, twining themselves round, tight. She was anchored to the earth.

"I didn't tell you my name," he said.

"And why would you need to? Look at you. Do you even

know that you stand like him? That your voice lilts like his? That you have the same arrogant tilt to your head, the same way of keeping to yourself, the same way of looking right into a person?"

Sam knew who she was describing; he just didn't recognize himself in it.

"That's right," she said. "I knew Flaxfield longer than you ever did. I knew about you before you knew about yourself."

"That doesn't mean I should trust you."

"You stay here if you like. Or run away with your dragon. I don't care. But I need to go to my father. He's in danger. Now set me free." ||

# Starback flew high above Smith's house

and the forge. There was no way in or out. The kravvins formed a circle, three deep, all around it. They were chanting.

Sam and Winny kept their distance.

Sam leaned on his staff, his eyes closed, his hands tight on the smooth bark. Winny rubbed her wrists. The roots had gripped her tightly.

"What are they doing? Are they attacking?"

Sam barely moved his head, just enough to signal no. Winny's voice was distant for him, faint.

Starback banked to the left and returned. Sam waited until the dragon had settled on the stubble and folded his wings before he opened his eyes again. When he did, Winny saw that blood seeped out from the side of his left eye.

"Do you see what the dragon sees?" she asked.

Sam stepped back, finding his feet again and letting the staff tilt without his weight. He brushed his sleeve against the blood.

"I am the dragon," he said. "Don't ask any more."

Winny waited.

"They're just standing there. All around the house. Not too close. They haven't crossed the line of the yard and the garden."

"Is my father safe?"

"I couldn't see him."

"If the house isn't burned down and they're all outside, something's keeping them away."

"Yes," Sam agreed. "Do you know what it is?"

Winny pointed to the locket.

"What about that?" she asked.

Sam opened it. They bent their heads together and stared at the looking glass. As they did, a noise went up from the Kravvins. First, a single voice, harsh, carrying.

"Kill. Fire. Kill. Fire."

The shout was taken up by the next and the next, until it ran round the circle, rising and falling, a wave of hate. They scratched the ground with their sharp legs in time to the chant. The raucous mixture of chant and scrape set Sam's teeth on edge.

"I can't see him," said Winny, looking into the glass.

Sam snapped the locket shut.

"It's a good thing," he said. "If they'd got him they wouldn't be out there, would they? They'd be running through the house. Like at the village."

"What do they want?"

Sam gave her the sort of look Flaxfield used to give him.

"You know," he said. "Better than me. Don't you?"

Winny nodded.

"So don't ask me. I'm not stupid."

"Sorry."

"How did you do it?" he asked. "How did you get the chain from halfway into the Finished World?"

"You'll have to ask my father that," she said. "When we've got rid of the kravvins."

Sam glared at her.

"If I knew why they were attacking him I might be able to work out how to fight them," he said.

Each glared at the other. Neither seemed ready to back down. Sam wondered how long it would have lasted, how great her stubbornness was, and if it matched his own. Before it was put to the test the sound of crunching twigs announced the arrival of someone from the forest.

Sam swung round, ready to face more kravvins. Winny drew a short dagger from her tunic. Even at a moment of possible danger Sam couldn't help noticing the simple beauty of the knife, its balance and form, the way it fit perfectly into her hand, the intricately etched decoration on the blade. He noticed, too, the easy and familiar way Winny held it, ready for use. The glint of late sun from the blade.

"I don't think you need that against a roffle," he said.

Winny almost smiled.

Megatorine waved at them. Winny slipped the blade out of sight.

"This isn't finding you a tailor," said Megatorine. "Who's this?" He nodded to Winny.

"Why are roffles so deceitful?" she asked.

"Why does a rabbit paint a windmill?" asked the roffle.

"Do you know him?" asked Sam.

"Ask him," said Winny.

Megatorine found a pair of spectacles in his pocket and put them on. He looked at Winny with an expression of concentration. Sam saw her face reflected in the glass.

"Does a wardrobe recognize a mixing bowl?" he asked.

"I've got an idea," said Sam. He grabbed the roffle's shoulder. "Is there a roffle hole over there? Near the house?"

Megatorine took his spectacles off, polished them on his sleeve and popped them back into his pocket.

"Is Solder in there with him?" asked the roffle.

"Who's Solder?"

The roffle looked at Winny.

"Is he?"

"No. Solder left without telling us where he was going."

Megatorine wagged his finger at her.

"Ah," he said. "Gone, is he? But no one leaves without you knowing where they're going, do they?"

Winny didn't answer.

"So Smith's alone there? No Solder?"

"He's alone."

"In that case," he straightened the straps of his barrel-pack and turned around, heading back to the forest, "I don't know if there's a roffle hole we could get to. Smith can look after himself."

They watched him till he was out of sight. The trees gathered him in.

"He could have got us in," said Sam. "Through the Deep World."

"Or he could have gone himself, and told my father we're here."

"Smith," said Sam. "Is that your father?"

"Yes."

"Is it his name, or what he does?"

"Yes." She kicked the earth. "Roffles. You can't trust them. Even the best."

The chanting and stamping rippled over them.

"It looks like they can't get to him," said Sam. "They're keeping their distance."

"For now. What will happen when night falls? It's close now."

"Why should that change anything?" asked Sam.

"Darkness always does. You know that."

She moved away from Sam. He felt the distance as sharply as he would have felt a slap.

"We can't get to him through the Deep World," she said. "But there's always the other way."

Sam pretended not to understand.

"The dragon could fly over them."

"What good would that do?" asked Sam.

"You tell me."

"All right," said Sam. "But I'm going to lie down. Watch the kravvins. Make sure they don't come this way."

He laid his staff on the stubble, lay alongside it, as though they were aligned together to some arcane agreement. He spread his cloak over himself. Winny could still see him, but only because she knew he was there. If she had walked across the field she would not have noticed him. Perhaps even had she stepped on him she would have felt only a slight rise in the level, never have thought it was a person. He was not invisible, it was just that he couldn't be seen.

Starback flexed his legs and jumped into flight.

Dragon and boy. Boy and dragon. It was still new to Sam.

The dragon circled the ring of kravvins, diminishing the distance each time, gathering them in as with a loop of twine.

The kravvins' eyes were fixed on the house, the scribble of smoke. They scraped sharp legs, chanted rough demands.

"Kill. Fire. Kill. Fire. Kill."

The dragon felt the vibrations like tremors of fever. They unbalanced him, rocked his flight, blurred his eyes, gripped his throat.

He stopped circling, tilted and dived. He crossed above the line of kravvins. It was like breaking through a wall of slime. He felt himself covered in a soft layer of hate.

As he broke the circle the chanting and scraping stopped. Instantly. All heads looked up. Smooth faces glowed in red light. As a single creature, they all hissed. Starback reeled, righted and found a way to land as far as possible from the ring of kravvins.

The door opened.

"Come on. In. Quickly."

Starback slipped through and heard the door slam after him.

Smith wore the leather apron he used at the forge. His sleeves were rolled up. He grasped a short, heavy hammer in his left hand.

"Can you talk?" he asked.

Starback turned his head away.

"That could mean anything," said Smith.

Starback moved to the window and looked out. The kravvins seemed to have moved nearer, the circle tighter. They had stopped hissing, and scratched their legs now, with an ominous delicacy, the sound more like a low scream.

"Can you hear?" asked Smith. "Do you understand what I say?"

Starback looked over his shoulder, raised his head and spat a jet of fire.

"I'm going to tell you," said Smith. "Understand?"

A smaller jet of fire.

"I'll take that as a yes."

Smith stood next to Starback and they looked out of the window together, fixing their eyes beyond their own reflections and on to the kravvins.

"I don't know what they're doing," said Smith. "And I don't know what they want. I don't know if they know what they're doing."

Opposite the front door, thirty paces away, a small clump of kravvins formed in the circle. The scraping grew louder. It was a struggle. They were fighting. The winners of the struggle pushed a kravvin into the circle. The creature staggered forward, screeched, tried to turn back, was pushed again, harder. It advanced two, three paces, screeched again and exploded. Before the pieces of the dead kravvin had hit the ground the whole circle snapped tight, up to the place where it had died.

"Kill. Fire. Kill. Fire. Kill."

"Well," said Smith. "There's an answer for you. They want fire. And they're getting closer."

On the stubble, Sam stirred beneath his cloak. He moaned. A dribble of smoke fell from his nose.

"Look at them," said Smith. "They're made of fire. You can see it. Red as embers, smooth as flame."

Starback leaned in towards the smith. He smelled the sweet leather of his apron, the scent of smoke in his hair. He responded to the solid bulk of the man.

Another knot. Another kravvin sent staggering in. Another scream. Another explosion. Another two paces advanced. Another surge of chanting.

"They're like ants," said Smith. "Look at them. They sacrifice their own to get what they want. It's only a matter of time before they get to us."

He moved back and raised the hammer.

"You fly off," he said. "While you can. Thanks for coming, whatever you are, but escape now. Before it's too late."

He opened the door and stood aside for Starback to pass. The dragon stepped through. He flicked his tail against Smith's legs, gently.

"Thanks," said Smith. "If you can bring help, I'll be grateful. But don't stay here to be killed with me."

Starback leaped forward. Instead of rising into the air he ran full pelt towards the kravvins, fire flooding from his open jaws.

"No!" shouted Smith.

Sam writhed and groaned. Winny crouched beside him.

"Are you all right?" she asked.

She put her hand to his forehead. It was too hot to touch. She jerked away.

"Sam."

He rolled to one side, smoke pooling round his mouth and nose.

"No!" shouted Smith. "Don't."

Starback charged the line of kravvins.

The chanting billowed and quickened.

"Kill. Fire. Kill. Fire. Kill."

Sharp legs stabbed at him, broke off, stabbed, snapped.

The line broke. He roared fire. Kravvins swelled up and spattered, exploding with wet, stinking slime and shattered shells.

He was trying to clear a way for Smith to escape, a breach in the wall of beasts. As many as died were replaced by others, as the water closes over a stone.

There was no breach, no escape.

Starback sprang up, swirled round, flicking his tail to scythe through the nearest kravvins. He darted back, joined Smith and waited for the circle to reform.

Two by two, three by three, four abreast, the kravvins followed him.

"You've broken the barrier," said Smith. "They're coming in. This way!"

He ran to the wide door of the storeroom. Starback swooped over his head and darted ahead of him. Smith slammed the door shut and bolted it.

Starback heard their legs jabbing the door, heard them scurrying up the walls, over the roof. They were all around now.

"Come on."

Smith led them through the maze of stacked scrap metal. Starback was dizzy with the effort of attack and retreat, sickened by the drumming of the kravvins' feet on the walls and roof. When the first kravvin broke through and fell from the ceiling he roared in fury and fear and leaped high above the stacks, engulfing it in fire. The kravvin popped and fell, and others followed. The walls and roof were breached. The kravvins were everywhere. Starback saw Smith run through another door. He swooped down to follow and Smith slammed the door shut before he could get through. A krav-vin was trapped in the slammed door, legs caught, screaming with pain. Starback spread wide wings and landed, feet first, on the trapped creature, tearing at it with his claws, disgusted by the pus that oozed from the split shell. He reeled back, flipped, and flew along the stacks and straight through another door, where he found himself in a small room that went on for ever, facing an endless image of himself repeated and reflected in a thousand mirrors. ||

# Tim found himself dropping to his knees

and loping along the corridors at night when everyone else was asleep. He liked to sniff in corners and push his face into angles where walls met the earth. The sweet stink of other dogs attracted him. He took off his shirt and lay on his back, writhing against pebbles to scratch himself. He let his tongue loll out to catch the moist cool air of the dark garden.

In the mornings he was exhausted. Scents of the night made him retch. There were bloody lines on his back. His skin stuck to the sheets and when he eased himself away the cuts opened up and bled more.

Smedge came to him, smiling.

"How are you feeling? You look tired."

He put his hand on Tim's arm. Tim flinched and pulled away. Smedge frowned.

"Don't hit me," said Tim.

Smedge smiled.

"Have I ever hit you?"

"No."

"Then why do you say that?"

Tim cringed, turning half-sideways, keeping his eyes on Smedge in case of an attack.

"I don't know. I just said it."

Smedge raised his hand.

"Come here," he said.

Tim approached, in small steps, head bowed.

Smedge put his hand on Tim's shoulder.

"Good boy," he said. "There's a good boy."

Tim was amazed to find that he was grateful for the touch, relieved. Smedge tousled Tim's hair and Tim felt an overwhelming need to scratch behind his ear.

"There's a good boy," said Smedge. "Now run off and wash yourself." He pulled a face indicating disgust. "You've been rolling in something."

Tim felt sad when Smedge took his hand away, abandoned. He jogged to the bathroom and washed all over, standing up in front of the jug and basin.

Clean, and in fresh clothes, Tim felt a surge of anger and shame. Smedge and the others had gone to classes. The dormitory was empty. Tim was missing a lot of lessons these days, being so tired in the morning. He dragged his bedclothes into something like tidy and lay down and slept.

He was thirsty when he woke, and hungry. His head ached and his back tingled from wounds closing over.

He rolled over and groaned.

"Feeling bad?" asked Smedge.

Tim moved to see him sitting on the bed.

"How long have you been there?"

"I can make you feel better," said Smedge.

"Why are you watching me?"

Smedge's hand was so fast that Tim didn't see the smack coming. It stung his face and jerked his head to the side, hurting his neck. He curled up, hands protecting his head, and made a quick spell to send Smedge a neck pain to match his own.

Smedge laughed.

"Is that the best you can do?" he said.

He batted the spell away and Tim's pain doubled. He yelped.

Smedge grabbed Tim's wrist, pulled his arm away from his head and spattered a series of slaps on to him, palm open, heavy and hard. They thudded into Tim's head, sending it bouncing off the pillow and back into Smedge's hand, blow after blow.

Smedge stopped, let Tim relax and gave him a final, reeling slap that drove Tim's face against the mattress.

"Magic's a good weapon," said Smedge, in a very calm voice, as though he was a teacher, instructing a class. "But you should never use it against someone with stronger magic. It will only hurt you all the more. And sometimes," he continued, "it's just so much nicer to use your hands."

He raised his arm again. Tim cowered.

"With your hands," said Smedge, "you can feel the slap landing."

Tim waited for the next attack.

"Come on," said Smedge. "Get up. There's work to do."

Tim uncurled and slid to the floor. He stood and faced Smedge, keeping out of arm's length.

"I don't want to be a dog any more," he said. "I don't want to be your dog."

"That's a pity," said Smedge. "Because that's just what you are. Now, come with me."

"I'm going to lessons. Stay away from me."

Smedge moved closer and raised his arm. Tim was taller than Smedge, stronger; he braced himself for the fight.

Smedge paused, smiled, lowered his arm.

"Down, boy," he said.

Tim felt the spell overwhelm him. He struggled. It took tight hold. He gathered all his magic and resisted. Sweat shone on his forehead. His chest hurt.

Smedge was relaxed and amused.

"It's so funny," he said. "Like watching a baby trying to lift a farm cart."

Tim stumbled and fell. His claws rattled on the dormitory floorboards. His tail swished against the bed. Smedge clicked his fingers.

"Come on, boy."

Tim trotted after him and was pleased when Smedge stroked his ears. He wagged his tail and licked the back of

Smedge's hand.

At the great gate of the college Smedge pushed a jerkin into Tim's face. It smelled of Tamrin.

"Go find," said Smedge. "Off you go. Find her. Bring her to me."

Tim bounded off, nose to the ground, delighting in the many scents of the market and the countryside, and always following the scent of Tamrin. How pleased Smedge would be when Tim found her. How pleased Tim would be when Smedge called him a good boy again.

Smedge watched him disappear. He skirted the walls of the college, found back streets, the town middens, the earth closets. He crouched, silent, simple. The creatures of the dank alleys, who had scurried away, stopped noticing him and returned. When all was still he snapped out his arm and seized a rat. He bit off its head, sucked at the neck, tore the stomach open and ripped at it with yellow teeth. Pleasure of rat flooded through him. He shrank, shifted and shaped himself into rat and set off for Boolat with news.

Vengeabil watched Tim disappear, too. The old storeman leaned on the parapet on the tower of the college.

"You'll need keeping an eye on, young Tim," he said. ||

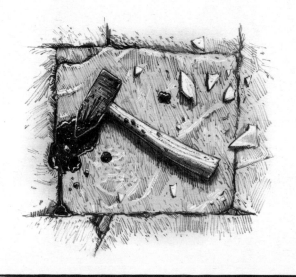

Part five

# DOUBLEDEATH

# Dragon looked at startled dragon.

Glass reflected steel. The image bounced off the surface and rebounded over and over again.

Starback arced his back, reared up and flexed long talons.

The air was thick with reflected light. The mirrors caught it, threw it back, tossed it with pitiless mimicry, till it meshed and trapped Starback in its net.

The door slammed open. The first kravvin moved into the perplexed space. It hesitated, saw itself, stepped back, recovered and scurried in.

Another followed and another. Starback wheeled, spewed fire and spattered them, staining the nearest mirrors. Reckless of death they poured in, clambering over the ruins of the first. There was not enough fire in the world to destroy them all.

They crammed into the doorway, forbidding escape. They swarmed on the floor, grabbing at Starback. Sharp legs prodded and pierced his skin. Sharp spit from blank mouths stung his eyes. He flapped and rose up and sought an escape.

He looked at himself in a large mirror, trapped and tormented, frightened beyond fear. For a moment it seemed to Starback that, instead of looking at himself, he looked at Sam.

The illusion passed and he saw himself again.

The reality passed and he saw, through the reflecting surface, a room, a route.

With a shriek of anger and pain he flew directly towards the sheet of polished steel, ready to crack his head open on the cold resistance rather than submit to the fury of the kravvins.

Tamrin screamed and the figure stepped through the mirror into the room and seized her.

"Stop. Who are you?" she shouted.

The grip wrenched her wrist. She screamed again, in pain.

A shower of flame sprayed her face. She tumbled down. The figure fell over her and landed beyond.

The creatures behind the glass pressed their no-faces against it. Were they looking through? Could they see her? It seemed they couldn't pass.

She wheeled her feet, not knowing which way to escape.

The bloodied tailor lay in one way, wet-gasping, eyes wide and weak.

The mirror lay another way, with monsters clawing at the fragile barrier.

The other way lay a hunched form, with scaled skin, fierce talons, smoke-wreathed and unknown.

She clambered to her knees and looked at it.

The smoke began to clear.

The face emerged.

Sam.

Winny watched helplessly as the kravvins broke the barrier and surged forward, attacking her home, her father, and Starback.

She heard the hissing, the screams, the rattling feet on the storeroom. She watched the red army devour the building. Saw the roof torn open, the door penetrated.

"Sam."

She only dared make an urgent whisper, like a child in the night, desperate for attention, fearful of being heard calling.

Sam moaned and twitched. He flung off the corner of his cloak in his sleeping frenzy. A tongue of flame licked his lips.

"Please, Sam," she said. "Please. They're being killed."

She leaned over to shake him.

The shattering sound of a thousand windows ripped the air.

Winny jumped to her feet, looked back at the house. It was embraced by a rainbow of light. Numberless shards of glass showered down over the storeroom, catching the lamplight and breaking it into a shout of colour.

She held her gaze until the glass settled, the colour faded and fled. She turned back to Sam.

"Sam?"

The boy had gone.

Starback crouched, teeth bared, nostrils wide, eyes of polished yellow stone.

He sprang up, tested his wings, soared high, swooped down, and settled by her in a fret of smoke and flame.

"Where's Sam?" she shouted. "What's happening?"

Tamrin couldn't decide if it was a cloak or wings that covered Sam. She edged nearer.

"Sam?"

He opened his eyes.

She touched his cheek.

"Sam."

He gasped. She drew back to avoid being licked by the flames.

He sat up. The wings decided to be a cloak. The talons and scales had been only a trick of the half-light.

He looked at her, shook his head, closed his eyes, looked again.

He started to lie down again, exhausted.

Tamrin shook him.

"Sam. Wake up."

He struggled to sit upright. She helped him to steady himself. He looked at her, looked around and let his eyes settle on something just behind her. Tamrin looked over her shoulder.

Shoddle was grasping his throat with both hands. Blood flowed from between his fingers.

"What's happened?" asked Sam.

"I stabbed him. In the throat." She held up the scissors. "It was an accident."

Sam managed to stand.

"Can we help him?" he asked.

Tamrin indicated the mirror. A legion of kravvins clawed at the polished surface.

"Him first," said Sam.

Shoddle mouthed sloppily at them. The words drowned in blood. Only the expression on his face revealed his thoughts.

"He doesn't like you," said Sam. "Why's he dressed in rags?"

Shoddle's neat suit was exposed as a jumble of stitched sacking.

"Never mind. He's going to die. And I need him to talk to us."

Sam ripped Shoddle's left sleeve away and, moving the tailor's hands to one side, slid it beneath them, winding it round his throat. He leaned back, fingered the weight around his neck, as he always did when he was concentrating.

"Give me the scissors," he said.

Tamrin didn't like to hand them over.

"Come on."

"Can't I do it?"

"What?"

"Whatever you want them for."

"Give them to me."

Tamrin set her mouth into a hard line.

"You never used to be so bossy."

Sam smiled.

"It's good to see you again," he said.

She couldn't stop herself from smiling back.

Shoddle beat his fist against the floor and made a wet noise of contempt.

Tamrin handed them over and felt as though she was betraying herself.

Sam closed the scissors, held the handles in his fist, and, before Shoddle could flinch away, thrust them into the tailor's neck.

Tamrin shouted.

Sam felt sick.

Shoddle shrieked, spraying blood over them both. His hands unclenched. He relaxed. The blood had stopped flowing. It seemed to Tamrin that his pain had gone.

"That won't last for long," said Sam. "Now, if you want me to do something better you'll have to talk first."

Shoddle was instantly sly and aggressive, now that the danger was, for the moment, tamed. He looked at the mirror.

"Come on," he whispered to the kravvins. "Come and get them."

"Stop that," said Tamrin. "Or I'll pull out the scissors and watch you bleed to death."

"You would, too," said Shoddle. "I think you would." He looked at Sam. "You wouldn't, though."

"Maybe," said Sam. "But I wouldn't stop her."

Shoddle leaned back.

"I'm too tired to tell you now," he said. "Finish the job and I'll tell you."

Sam walked over to the window and looked at the stars.

"Pull the scissors out," he said to Tamrin. "We're wasting our time."

Tamrin took them by the handle.

"No!" Shoddle screamed.

"Tell us," said Tamrin. "Who am I? And where did I come from?"

"I was sent for," said Shoddle. "To make new clothes, expensive ones." He wasn't spitting blood any more but his voice still gurgled. "It was not much of a journey, the way soft, the roads good. And the house. When I saw the house—" He tried to rub his hands together but it made him topple over and Sam had to help him to sit upright again. "You've got your hands wet," Shoddle laughed. "Straighten these scissors, will you?"

Sam walked away.

"No? All right. To say it was a big house would not be enough. It was big, and it was fine, with enough rooms for a village to live in. A small village, anyway. And it had a moat, with a little bridge, and there were chimneys shaped like willow catkins. Come to think of it, there were willow catkins on the trees when I got there, so it must have been spring. And I knew I could make a lot of money, at a house like that."

"Why would they send for you?" asked Tamrin.

Shoddle spat a gout of blood at her.

"Because I'm good. I'm a great tailor. That's why. Better than you'll ever know."

"You should have stuck to that," she said. "And not tried to cheat with magic."

He spat again and missed her this time.

Sam looked at the stars.

"Go on," he said.

"I had a cart," said Shoddle, "and a pony to pull it. I had bolts of cloth, silk and worsted, linen and fine cotton. I had lace and I had damask. I had brocade. There wasn't a coat wanted that I couldn't make. The servants carried it all in and looked after the pony and cart. I had a room to myself, as grand as you could want."

"Why didn't they come to your shop?" asked Tamrin. "Why would they want you to be with them in their house?"

"Folk like that don't go to shops. They bring shops to them. Besides," his face took on the sly look again, "they were the sort to keep to themselves. They liked secrets."

"Secrets?" asked Sam.

"All in good time. I have secrets to tell. The lady of the house, she was expecting. The baby was due very soon. I measured the man and took his instructions. Three coats. Three. And leggings and more. I told him it would take a month to do it all. Should I come home and have it sent? He wanted me to stay, so I could make fittings, a tuck here, a dart there. Perfection. I was there best part of a week, and the first jacket was ready for fitting. He came and tried it on, and I made the adjustments. I wanted him to look at it, but there wasn't a mirror in my workroom. I asked to go to another room, and he brushed me away, saying it wasn't needed. He could see well enough and it felt right."

Shoddle paused in his story to look at the mirror to his side. The kravvins still pressed against it, almost motionless now, silent, watchful. The edges had grown blurred.

"Can they see us?" he asked.

"Go on," said Sam.

Tamrin didn't like the way the story was going. When she heard of the woman expecting a baby she felt sure it was her mother and equally sure that it wasn't. She didn't feel like the child of a rich woman in a big house with a moat and servants. She tried to see if Sam knew that this story was going to be about him as well. He gave no sign.

"Once I saw that there were no mirrors in the house I grew curious. I searched everywhere. Not one. Not in a chamber. Not in a bedroom or a parlour. Not in a corridor. Not a looking glass on a dresser. Even the servants were not allowed a reflection of themselves.

"Above the servants' rooms there was an attic. I must have been careless. I thought no one had noticed my curiosity. The attic was locked, but needles can do more than sew, and I was soon through the door. You've seen attics before?" he asked.

Sam ignored him.

Tamrin told him to get on with his story.

"Attics," said Shoddle, "embrace lost lives. They hold all the remains of people long gone. Toys and books, unfashionable furniture, dresses too small for women grown stout, letters and bills, boots and shoes, things too precious to throw away, too useless to leave lying around. Not this attic. This attic was empty, quite empty, save for one thing."

He stopped and put his hand to the scissors.

"Go on," said Tamrin.

"I have a pain, in my throat," he said, his voice growing hoarse.

"No you don't," said Sam.

Shoddle glared at him.

"How do you know?"

"Because I have the pain in my throat."

Tamrin had been giving all her attention to Shoddle. She looked now at Sam and understood how he had made the spell to staunch the blood and take away the pain. She saw sweat on Sam's forehead; his lips were blue. She kicked Shoddle.

"Get on," she said. "Hurry up or I'll pull the scissors out and let you die."

"What was in the room?" whispered Sam. "The attic?"

"What do you think?"

Tamrin couldn't look at him any more. She stood and joined Sam at the window. She had never seen so many stars. Lowering her eyes, she saw Solder in the street, sitting on his barrel, looking up at her. He waved, not his usual, cheery wave, a tentative question of a wave. She nodded. He half-smiled and folded his arms.

Shoddle coughed. When Tamrin looked round she saw he had sent a fine spray of blood over the gleaming metal of the mirror. The image faded. The kravvins dissolved.

"That was there," said Shoddle. "That mirror. It was covered with a length of cotton cloth. Poor stuff, but thick enough to keep the light from it. I didn't know then, of course, what it was. I put my hand to pull the cloth away and look at it. The lady of the house screamed at me to stop. She had followed me up there. It took her longer to climb the stairs, what with her belly big and her legs tired.

"As soon as she told me to leave it alone I tugged at it, before she could get near and stop me. She ran at me and as the cloth fell she stood full in the path of light. Where there had been one there were two. Her reflection was pin perfect. The shine and smooth of the metal were beyond imagining."

He struggled to his knees, hand at his neck, fingers in the loops of the scissor handle.

"You tell me what happened next," he said.

"You tell it," said Sam.

"I won't. If you want to know, you say it. I'll tell you if you get it wrong."

"She fell," said Tamrin.

"They carried her downstairs," said Sam.

"Her baby started to come."

"They forgot about you."

"Yes, they forgot about me," said Shoddle. "Clever of you to think of that."

"The baby was born," said Sam.

"It was a girl."

"It was a boy."

"It was twins," said Tamrin.

"Stop there," said Shoddle. "You know that's not true. Remember the story."

"Was it a girl or a boy?" asked Sam.

"Yes," said Shoddle. "It was a baby. I never heard what. She was delivered of only the one. They were clear about that."

He fell back again.

"My throat does hurt," he complained.

"It really doesn't," said Sam. "You'd know."

Sam and Tamrin turned together to face Shoddle. They left their examination of the stars and looked inward. They moved forward, two steps, and stood directly in front of the mirror.

Sam looked at his reflection in the polished metal, and he saw Tamrin. Tamrin looked at herself and saw Sam.

Sam reached out his hand to the mirror and his fingertips touched the outstretched fingertips of Tamrin. Tamrin pulled a face and Sam's reflection pulled a face back at her.

"That's right," said Shoddle. "When the house was still and the dark had come I crept to the room and looked at the child. There were two of them. Just as in the first time of magic. Two babies where there had been one."

"Which one did you take?" asked Tamrin.

"You, of course."

She rushed forward and kicked him in the stomach. He bent double and coughed blood.

"Which one? Tell me. Did you take the baby that was born or the second one, the reflected one?"

She had to wait while Shoddle coughed out his recovery. He raised a look of hate at her.

"You'll pay for that," he said.

"Which one?" she shouted. "Which one am I?"

She had never hated anyone as much as when he gave her the self-satisfied smile that she knew meant he was speaking the truth.

"I don't know," he said. "I didn't care then, and I don't care now. I just took the one that was nearest. I took you and I took the mirror and I put you both on my cart and brought you here."

Tamrin went back and stood next to Sam. Their reversed images stared back at them.

"One of us isn't real," she said.

He pointed to Shoddle, hunched in a wounded crouch, blood-smeared, scissors sticking out from a sack bandage.

"You think that's real?" said Sam. "Cover the mirror."

There was a lot of catching up to do, news to share, stories to tell. Solder was halfway up the stairs when they left the room, come to look for Tamrin. Jaimar was waiting for them. She had tidied up till there was nothing left to tidy and then she tidied some more. She hugged Tamrin most and longest. Solder skipped out of the way of her arms and she seized Sam and hugged him even though she didn't really know who he was.

"But you're welcome," she said. "You must be hungry."

"I couldn't eat anything," said Sam.

Tamrin shook her head.

"That's very kind," said Solder. "Bacon and eggs is good at any time, I find."

Tamrin told Sam about the accusations of bullying at the college, about the kravvin attack, about Winny and Smith. Solder interrupted at inconvenient moments to explain his own part in the story.

Sam gave her his account of the journey, and the moment when he had burst through the mirror.

"You mean you were the dragon?" asked Tamrin.

"Sort of. I mean, yes."

"And where's the dragon now?"

She watched the worry cross Sam's face.

"That's just it," he said. "No matter how far away he is I'm always there in him. I can always see what he sees, hear what he hears. I can switch from me to him and back again. But since I crashed through the mirror I can't find him."

Tamrin hesitated, then she said, "But can you switch to—"

"It's late," said Sam. "We need to talk more tomorrow. And we need to make sure Shoddle is properly dealt with."

Tamrin took the hint and shut up. When Sam said they should go back to Shoddle's and sort things out she agreed without question and suggested that Solder could finish his eggs and bacon while they were away.

He waved a cheerful fork at them and Jaimar told him to mind his manners before she told Sam and Tam to be careful.

They didn't speak in the street. Sam pushed the tailor's door open and let Tamrin go through first. The bell jangled.

Nothing remained of the appearance of a thriving business. Piles of sacks were everywhere. The walls were grey with dirt, yellow with neglect, black with mould. Only the solid wood of the tailor's bench was unaffected by the unravelling of the magic. It shone with the deep polish of long use. Shoddle lay on the bench, stretched out, covered with sacks, his head to one side in a crazy posture of surprise.

Sam had removed the scissors and staunched the wound. He had not been able to repair the damage to the tendons in the neck, and Shoddle's head hung to one side, flopping like a spaniel's ears if he turned. Not that he could sit or turn, fastened as he was with the bonds of sack.

Sam tested a knot.

"He's safe enough," he said. "For now."

"I'm safe enough," said Shoddle. "I'd look to yourself, if I were you. There's no safe place for you."

Tamrin leaned close to him, ignoring his stinking breath.

"Who were those people?" she asked. "Where did they live? What happened to them?"

"Gone," he said. "Long gone. I told you. I went back, just the once. The house wasn't even there. I don't think it had ever been there."

Tamrin pushed the side of his head so that it lolled in the other direction. Shoddle yelped.

"Don't hurt him," said Sam.

"He's a liar."

"I know. But sometimes even liars tell the truth."

"How can a house just disappear?"

Shoddle laughed so loud that he coughed and cried out in pain.

"Leave him," said Sam.

He led Tamrin upstairs. The mirror was veiled. Sam walked around it, looking at it from the back.

Tamrin kept to one side, careful not to be in line with the surface, even obscured. Positioned in this way they couldn't see each other.

"Go on," said Sam.

"I'm afraid to."

"You don't have to."

"Yes, we do," said Tamrin. "You know we have to."

"I'll close my eyes," said Sam.

"I'll leave mine open."

"Ready?"

"Yes."

And they switched.

Sam looked through Tamrin's eyes.

Tamrin opened Sam's eyes.

Now she was looking at the back of the mirror and he was looking at the veiled front.

An observer would have seen no change, no difference.

"Back," said Tamrin.

They switched.

She gasped and walked away, over to the window.

"It's terrible," she said.

Sam stayed where he was, unable to see her.

"As long as I can remember," said Tamrin, "I've wanted to know who I am, where I came from. I knew I was a twin. I felt it. I knew it. And I wanted to know about that. And then you came along last year, to the college, and I knew it was you."

She waited for Sam to say something and carried on when she found he wasn't going to.

"And you didn't know you were a twin," she said.

"I'm not."

"No, you're not. You're me."

"You're me."

"I can't remember what you can remember," said Tamrin. "If I was just you, I'd know everything that you know, wouldn't I?"

"This is new to me," said Sam. "I don't know all the answers. Ask a different question."

Tamrin moved back to the front of the mirror.

"What's this?" she said. "Where's it from?"

"I'm just going to try something," said Sam. "See what you think."

As Tamrin looked at the mirror she began to see it from the back as well as from the front. It was difficult to fix the images at first. She tried to separate them and lost them both. She was seeing through her own eyes and through Sam's both at the same time.

"Stop looking," said Sam.

She allowed her eyes to relax and saw both sides clearly. It lasted just a few seconds then flipped back to seeing just the one side.

Sam walked round and joined her.

"How do you do that?" she asked.

"I learned it by looking through Starback. It gets easier the more you try, but it always takes some effort."

"Will I be able to see as Starback?"

"I don't know. Perhaps."

"Go back."

Sam went back behind the mirror.

"I'm going to do it," said Tamrin.

"Look out of the corner of your eye."

Tamrin found the way to do it and she saw as Sam did.

"That's enough," she said.

He joined her again.

"So we can switch," she said. "And we can overlap. Is that right?"

"I think so. That's sort of what it's like with Starback."

"I don't know if I like it."

"It's odd. But you get used to it."

"I don't want to switch again. Not for a while."

"Talk about the mirror," said Sam.

"We don't have to."

"No?"

"No. We know what it is."

"Say it."

"It's the very first mirror ever. It's the mirror that brought magic into the world."

"It can't be."

"You know it is."

Sam put his hand to his throat, to help him to think. The pendant had gone. He scrabbled around.

"What's the matter?"

"It's gone. I've lost it."

He dived back round the mirror, on his knees, hands wildly sweeping the floor.

"What? What have you lost?"

"It's a leather cord, with a metal weight on it. A dragon's head."

He banged his shoulder against the stand holding the mirror. It lurched forward and Tamrin grabbed it and righted it.

"I can't lose it. I can't."

"Calm down."

Sam, still crouched, pushed the mirror aside and glared at her.

"Don't tell me to calm down."

Tamrin closed her eyes and made the switch. She felt a surge of panic, a sense of loss, a rage of having done something terribly wrong. It was going to be hard, feeling as helpless and angry as Sam. She layered her sense of calm over his agitation.

Sam stopped shouting, stopped flailing for the seal. He stood and touched his hand on the frame of the mirror.

"See," said Tamrin. "Here it is."

The leather thong was round her neck. The weight hung at her throat.

"You took it."

He grabbed. She stepped back.

"It came to me," she said. "When we switched."

"Give it back."

"All right. Don't get angry."

She untied the knot and held the pendant out to Sam. He tied it round his neck.

"Sorry," he said. "It's very important."

"Are you all right now?"

He smiled.

She felt a heaviness at her throat. She raised her hand. The seal was back. Sam put his hand to his throat. It was gone.

"Did you do that?" he asked.

"No."

"Give it back."

"There's no point."

"Give it."

She handed it over. He tied the leather and gripped the iron weight in his fist.

Tamrin felt it return.

"I can't let it go," said Sam. "This can't happen."

"Perhaps it will come back."

Sam thumped the side of the mirror.

"Careful."

She felt Sam's anger flooding her. She closed her mind to it, tried to shut it out.

"If it is the mirror," she said, "we need to take it. We can't leave it here."

"It isn't."

Tamrin walked to the window.

"See the stars."

"Are they saying anything?" asked Sam.

"Of course."

He looked up with her.

"Can it be the mirror?" he asked.

"Can it be anything else?"

"No."

"We have to take it. Make it safe."

"Where?"

They kept their eyes on the stars.

"You met Winny," said Tamrin.

"Yes."

"It's the mirror Smith is looking for. It's why she goes round collecting old metal. We should take it to him."

Sam laughed.

"We should. It's where it belongs."

She felt Sam open his mind to her. She knew his thoughts, his doubts.

What did they know of Smith? How could they trust him? How could they trust anyone? And besides — with a shock of recollection — Smith was under attack from the kravvins, perhaps dead already. And the room of mirrors reflected the blank red faces of pure hate.

"Don't," said Tamrin. "Get out of my thoughts. Don't take me over like that."

"I didn't," said Sam. "It just happened."

Tamrin couldn't take her eyes from the sky, the black emptiness, the confused chatter of the stars. She was losing herself, sinking into another mind, another person. In a jagged lapse of sense she found that she wasn't even a girl any more. Bewildered by male strangeness she dragged herself back.

"You know the way?" said Sam. "To Smith's?"

"Yes."

"We have to go there. See if we can save him."

"What about Starback?" she asked.

"That too." ||

# The woman, Winny, was screaming

at him. Fireflash and flight. Shards of glass grazed his scales. A rain of fragments. Blue and green of spread wings. He leaped and shook himself like a wet dog. The glass spun from him, bright as starlight.

"Stop."

Starback let the earth touch his feet.

The woman, Winny — yes, Winny — huddled away from him, arms upraised, her scarf dragged round her face.

"Stop it," she said.

Starback kept still.

She drew back the scarf.

He had shot splinters of glass at her. Her face was red with specks of blood, spreading, dripping. She wiped her sleeve across her face. The bleeding stopped.

He breathed an apologetic wisp of flame towards her.

"Never mind me," she said. "Look."

Starback followed the line of her finger and he remembered.

The smith. The storeroom. The ceiling pierced. The kravvins. The chase. The mirrors. The flight into his own reflection.

Sam had gone. Starback opened his mind to Sam and there was nothing. No boy any more. Alone again.

He skimmed the air, low over the stubble. Winny ran behind, hopelessly outpaced.

Smoke from the forge chimney. Something different about it. Something wrong.

Starback, flying low, banked and went around the storeroom, ignoring the breached door. He flew to the other side, the outer door of the forge. All the kravvins had swarmed the other way, straight after him and Smith, so the door was clear. His claws grasped the clinker path. He hunched and moved towards the door, low, not from fear but for purchase, to spring forward and attack.

The smoke stank. He raised his head and looked up. The grey was streaked with red.

Winny had made good ground and was nearly at the gate.

Starback couldn't wait for her.

He pushed through the door, ready to take on the army of kravvins if there was any hope for Smith. Ready to find Smith dead at his forge.


"You'll be safe here till we get back," Sam said to Shoddle.

With the tendons and muscles sheared by the scissors, the tailor couldn't move his head to look at Sam. Only magic kept him alive.

"Can't you put this right?" he shouted.

"I don't know." Sam moved so that Shoddle could see him clearly. "And I don't care. I'm not going to waste magic on you now. I've got other things to do. More important things."

Even in his helpless state Shoddle couldn't stop his vicious tongue.

"You're not the only one with magic, you know."

"I know."

"I've got a friend with more magic than you. He'll fix me up. And then he'll fix you."

Sam shrugged.

"No you haven't," he said. "You'll wait here till I get back. Then I'll decide what to do."

"I'll starve. I'll die of thirst. I'm thirsty now."

"I've taken care of that," said Sam. "You'll last long enough."

"What if you don't come back?"

"Then you'll die."

Sam could still hear Shoddle's raving when he closed the door. There was no key. As he made the sealing spell Sam remembered using it once before, on the door of Flaxfield's study. He longed to be there now. To sit in the panelled room with its walls of books and the ash tree outside the window, the blue and white china, the oak table.

"He has got a friend," said Tamrin.

"Yes?"

"Yes. It's Smedge. I'm sure of it."

Sam checked the sealing spell at the name of Smedge.

They had met at the college a year ago. He remembered that boy with loathing.

"This will keep anyone out," he said.

Tamrin put her hand to the door. She pushed and it opened.

"Except me," said Sam.

Tamrin sealed it again and they looked at each other.

"This is going to take a lot of getting used to."

Once he realized they were not coming back Shoddle settled into a vengeful silence.


Solder was ready for a quiet night and an early bed. Jaimar hugged them both this time. She was beginning to understand something of what was happening, though they had not told her who they really were.

"You can't go now," she said. "It's dark."

"Easier to travel in the dark," said Sam.

"You stay here," said Tamrin to Solder.

Sam could see she was ready for an argument and a little disappointed when none came.

"All right," agreed the roffle. "Let me know how you get on."

Just like a roffle. Sam had little time for them, after the treachery of Megatorine. Which reminded him.

"Do you know a roffle called Megatorine?" he asked.

"Megantople? Yes, he's a very famous roffle."

"I said Megatorine."

"Oh, sorry. Perhaps if you spoke a little louder. And you're not very clear, you know. Have you thought of having lessons?"

Sam started to make a spell to tip gravy over Solder as the young roffle seemed to like eating so much. He stopped himself and spoke very clearly and slowly.

"Do you know a roffle called Megatorine?"

"Have you noticed," said Solder, "that all roffles, well, all men roffles, have names that begin with Mega? Take me, for instance," he said. "Although you call me Solder, my real name—"

"Just answer the question, will you?"

Solder looked astonished. It was a good look and Sam would have admired the artistry if he hadn't been so frustrated at wanting an answer. Jaimar touched his sleeve.

"I think he has answered," she said. "It's a roffle's answer."

She insisted on making them food for the journey.

"And you can tell me all you know about Winny," said Sam, partly to make time pass on the journey, partly to keep from thinking or talking about the mirror and what it had shown them about who they were, and partly because he really needed to know about that strange woman.

He let Jaimar hug him and opened the door as Tamrin dodged out of the way of a hug.

It was good to be a rat, but it made for slow progress. Smedge was reluctant to change. Of all creatures he liked rat best. On the other hand, Ash needed to be told what was happening. He changed to fox, to keep his nose full of the scents of earth and his feet on the ground. It was faster. Not fast enough. So it was as a crow again that he landed on the high wall of the Castle of Boolat.

"Here again," rattled Bakkmann. "Can't stay away. Want some more fun?"

"I've got news," said Smedge, melting back into human shape.

"She likes good news," Bakkmann clattered. "I wouldn't want to be the one who brings her bad news."

Smedge kicked out at Bakkmann, snapping a leg.

Bakkmann scuttled away, hurt, because she had once not been as she was now and remembered what pain was. The leg would grow again. So would Bakkmann's hatred of Smedge.

Ash was in the dungeons, playing with prisoners.

"Remember this one?" she asked Smedge.

"Is it the old wizard?"

"Axestone?" said Ash.

"That's the one."

"No. This is the dark one, Khazib."

Smedge poked the figure with the toe of his boot.

"Doesn't look like him."

Ash shimmered. Smedge wondered again just how substantial she was. He thought he could put his hand right through her. To Khazib she was substantial enough. Ash held a tooth between her thumb and forefinger.

"I pull them out," she said to Smedge. "And they grow back, so I can pull them out again. Don't I?" she asked Khazib.

Smedge remembered Khazib as a tall man, with skin the colour of winter ale. Strong and upright. With a subtle magic that was like a distant music. This grey waste of life on the filthy floor seemed to be a different creature. It was only when Khazib spoke that Smedge recognized him.

"Magic always has its returns," he said.

"What?"

Did Ash demand that he repeat it because she had not heard, or because she dared him to say it again?

"Magic always has its returns," he said.

Smedge felt afraid of him. Of this! This broken prisoner. He kicked him hard in the face.

"Careful," said Ash. "The teeth grow back, but they're slow. And I want to pull more."

Khazib shifted his position. He felt inside his mouth with his finger and cleared fragments of teeth.

"Magic doesn't forget," said Khazib.

Smedge left the cell. Ash didn't bother to lock the door. Khazib couldn't escape just by walking out.

"What news?" she said.

Smedge explained about Tim and the hunt for Tamrin.

"They had a special friendship," he said. "I thought about it. The bonds of trust will draw him to her. He'll find her."

"Why didn't you just go and look for the tailor? You know where he lives."

"I don't think that's where she's going," said Smedge. "And even if it is, it's how she gets there. Who she meets on the way. That's what we need to know."

He was pleased with the small expression of surprise and approval that crossed Ash's face. She made no attempt to praise him.

"You could have done it," she said. "You make as good a dog as he does."

Smedge's pleasure melted.

"No," he said. "She spread magic behind her, hiding her way. It's the friendship that will find her out."

"Friendship," said Ash. "Weakness. We'll use it."

She gestured for him to leave her.

"What about the tailor?" said Smedge. "I could go and see him."

"Would you like that?"

Smedge wondered what he liked. He liked playing with the prisoners in the cells. He liked smacking Tim. He liked hurting the little ones in the college. He especially liked the hurt he saw in Tamrin when she was accused of bullying and lying.

"Yes," he said. "Yes, I would like to go and see the tailor."

Ash laughed.

"He won't like it," she predicted.

"No. He won't like it at all. I'll go there, shall I?"

"Do that."

Ash watched Smedge through the gate. When he was out of sight she crooked her finger for Bakkmann.

"I want him watched," she said. "Send kravvins. Keep a distance, but follow him."

Bakkmann clattered with anxiety.

"No one will be eaten," warned Ash. "No one. Unless I say so. Tell the kravvins."

She left Bakkmann to gather a squad together.

It was the hissing that was so horrid. The kravvins hissed at Smith. They hissed hatred. The fire in the forge hissed as the air drew up and fanned the flames. The hammer hissed through the air as Smith swung it, his thick arm tight with effort.

And when the hammer struck a kravvin's head it hissed. But the worst hiss of them all was the high sizzle when Smith flung the kravvin on the fire. The red shell shattered and the pus fried.

It had been a hard battle. Smith was wet with sweat. The kravvins were giving up. Even their mindless swarming was beginning to fail against the remorseless attack of the hammer and the fire.

Their faces bore no expression. It was their posture, their gestures that suggested amazement and disappointment.

"Kill. Kill. Kill."

Starback listened. They had stopped chanting "Fire". All that remained was the desire to kill.

"Hello," Smith sang out. "Come to help?"

Starback drew in his breath and spat out a huge gout of fire.

The kravvins shrieked with pleasure.

"Kill. Fire. Kill. Fire."

They surged towards him.

"Stop!" shouted Smith. "Not that fire."

He swung the hammer, smashing two at once and hauled them into the forge.

"Get out," he said. "I'm fine."

Starback didn't like to leave the battle. He hesitated.

"Out. You'll make it worse."

The dragon collided with Winny, coming into the forge as he left. She dodged round him and stood next to her father.

"Take this," he said, offering her a length of iron that had been in the furnace.

She slipped on a leather glove, grabbed the end of the rod furthest away from the glowing heat and brandished it at the kravvins.

They flinched.

She jabbed.

She thrust it in the neck of the nearest one.

It grabbed hold. Its hands popped. Its neck exploded. It fell and smashed like an egg.

She jabbed again.

Hot iron.

Hammer

Hot iron.

Hammer.

Furnace and fire.

The kravvins fell back.

"Kill. Run. Kill. Run."

They made one last surge to attack.

Smith swung his hammer.

Winny jabbed the glowing iron.

The kravvins retreated, turned and fled.

Starback edged back in.

"All right," said Smith. "It's clear now. Come on."

Starback sniffed the forge. Dragons know about fire.

"That's right," said Smith.

Starback looked at him.

"Sorry," said Smith. "Thank you for your help. It was brave of you."

Starback flicked his tail and let the end of it touch the fire in the furnace.

"Careful," said Winny.

"It's all right," said Smith. "He knows what he's doing. Don't you?"

Starback pushed his tail deeper into the hot coals. It was cool. Cool as a stream in autumn. Cool as cloud.

Smith laughed.

"There's fire," he said, "and there's dragon fire. They're different. And then there's my fire. That's different again."

He put down the hammer and wiped his hands on his leather apron.

Winny put the glowing iron into the bucket of water by the forge. It died in a new hissing. A comforting hiss.

"It's not even like the fire that other smiths use," Smith continued.

He leaned over and put his arm round Starback's neck. It was an intimacy that no one would dare to offer. Starback started to recoil, thought better of it and enjoyed the strong gesture of friendship.

"Shall I call you Sam?" asked Smith.

Starback gave him a surprised look.

"Best not to," said Smith. "Anyway, my fire is not like any other fire you'll ever know." He stirred the coals with a poker. "This furnace goes straight down to the Deep World. It's a gate. A link. A bridge. This is roffle fire. And what you make with this fire stays made."

"You shouldn't be saying this," said Winny.

"He needs to know. Sam needs to know. Those kravvins. They're made of fire. Somehow. They were drawn here by the fire. You know they were."

"Boolat," said Winny.

"Boolat," he agreed. "And Ash. We're going to have to deal with them now. And we'll need help. We need your help," he said to Starback. "And Sam's. And, by the stars, we could do with Flaxfield's help, but that's gone from us now."

Starback let his head droop.

"Sorry," said Smith. "Do you miss Flaxfield? We all do."

Winny touched Starback's head.

"I miss him," she said. "Awkward and difficult though he was. I miss him, too."

Starback drew back from their touch. He wanted to be away from them. He wanted to be with Sam. And, in a way that he didn't understand and that was quite new to him, he wanted to be with that girl, with Tamrin.

"Let's clear this mess up," said Smith. "And then we'll see what to do next." ||

Part Six

# DOUBLEBORN

# Sam came to a sudden halt

to stop himself from bumping into Flaxfold.

"You can close that door," she said. "You're not going anywhere."

"What are you doing here?" he asked.

Flaxfold shooed them back inside.

"And why shouldn't I be here?" she said. "Hello, Jaimar.
How's business?" She ran her finger over the carved foliage
of the door frame. "This is nice work."

"Flaxfold," said Jaimar. "Welcome. I wasn't expecting
you."

"Good. Now, who's this? Tamrin? And a roffle. What's
your name?"

Tamrin scowled. Solder waved and grinned.

"Solder," he said, after only a slight pause to swallow what
he was chewing.

"You needn't bother with your roffle talk with me," she
warned him. "I know better than that."

She shrugged off her cloak and hung it on a hook. Her fingers found a wandering strand of grey hair and she tucked it in.

"Now," she said. "Let me see Tamrin. Come on, girl. Let's have a look at you."

Tamrin turned her back on Flaxfold.

"You haven't said why you're here," said Sam. "And how do you know Jaimar?"

Flaxfold sat at the table next to Solder. She looked around, taking stock of the room, noting changes, approving the cleanness and the neatness.

"There's not a better place for a tired traveller to stop and eat within a hundred miles," she said.

Jaimar put her hand to her mouth.

"I'm sorry," she said. "I'll get you something."

"Oh, that's all right," said Flaxfold. "I don't want to be any trouble."

Sam marvelled at the way that Flaxfold, while looking so insignificant, could take over and organize any room she walked into. He wished that Tam would come and say hello. She was standing by the door, concentrating on the frame, the leaves and tendrils, the stems twining up and over.

"That's lovely work," said Flaxfold.

Tam ignored her.

Flaxfold coughed, gently. Tamrin stepped back and exclaimed.

"Something wrong?" asked Flaxfold.

Sam moved next to Tamrin to see what she was looking at.

A smooth brown mouse scampered along a twig. It had no fur, but was carved from dark oak, the grain of the wood patterning its body. A snail, paler, carved perhaps from walnut, slid along a leaf. A wren and a ladybird, another mouse and a caterpillar. The foliage that Tamrin had created was alive with wooden creatures, beautiful in their detail, supple as silence. They hopped and slid and clambered, in and out of the leaves. And in the top corner, half-hidden, a green man grinned out at them, its face all leaves and twigs.

"Are you doing this?" asked Tamrin.

"Ah, that's better. I can see you now. And you're not bad-looking. Not at all. At least, you wouldn't be if you weren't pulling that face at me. Anger does you no favours, Tam. Now, if only you'd—"

She stopped and stared. Sam had turned as well. And now the two of them stood side by side, facing Flaxfold.

"Oh," she said. "That's the way of it, is it? That's the way of it."

"What?" said Sam.

Flaxfold's face was creased with surprise.

"I didn't even think of that," she said. "Not that. No. I didn't think of it."

"Didn't think of what?" asked Sam.

Tamrin stepped up and stood over Flaxfold, her face set hard with anger and curiosity.

"What?" she demanded.

Jaimar came through with a bowl of lentil soup and warm bread.

"Ah, food," said Flaxfold. "Thank you."

Tamrin pushed the bowl away from Flaxfold.

"You're not eating anything until you tell me what you mean. What didn't you think of?"

"I really think I preferred it when you wouldn't look at me," she said. "Sam, please will you look after Tamrin until I've eaten?"

Sam took Tamrin's arm to move her away from the table. Tamrin shook him off. He felt a jolt and fell back. He couldn't see. A pain shafted through his head. He called out and put his hand to his eyes. The blackness cleared. He glared at Flaxfold, hating her. He had a memory of dark corridors and lonely days, of being ignored and jeered at. He saw Smedge's face, calm, composed, attacking him with cool precision. He felt lost in a sea of loneliness. He was Tamrin. There was little of Sam left in his mind. He wanted to strike out at Flaxfold, make her talk to him.

The moment passed. He returned to himself, but not without some remnant of the experience, some memory of the feeling. He was more than Sam now. Something extra had been added to him. And he was less than Sam. Something had been taken away. Some element of the singleness of being himself had gone, for ever.

He looked at Tamrin and saw that she was shocked, too. The mixing had taken place in her as well.

Jaimar stared at him. Solder looked curiously. Flaxfold spooned soup from the bowl and broke off a hunk of bread.

"You two had better go and talk for a while," she said. "Then I'll tell Tam what she wants to know, when I've eaten."

They couldn't talk. They sat apart, at a separate table, silent and subdued. They looked at each other and looked away. Sam wondered — that is, Tam wondered — that is, they wondered, which of us is first and which reflected?

At last, Flaxfold put down her spoon.

"Sit with me," she said. She spoke first to Tamrin. "You're wearing the pendant."

"I couldn't help it," said Sam. "It goes to her every time."

"So it does," said Flaxfold.

Tamrin held it in her hand. Sam felt the comfort of its weight.

"How did you find out?" asked Flaxfold.

"What did you mean," asked Tamrin, "when you said you never thought of that?"

"We both know the answer to that," said Flaxfold. "Now, how did you find out about yourselves?"

Sam looked anxiously at Jaimar and Solder.

"You needn't worry about them," said Flaxfold. "Whatever's brought the four of us together means you can speak freely with them here."

"Five," said Solder.

"Carry on," said Flaxfold.

Sam explained about the tailor and the shop and the mirror.

"And the mirror is there?" she asked. "Now?"

"Yes."

Flaxfold stood quickly.

"Then we've no time to waste," she said. "Take me there."

Solder hopped off his barrel and shouldered it, ready to follow.

"You stay here," said Tamrin.

"He'd better come along," said Flaxfold. "We don't know why he's got involved. Best to wait and see."

Jaimar hesitated.

"Do you want to come along?" asked Flaxfold.

"Not really."

"Then stay here. That's what's chosen you. We'll be back."

She gave her a quick kiss on the cheek and led them out.

Shoddle's bell rang out, louder in the darkness than in the daylight. Flaxfold hardly gave the tailor a second glance.

"Is this the staircase?" she asked.

"Hey, you. What are you doing?"

Shoddle couldn't see them. His face was turned to the wall. Flaxfold paused, crossed to him and put her hand to his cheek, moving him so that he could see her.

"Couldn't you mend him?" she asked.

"Yes," said Sam. "But he's not in any pain, and I thought it would keep him safe for now. Otherwise we'd have to lock him up or something."

Flaxfold kept her hand on Shoddle's cheek.

"Do you think it's right to leave him like this?"

"Not for ever," said Sam.

"I don't see why not," said Tamrin. "After what he's done."

Solder kept his distance.

"It's not just what he's done, it's what he might do," said Sam.

"Might do? Might do?" Shoddle's voice was like the scrape of iron on cobbles. "I will do. Mark me, I will." He spat at Flaxfold. She moved aside to avoid it.

"Ah, well," she said. She took her hand away and Shoddle's head lolled back. "I suppose you're right. We can leave him like this for now. But I don't like it. We'll make better arrangements soon."

She headed towards the stairs.

"Come to see my mirror, have you?" Shoddle taunted her. "I think there's something there for you to fear."

He laughed until blood trickled out of the corner of his mouth.

Sam watched Flaxfold's face and he knew Shoddle was right. Flaxfold was afraid of what she might find upstairs.

"Come on," she said, and led them up. ‖

# The dog was tired and panting

when Smith called him over and poured some water into a bowl.

"There you go, boy," he said, scratching the dog's neck.

Tim enjoyed the hard fingers against his skin. He arched his back, flicked his tail and lapped the water. It splashed round the edges and he pushed the bowl with his nose to show he wanted more.

"In a minute," said Smith. "Don't drink too much, too soon."

"Who's this?" asked Winny.

Starback ignored them and sprang up into the air, circling the house, glad to be freed from the weight of walking. His wings bore him up.

Tim raised his head and looked at the dragon. He snuffled at the doorpost and slipped inside the house. Scents of Tamrin were everywhere. He raced round, trying to find her. She had been here, and here, and upstairs. He slipped on the stairs, still not used to four legs unless it was on level ground.

Not there either. He clattered down and found that Smith had set out a bowl with meat in it.

"Here you are," said the man.

Tim dipped his head and gobbled it up.

It hadn't been a long journey, avoiding roads, and he made good time, but it seemed too long since he had last eaten. He knew he could have killed something and eaten it, a rabbit, or maybe a bird. There was too much Tim left and too little dog for him to want to do that.

The meat all eaten he raised his head to look around. Smith slipped a chain around his neck, looped through a ring. Tim skittered backwards. He was too late. The chain had circled his neck. He pulled away. The chain slid through the loop and tightened. Smith fastened it to a leather leash. The more Tim pulled the tighter the chain gripped. When he stepped forward it slackened off.

He hurt his throat before he gave up and settled close to Smith. The man had not pulled Tim towards him at all, content to hold the leash and let Tim discover how to be comfortable.

Tim licked Smith's hand. It tasted smoky, better than Smedge's. He looked up into Smith's eyes and wagged his tail.

"Where are you from?" asked Smith.

"He's not a stray," said Winny.

Tim looked from one to the other. He tugged at the leash. The chain bit into his neck. He relaxed and moved back to be close.

"No. Not a stray," Smith agreed. "Are you, boy?"

Tim licked his hand again.

"And you're looking for something. Yes?"

Tim wagged a confirming tail and tugged again, gently this time, to indicate that he wanted to move. Smith stood and allowed Tim to lead him. Tim picked up Tamrin's scent again at the door and tugged hard. Smith followed as far as the edge of the path, just where the ring of kravvins had formed.

Tim shuddered and drew his nose from the ground when he reached the kravvins' mark. He jumped over it and picked up Tamrin's scent again. It was a funny business, being a dog, especially following scent. Tamrin's scent was mingled here with Vengeabil's. Only the storeman's scent was even stronger. As though he were there.

Tim raised his head and looked around him, as though he expected to see Vengeabil.

"Tamrin, is it?" asked Smith, recalling Tim to his purpose.

Tim cocked his head to one side. This man knew her?

Smith rubbed the side of Tim's neck. He pressed back against him, wanting more. His hand was heavy, reassuring. Not like Smedge's hand at all. Tim had longed for approval from Smedge, yet he knew that it was mixed with the threat of another smack. He didn't think Smith would hit him.

The memory of Smedge was fading. Tim pulled again, resenting the chain, the leash. Smith allowed him a little slack, but not much.

"Are you looking for her?" asked Smith.

Tim strained against the leash.

He did want to find her. And that was a problem. He started to wish he was a boy, not a dog, and could think like a boy. Then he reflected that he hadn't been very good at that anyway. He wanted to find Tamrin for Smedge. But now that Smedge was far away he didn't want to find her. But he wanted to find her for himself, to see her, to say sorry, to try to explain why he had lied about her. But he didn't want to lead Smedge to her or go back to Smedge and betray her again.

Better not to look after all.

"Take us to Tamrin," said Smith. "Take us there."

Tim leaped up and tried to lick Smith's face.

He bounded ahead, Smith playing out the leash, his head low, Tamrin's scent in his nose.

"Fast as you can," said Smith. "I think time's running out." ‖

# Bakkmann assembled fifty kravvins

and made them understand what they were to do.

They had no minds, no intelligence. They could speak, and understand speech, up to a point. They couldn't think, beyond following instructions, and they often forgot what they were doing, unless they were just sent out to kill and collect.

Bakkmann did her best to instruct them. She felt that Ash was letting her impatience blur her judgement. These red killers were as likely to eat the tailor and everyone around him as they were to do any good.

"Don't kill anyone," she warned them again.

"Not kill."

"Kill."

"Not kill."

Bakkmann clattered annoyance, and as her frustration grew so did a small idea of escape. She summoned another twenty kravvins. There were enough and to spare; a few more wouldn't be missed. Bunching them together she put herself in the centre of them and marched them towards the gate.

The vanguard went through without a problem. It was only as Bakkmann approached that the magic lashed out at her to prevent her exit.

Kravvins to her left and right shrieked and exploded. She hunched herself as small and tight as she could against the perfection of the pain. She pushed forward. It was the kravvins' nature to keep together and as the first ones died others swarmed to take their place, keeping Bakkmann surrounded. They absorbed the attack and, to her astonished joy, she was through the gate and in the open. Ash was locked in still. The seal was meant for her and was stronger for her.

Bakkmann's thoughts went to Smedge, and following him, and finding him.

Sam was the second one into the upper room. Flaxfold, then Sam, then Tamrin, then Solder. Shoddle's voice followed them up.

"You'll be sorry. Go on. Have a look at it, old woman. See what it makes of you."

Solder shut the door on the shouting. It persisted as an inarticulate rumble of spite.

The mirror was clothed with the length of cloth.

"Stay away from it," said Flaxfold.

Solder stood right in front of it. The others kept to the side so that even if the cloth fell they would not be reflected.

"Come away from there," said Flaxfold.

Solder ignored her. He shrugged off his barrel and sat on it, kicking his heels against the hard leather sides.

"I looked in a mirror in the Deep World," he said. "And do you know, if you look very closely you can see your own eyes reflecting yourself over and over again. You should try it."

"Don't move," said Flaxfold.

"You told me to move away."

She clicked her tongue.

"I mean don't move any nearer. Move away."

"Make your mind up."

Sam thought about a spell to make Solder shift himself. He could make the top of the barrel too hot to sit on.

"Don't do that, Sam," said Flaxfold.

"How did you know?"

She smiled.

"I've known you all your life, as good as," she said. "I can see what you do before you do it."

"Always?"

"Mostly."

Tamrin took Solder's arm and he hopped off the barrel. She led him to the window.

"Can you keep a lookout here?" she said. "In case anyone comes."

Flaxfold made sure Tamrin saw her smile of thanks. Tamrin ignored it.

"There's to be no magic in here," said Flaxfold. "Not in

front of the mirror."

"Is it the one?" asked Sam.

Flaxfold nodded.

"I always thought it was just a story," he said. "Not true."

"How did you think the magic started, then?" she asked.

"Does it matter, as long as there's magic?"

"Most of the time, no," admitted the old woman. "What matters is what you do with the magic, not where it comes from."

She spoke quietly. The tailor had stopped shouting. The house was silent around them.

"But I think it matters now," she added. "Come. Tamrin. Take my hand, girl. Please."

Tamrin hesitated. Sam joined his mind to hers. She brushed him aside and held out her hand. Flaxfold's hand was warm, dry, stronger than Tamrin had expected.

"We must be friends," said Flaxfold.

Sam felt the warmth of the woman's touch.

Solder leaned towards the window, looking down. This was about them, not him.

"There have been three moments when magic was born or changed," said Flaxfold.

She put out her other hand and took Sam's.

"There was the first moment, when this mirror created magic. When reflection and reality collided and magic sprang out."

"Are you sure it was this one?"

"What other could it be? It made you two what you are, didn't it?"

"Yes." They spoke with one voice.

"It was hidden away," she said. "It should never have been found. The tailor meddled."

Tamrin tried to take her hand away. Flaxfold held her tight.

"One of us would never have been," said the girl, "if the mirror had been hidden properly."

"That's true. And you two are the second big moment in magic. You are the second making. And no one knows what you will bring."

"That's two," said Sam. "What's the third?"

"The third came second. It was when an old, tired, dying wizard called Slowin stole the name of a young girl and stole her magic. The firestorm that it caused nearly killed him, but he survived. He survived and became Ash. Your enemy. The one who comes to you through the Finished World. She's hungry and she's eager. She wants to be free. This time we have to hide the mirror for ever. If Ash were to stand in front of it I can't think what horrors she would release. If she ever owned it then nothing could stop her."

She squeezed their hands.

"I'll always be glad that it made the two of you," she said. "But it must never be seen again. If she ever found out where it was she would never rest till it was hers."

"She never shall," said Sam.

"I think she will," said another voice.

The door had opened silently. A slim, soft figure filled the doorway. The bloodied face of the tailor watched over his shoulder.

"Now you'll see some magic," he cackled.

The kravvins surged on with the speed of stupid rage. It was their nature to hate.

All of the hard-shelled creatures that served Ash had descended from drops of her own blood, shed when she had been a different person. Before the fierce magic she had summoned had transformed her from a man to a woman, from a wizard to a wraith, from a person to a shape.

The takkabakks and the kravvins, the tiny black beetles that burrowed in the earth, the dozens of other kinds that swarmed through Boolat, all of them found their origins in the droplets of blood that had spilled from that one who became Ash hundreds of years ago.

Only Bakkmann was different. Bakkmann had been the servant who stood alongside Slowin when the storm of wild magic hit. Bakkmann had been transformed, too, into this creature of shell, of shock and scream.

And now Bakkmann led the kravvins. Now they had a mind and a purpose and an aim.

Their sharp legs consumed the distance. They didn't crawl, they scurried.

To Shoddle. To Smedge. To slaughter. ‖

# The slim figure stepped into the room

leaving the tailor to limp after him, head wobbling, mouth gaping, blood spattered all over his face.

"Who are you?" demanded Tamrin.

"And how did you get in?" added Sam.

"He came through the door," said Solder. "While you were talking."

"Why didn't you warn us?"

Solder shrugged.

"You told me to watch," he said. "You didn't tell me to say anything."

"You don't know me?" said the figure.

He breathed in, very deeply. His black jerkin, leggings and heavy boots shifted shape and became a college uniform. He lost height and breadth. He had entered the room soldier-like, taller than the others. Now he faced them as Smedge.

"And we were such friends, Tam," he smiled. "How could you not know me?"

Shoddle lurched towards them. Smedge had done something to the tailor's neck to help him keep his head upright and move it from side to side, but it was a botched job, like a crooked shelf. It jerked and twitched.

Before Sam could stop her Tamrin hurled an attack at Smedge. Floorboards buckled, split, shot up and flew towards him. By the time they reached him they had become arrows, slender, fletched, and with cruel, barbed heads.

Sam raised his hand to counter the spell. It was too sudden, too sharp to stop. The arrows found their target.

The first to strike drove itself into his right shoulder, sending him staggering back with the force of its blow. Five, eight, more followed, piercing his chest, his legs, his stomach, and, rocking him almost to his knees, one thrust into his throat and stuck out the back of his neck.

Shoddle screamed.

Tamrin laughed.

Sam felt a driving pain in his chest. He looked at Smedge and he hated him with a spinning hatred that he had never felt before. Tamrin's fear and loathing of the boy took over his mind and he felt the shame of being falsely accused, the rage of being a victim, the fear of further attacks, the triumph of winning a fight. He loved the sight of the wounded Smedge and he felt the sick terror that he might just have killed him.

Smedge sank to the floor.

Sam grabbed his thoughts back from Tamrin. His mind

had brushed alongside hers and now he drew back to be himself alone.

Tamrin glanced at him, a shy, embarrassed look, as though he had caught her undressed.

"That was a mistake," said Flaxfold.

Shoddle pointed a trembling finger at Tamrin.

"You'll pay for that. That's murder. Magic or not. It's all the same."

He put his hands to the sides of his head to control its spasms.

"I didn't mean to kill him," said Tamrin. "I just lashed out."

"He's not dead," said Flaxfold. "Nor dying."

Smedge lay still. Blood pooled on the floor around him.

"Look," said Solder. "It's green."

The arrows sagged and dropped away from his body. Smedge was melting, losing definition.

As they watched Smedge disappeared and became a squat, wet shape, rounded and shining in the candlelight.

"Ugh," said Sam.

"It stinks," said Solder.

The tailor drew in breath and smiled.

"Like fresh bread," he said.

"Worse than slurry," said Solder.

"What is it?" asked Tamrin.

"It's Smedge," said Flaxfold. "Without art or disguise."

"You mean he's not a person?" said Sam.

Flaxfold crossed her arms.

"Not at all," she said. "I recognize him now I see him like this."

The green slime twitched, heaved and re-formed into slug-like form. It slid towards Shoddle, slurping against the floor. The tailor reached out a hand and stroked it.

Sam shuddered at the strings of sticky slime that attached Shoddle's hand to the huge slug.

The tailor sniggered.

Slug to toad, and then to monstrous things with teeth and claws and spit and spew, the creature was changing shape, searching.

"What's it doing?" whispered Tamrin.

"Finding itself again," said Flaxfold. "Your magic was too strong for him. You took him off guard." She gave Tamrin a severe look. "Magic's not for killing," she said.

"Not for killing that?"

"Not even that."

The thing that was Smedge had found the shape of the boy again, more or less, with gaps in the face and the wrong teeth and still a thin coating of slime. Grabbing Shoddle's hand he hauled himself upright and fixed them with a steady stare. One eye didn't seem to work and was not fixed entirely in the socket. When he spoke, green slime dribbled down the side of his mouth.

"Thank you," he said, to Tamrin.

Sam prepared himself to fight.

"What?" she asked.

"Thank you." He swallowed, disgustingly, and coughed. "Now I don't care what I do. Now we know each other, don't we?"

He moved towards them, hands outstretched. Sam flinched away. Tamrin stepped back. Solder scooted over to the window and tucked his feet underneath him on his barrel. Only Flaxfold stood firm.

He stopped, tilted his head to one side.

"You don't want to shake hands?"

Sam moved towards Tamrin. Their shoulders touched and he lost himself again for the moment in the strangeness of her thoughts. They looked at each other and he knew that she had brushed her mind against his.

Smedge started moving again. He was almost within reach of the mirror.

"Stop there," said Flaxfold.

Smedge dipped his head and carried on. His fingers found the fabric veiling it.

"That's it," screeched Shoddle. "That's it."

Flaxfold stepped aside. Sam thought she was fearful of Smedge, then he wondered if it was the same disgust that moved her. She stepped back, behind the mirror, leaving the way clear for Smedge to take control of it. She was afraid. So afraid of her own reflection that she gave way to Smedge.

His fingers clutched the cloth.

"Shall I?" he asked.

"Go on," shouted Shoddle. "Let's see the mirror."

Sam didn't know what to do. If he grabbed Smedge the cloth would come with him.

"Let's see the mirror," Shoddle shrieked.

Sam felt Tamrin's disgust at the gibbering tailor. He felt his own dread of what would happen if the mirror should be unveiled.

Smedge fondled the cloth.

"Oh," he breathed. "Oh, yes." He lifted the cloth a little and put his head between it and the reflecting surface. "Come on," he said. "What can you make of me?"

"Stop him," said Sam.

Flaxfold moved further into the shadow.

Smedge, his head beneath the cloth, his face against the mirror, shimmered and stood back. He shifted shape. Sam's eyes were confused by mist and movement. When they cleared he saw, sharp-set for the first time, the slim woman in the grey dress who had hunted him.

"Ash," he said.

She smiled.

"I've come for this mirror," she said. "And I've come for you, Sam."

Smith and Winny spoke little as Tim raced them towards Tamrin and the tailor's shop. After a few miles Smith slipped the leash and allowed Tim to run ahead, judging, rightly, that he would not run off altogether.

Tim's mind was a confusion of perplexity and delight.

He longed to see Tamrin again, though he feared to explain to her what he had done to betray her. He longed to lead Smith where he wanted to go, longed to please the man. Somewhere, lost in the doggy depths of his mind, he still longed to please Smedge, though the thought of the other boy made him cringe. More than that, the thought of Vengeabil filled him with regret, and anxiety. He could never go back now. Never face the old storeman who had trusted him. Thoughts of Vengeabil flooded through his mind and, for a foolish moment, he felt that the man was watching him.

To throw the thought out of his mind he tossed back his head and howled, and ran in a huge circle. He loved the chase, the scent, the air in his lungs, the disappearing miles.

Smith loved the chase a great deal less. Breathing was growing hard. His legs ached. He stopped to recover. Tim lolloped back to join them.

"Are you all right?" asked Winny.

Smith could only nod in reply.

"If you weren't carrying that it would be easier," she said.

He looked at the hammer he was grasping and frowned.

"I know," she agreed. "I'll carry it for you for a while."

Smith shook his head, but she took it from him.

Tim rushed round their legs, yelping encouragement.

"All right," agreed Winny. "But run right ahead. See if you can find a stream or something and wait for us there. You need a drink."

The stream, when they reached it, was on the edge of the town. Tamrin's scent was strong and fresh here. And there was Vengeabil's scent again. Tam must have spent so long in his kitchen that she even smelled of it. Tim bounded with pleasure and couldn't stop himself from leaping up and licking Smith's face when the man at last arrived.

"We're close, are we?" he asked.

Tim yelped.

"I'll take the hammer, then," he said.

Winny handed it over. Tim noticed that her hands were large, strong and used to the weight. She wasn't tired, either.

"Where's Starback?" asked Winny. "Why isn't he with us?"

"We'll go carefully from here," said Smith, putting Tim back on the leash.

Tim was surprised at how comforted he was by the restraint. He looked over his shoulder, towards Canterstock, so many miles away, and towards Vengeabil, who had helped him and whom he had let down.

"No," said Winny. "Let him run. Time's short and he's faster than us."

The kravvin army approached from the other side of town, and at a much swifter rate.

They had come further, but faster. Bakkmann, who thought to lead them, found herself challenged to keep up. They wouldn't stop, even when she tried to make them. She clattered out her orders and they ignored her, streaming ever onward, towards the town, towards the tailor, towards Tamrin.

✠

Starback was a ship without a compass. Sam had gone. Just disappeared. These people were chasing a girl, but Starback needed to find Sam. Needed to be Sam again.

He rose high into the air, out of sight. First he would fly over Boolat, try to find Sam there. Then the college, perhaps. After that, Flaxfold's house. The inn. Anywhere. Everywhere. Until he found him.

For the first time, Ash stood before Sam's eyes, clear to see, not shaded by the edges of the Finished World. And Sam was astonished at how lovely she was.

He stepped nearer to her.

She smiled and held out her hand.

"Come to me, Sam," she said. "I've been waiting for you a long time. Come, now."

Her grey dress fell in graceful folds, nearly to the floor. Her outstretched arm was wreathed in a flowing sleeve that shimmered in the candlelight. Her hair framed the delicate features of her face, casting them into mysterious shadows. Her smile was kind. Her hand was open to him.

Why had he feared her?

"Come away," she repeated. "I'll show you magic. Magic you've never dreamed of." She lowered her voice to a whisper, as though speaking to him alone. "They've tricked you. They've told you lies. They've held you back, Sam. They're jealous of your magic. They hate you for being so powerful."

Sam couldn't take his eyes from her.

"You know it's true, don't you? They bind you. They tie you up. They chain you. They restrict you. You want to break free and use your magic and all the time they prevent you. They tell you magic is dangerous. They won't let you use it. That's right, isn't it? You have so much magic. So much more than they do. They envy you."

Sam nodded. It was true. They did.

"Don't listen," said Tamrin. "She's lying."

"But she isn't lying," said Sam. "It's all true."

"No. All she wants—"

Ash raised her arm and drew a circle in the air. The circle became a hole and Sam could see the sky above it, black and starless. Ash beckoned into the blackness. Beetles tumbled over the edges of the hole, falling like hailstones. They swarmed over the floor. They fell on to Sam's shoulders and into his hair. He flinched in disgust, then began to enjoy the delicate scrape of their legs, the tickling and the scratching.

They covered Tamrin, stifling her. She clamped her mouth shut to stop them running in.

"Take the mirror, Sam," said Ash. "Carry it out and come with me. To Boolat."

"Yes," said Sam.

"And we'll make more magic than has ever been imagined."

Sam nodded and moved to the mirror.

"You'll have to help me," he said. "It's too big."

Ash trembled. She snapped at him. "Use your magic. Quickly. Take it."

Sam put his hand to the mirror. It was cool to his touch.

Tamrin dragged the beetles away from her, clawed them from her mouth and eyes. She sprang forward and punched Ash full in the mouth. She waited for the horrid thud of fist on face, for the crunch of teeth, the spurt of blood.

Her fist went straight through the face.

"It's Smedge," she shouted.

Sam turned.

"It's not Ash," said Tamrin. "It's Smedge. It's a trick. Ash is still in Boolat. The mirror helped Smedge to look like her."

She gathered her mind into a concentrated spear and threw it at Sam, breaking through the barrier between herself and him.

For a moment she felt the sly invitation of Ash and wanted to respond.

For a moment Sam felt the sloppy repulsion of Smedge's face on his hand.

They were one and they were two again in an instant.

It was enough to break the spell. The beetles disappeared. Tamrin drew back her fist. Smedge put his hands to his head and kneaded it as a potter kneads clay, trying to re-form it into something like its usual appearance. The image of Ash had fallen from him and he was himself again.

Sam couldn't look at the others. He closed his mind tight shut against Tamrin. He glanced at Solder, who was standing on his barrel, avoiding the beetles. He looked at the floor and saw Flaxfold move from behind the mirror. He noticed that she still kept out of its direct aim.

"I'm sorry," he said.

"What happened?" asked Tamrin. "Smedge looked in the mirror and nothing really happened. It was just another shape shift."

"That's because he doesn't exist," said Flaxfold. She turned eyes of pity at Smedge. "He's not a person at all. He's just the excrement of the wild magic that Slowin summoned up all those years ago when he became Ash. There's nothing there to reflect."

Smedge snarled at her.

"I still hate him," said Tamrin. "I'm not going to be sorry for him."

"That's your choice," said Flaxfold. "He's done you great harm and means to do much more if he can."

"And I can. And I shall," said Smedge.

"They weren't real, the beetles," said Tamrin. "You're nothing. You're all tricks and pretend."

Shoddle, who had sunk to the floor and was leaning against the wall, raised his hand to his ruined head and cupped his ear. A horrid clacking of sharp legs on the cobbles outside. and thick voices.

"Here."

"Kill."

"Here."

"In."

"Kill."

"Up."

"Up."

"Up."

"Listen," he said. And he laughed. "They've arrived. Now we'll see some fun."

The front door slammed and the skittering legs mounted the stairs.

Sam put his hand to his head. Not them. Not now.

The kravvins surged through the door.

"Yes," cried Shoddle. "Come in."

Flaxfold grabbed Solder's hand and he hopped from his barrel.

"Get fire," she said. "Quickly."

Solder flipped the top from his barrel, plunged in and drew out a tinderbox. He struck it. The tinder flared. Flaxfold dragged off her scarf, held it over the flame and let it catch. She pulled Solder, Tamrin and Sam to the mirror and drew a line of fire on the floor in front of them, painting them into a corner. It was all done in an instant.

A kravvin stepped into the line of flame and exploded with a scream.

The room was alive with kravvins. Last of all, Bakkmann pushed through the doorway and surveyed the scene.

Sam saw that Bakkmann and Smedge knew each other.

Tamrin saw that Bakkmann and Smedge hated each other.

Another kravvin attempted the line and died with a sizzle of hot pus.

Bakkmann clattered a loud order to hold back. Their blank faces turned to her and Sam thought they would attack her. A part of his mind wanted to see them do it, wanted to see them destroy at least one of his enemies.

Beyond Sam's control, magic slipped from him. His thought took shape and slid down to the floor, where it crouched, lizard-like. It curled into a ball and rolled over the flames to the kravvins' side of the room. It scurried to Bakkmann and crawled up her boot. Bakkmann shook her foot and it fell off, landing on Shoddle. The tailor screamed. His head dropped to one side. The creature leaped to Shoddle's face and clawed at him. Shoddle shrieked and a kravvin turned its blank face to see what was happening.

"Get rid of it," shouted Shoddle.

The kravvin stepped forward, grabbed the lizard and squeezed it, killing it instantly, then took Shoddle by the neck, snapped what was left of it, cuffed his head aside. The head rolled to the wall beneath the window.

"Kill."

"Head."

"Kill."

They fell on Shoddle, tossed his body up and it smacked against the ceiling. Blood spurted from his neck. As the droplets fell they hardened into beetles the size of your thumb and when they hit the floor they ran in all directions.

Shoddle's dead face leered up at them. They covered it, a blood-red mask of legs and shells, and burrowed in, eating it clean in no time till all that was left was the white skull.

The kravvins didn't even leave the bones of his body. They crunched through everything.

The beetles, searching for more food, more fight, ran over and into the line of flame. They popped and sizzled, screamed and died, but they were winning. Their wet corpses began to smother the fire. The line was being destroyed.

Sam gripped his staff in both hands.

"No more magic," Flaxfold warned him. "You saw what happened last time. Magic will feed them."

"What can we do, then?" asked Sam.

He thrust the end of his staff into the chest of a kravvin that was trying to cross the line, through a small gap made by the beetles. The kravvin fell back but was not killed. It rushed at him again, and again he repelled it.

Flaxfold sighed.

"I don't think there's anything. Just get ready to fight as long as you can."

Tim turned his head over his shoulder and yelped to the others to catch him up. They were out of sight. He skidded round the corner into the narrow street and ran through the front door into the tailor's shop. Tamrin's scent was so strong here. He bounded up the stairs and crashed into the room.

The kravvins turned their faces to him as one and sniffed.

"Dog."

"Kill."

"Eat."

"Kill."

He planted his paws on the floor, slid to a halt and tried to run back.

A hand grabbed his neck. A kravvin. It hauled him off his feet, into the air, and was about to throw him up and dash him against the ceiling, killing him.

"No."

Smedge grabbed the kravvin's arm and dragged it down.

"Drop him."

The kravvin pushed its smooth face into Smedge's.

"Do it. Or Ash will be very angry."

The kravvin opened its hand and Tim fell to the floor. He slunk into the corner, his tail between his legs. He kept his head down, ready for a blow from Smedge.

Smedge put his hand to Tim.

Tim cowered.

Smedge stroked him.

"No. I won't hit you," he said. "Not just yet."

He looked across at the group in the opposite corner. Flax-fold had torn her sleeve off and lit it from the flames. She was rebuilding the barrier.

"Oh, that won't help you," he said. "It keeps your enemies out. It works against anything made by the wild magic. It kills kravvins and beetles and poor old Bakkmann, and even me. We're all from the wild magic."

Sam and Tamrin stood side by side. They searched each other's minds, like putting a foot into water to decide whether or not to plunge in. So far they had paddled in the shallows. Neither of them had been able either to open completely to the other or to allow the other in.

When Sam became Starback he gave himself completely to the experience of being dragon. He had not gone this far with Tamrin. Something held him back. Now he had a sense that they would be stronger together against Smedge than separately.

And he still could not give himself to it.

"But how about an old friend?" asked Smedge. He patted Tim. "An old friend could come to you there, I think."

He smacked Tim's head. The dog face disappeared and Tim looked out at them.

"No," said Tamrin.

"He's my dog," said Smedge. "My pet."

He slapped Tim's face and he became all dog again.

"Everyone hates you," he whispered to Tamrin. "Everyone. And do you know why? Because your friend Tim told them you were a bully. He did. He said you hurt people. Didn't you, Tim?"

The dog wagged a slow tail. He looked away.

"And now," said Smedge, "he's coming in there to get you. He'll bring you out. And some of you will be fed to the krav-

vins and some of you will be coming back to Boolat with me.
I wonder which is which?"

He put his finger to his face in mock puzzlement.

"We'll feed the kravvins first," he said. "That will stop
them from falling on the rest of you for food."

He ruffled Tim's neck.

"Get the roffle," he said.

Tim leaped up, through the flames, and seized Solder's
leg in his mouth. He dragged him towards the centre of the
room.

Solder yelled and struggled. Flaxfold grabbed Tim by the
scruff of his neck. Tamrin smacked him. Sam flung his cloak
over his shoulder, ready to attack.

"No magic!" shouted Flaxfold. "No magic. It will come
back to kill us all."

They held on to Solder and pulled against Tim. Tim
snarled and clamped his teeth into Solder's leg.

"Let go," screamed Tamrin.

She raised her hand to hurt Tim and found that she
couldn't. She couldn't damage the boy who had been her
friend.

"I'll turn him back," she said. "Back to Tim."

Flaxfold took hold of her shoulders.

"No magic. No. It will kill us all."

Smedge laughed.

Tim dragged Solder further from the safety of the barrier
of roffle fire.

"Let me go," Solder shouted.

"We've got you," Sam said. "We've got you."

"No." Solder beat his fists against Sam's face. "You let me go. You're killing me."

He was being pulled apart. Tim had magic enough to beat any ordinary strength Sam might have to save the roffle.

Solder slipped from Sam's grasp and slid through the fire, towards the hungry kravvins. They knew he was theirs. They clacked their legs with pleasure.

Until Smith came through the door, swung his hammer and took the head off the nearest kravvin.

Winny grasped the whole situation in a second. She crossed the room, slipped the chain round Tim's neck and dragged him clear. Solder slipped from his jaws and backed off, rubbing his leg.

"You can't hold him with a chain," Smedge sneered. "Come here, Tim."

He flicked his fingers.

Winny stared into his eyes.

"A chain made at Smith's forge from roffle fire," she said. "That will hold him."

Tim pressed himself against her legs and kept away from Smedge.

Winny scooped up the burning material in her hands and swung it round, lashing the kravvins that Smith hadn't already smashed with his hammer.

As soon as it hit them the burning scarf and sleeve sliced

through them and they burst like poppy heads in the sun. Bakkmann tried to attack Smith from behind. Tim darted at her and she lost her balance. Smith swung round, scythed his hammer and took Bakkmann's legs away from her, snapping them. She fell on to her back and couldn't right herself, the stumps waving in the air.

The last kravvin burst under Winny's attack with the flames. The floor was a shambles of shell fragments, legs and the soft grey insides of the dead creatures. Only Smedge and Bakkmann remained to do them harm. Bakkmann was out of the fight and had no magic anyway. But they moved carefully from their safe corner back into the room, keeping her under close watch.

Shoddle's skull grinned at them from the floor.

"Hello, Dorwin," said Flaxfold. "And Smith. You were just in time."

"Flaxfold," said Smith. "Good to see you."

Winny hugged Flaxfold.

"Dorwin?" said Tamrin.

"Dorwin. Winny. Tamrin. Tam. What does a name matter?" she said.

"Names are important," Sam told her.

"She knows that, boy," said Smith. "As well as anyone."

Tamrin confronted Smedge. "Bring Tim back," she said.

"Do you think so?" he asked. "It will need magic. What will the mirror do then?"

"I want to see Tim."

Winny slipped the chain from him. Tim's face emerged from the fur. His legs straightened. His tail disappeared. He crouched, stretched, stood. He hung his head and refused to look at anyone.

"Are you all right?" asked Sam.

Tim smiled at him.

"You've grown," he said. "Since last year, at the college."

"You were my first friend," said Sam. "The first I ever had."

Tim shrugged. He moved to stand next to Smedge.

"Not any more," he said.

"You can go now," said Smedge. "All of you. Go on."

Tamrin lunged at him. She knocked him to one side and seized Tim's arm.

"You're not going with him?"

"Yes. I am. It's what's left."

"You can't. You're not like him."

Tamrin felt tears coming. She pushed her hand against her face, hurting herself in her determination not to cry.

"How do you know what anyone's like?" asked Tim.

"But you hate him. You're my friend. You said you'd help me."

Tim looked her in the eyes.

"Things change," he said.

Smedge patted him on the head.

"Good boy."

Tim started to snarl at Smedge but it changed to a whimper and he nuzzled his head against him.

"Get out," said Smedge.

"We're keeping the mirror," Sam told him. "Go back to Boolat. Tell your Ash that she'll never find it. Tell her to stay where she is or she'll regret it."

Smedge put his hands to his head to shape it nearer to the real thing.

"You had better go," said Flaxfold. "There are more of us. You can't have the mirror."

She spoke with her usual quiet authority, and Sam gasped when Smedge argued with her. No one did that.

"Get out, old woman," he said. "I remember you. I remember how scared you were of the wild magic. I'm not scared of any magic. The wild magic made me. Let's see what it makes of you."

He grabbed the cloth covering the mirror and flicked it away. Flaxfold saw his plan and swung the mirror so that it was turned away from all of them.

Smedge laughed. He put himself in front of it and paraded before its surface. No reflection answered him.

"He's not there," said Tamrin.

"There, and not there," whispered Flaxfold, "as you two are two and one."

Smedge leaned down and grabbed a stump of Bakkmann's leg. He dragged the clattering creature to the mirror.

"No," she clattered. "No. No."

"Shut up. You're real enough. The wild magic changed you. It didn't make you. Let's see."

Smedge moved the mirror again. Bakkmann saw herself reflected back, not as a monstrous shape, half-beetle, half-human, but as the woman she had been before the wild magic had struck. She reached out her finger to touch the surface.

"All these years," she said. "All this time." She was crying. "I stood next to Slowin. Side by side when the magic struck."

Her fingers touched the bright metal.

And she exploded in a flower of flame.

She burned like a rush torch in tallow, with a steady, greasy light.

Solder moved his barrel as far as he could from the light and sat on it cross-legged.

As the flame flickered and died the central pillar of fire gathered into a clear shape. The last light faded.

"Side by side," said Ash. "We did. We stood side by side."

Where Bakkmann had died Ash stood looking at them. She looked at her reflection in the mirror.

"Come here, Smedge," she said. She took his hand. "You've done well. Very well. You brought me here at last."

She raised her arms above her head, breathed deeply and smiled.

"At last."

She surveyed the scene of death all around her.

"And you made everything so nice for me to come to," she said.

"What do you want, Slowin?" asked Flaxfold.

Ash whipped her head round and glared at her.

"Don't call me that," she said. "I'm Ash. Understand?"

"How did you get here?" asked Sam.

He was speaking to her face to face at last. He didn't know how he felt. Not fear, but something more elusive.

Ash put her hand to the frame of the mirror.

"Do you need to ask, boy?" she said.

"You should be in Boolat," said Flaxfold. "Locked away."

"Indeed," said Ash. "Come with me."

She spread her arms, pursed her lips and blew.

The room filled with smoke.

She blew again.

The smoke cleared.

The room was transformed. It was twenty, thirty times as big, round and tall, the roof open to the sky. A huge chimney.

"Just like home," said Ash.

"Sam," said Flaxfold. "You have to try now. This may be the moment that all was leading towards. From the day that Flaxfield took you in as his apprentice. From the day he died and we cast him to the river to take away. This may be what you were made for."

Ash opened her arms to him.

"Try me, boy," she said. "Try your magic. You've seen what mine can do."

Sam leaned his staff on the floor. He swept his cloak back to free his arms. He steadied himself on firm feet.

He cleared his mind and thought what substance Ash could be made of, where he could attack her. Slowin had been fire. Fire had remade Slowin. Sam would not use that.

He drew a line on the floor with the tip of his shoe. He scraped his foot back and stamped.

A spring of clear water bubbled up. Sam directed it with his staff. It ran towards Ash, gathering speed and strength. By the time it reached her it was a flood, surging over her.

She held her head high, let it roll back and allowed the water to sweep over her. The torrent was strong enough to uproot an elm. Ash stood firm. She put her hands in front of her, palms together. The water divided and passed her, and as it passed it turned to bright flame, licked the curved wall and ran up and out of the round opening at the top.

"You are the old magic," she said. "Wasted. Wanting. It will be a kindness to kill you."

Starback settled on the roof of Flaxfold's house, folded his wings and looked down the slope to the river.

Sam had gone. Perhaps dead. Perhaps so damaged by the switch through the mirror that he would never be part of Starback again.

The dragon crept along the eaves and slipped into the house through an open window. It was so clean, so bright, so nicely jumbled with the objects of everyday life. Starback curled up in an armchair, tucked his tail under his chin and stared at the carved oak dresser. The armchair smelled of Sam, and of Flaxfold, of soap and sleep. Underneath all the other layers of people in the house Flaxfield's distinctive scent remained; the persistence of memory.

Starback missed Flaxfield. The old wizard had brought him here when Sam was a sad child, and Flaxfield had made them friends.

Nothing had been right since Flaxfield had gone, and without him nothing could ever be right again.

He had lost Flaxfield, but he had Sam. Now he had lost Sam as well, and he had nothing but himself.

Sleep would take away the sadness, but sleep would not come. ||

# Ever since the day that Flaxfield had died

Sam had wondered what it would be like to be dead, and now he was going to find out.

Smedge hugged himself with pleasure. His shape ran through the gallery of creatures he had been in his journey from slime to servant of Ash. Sam's eyes were dazzled by the speed and variety. Like flicking the pages of a book of pictures. Ash clicked her fingers and scowled. Smedge formed into something like his school self, only taller and in the black jerkin and boots of a soldier.

Sam saw that Ash was excited. She was trying to be calm, to seem like a teacher controlling a class. But, as a nervous child will pick at its fingernails, Ash snapped off the tip of her finger and sucked at the bleeding end. It was a chance, a weakness, an opportunity.

Or it may have been.

Ash dropped the finger end on the floor, crushed it under her foot and said, "Enough." She raised her hands so that the sleeves of her gown fell back, revealing her arms. She opened her palms towards them and began to chant.

Sam felt his hands grow cold. Then he could not feel his hands at all. The staff fell to the floor. His head was heavy. His legs trembled. He leaned back against the wall to stop himself from falling.

He put out his hand to Tamrin, thinking her strength might strengthen him. She was as damaged as he was. Her face was grey and flaking. The skin peeled off like paint from a weathered door.

"Slowin!"

Sam recognized the voice. He couldn't remember where he had heard it last.

"What are you doing?"

Sam's head cleared.

The old storeman from the college stood near to Ash.

Sam gave himself over to despair. Just an old man who stumbled into trouble. Another one for Ash to kill.

Vengeabil brought his staff down in a vicious swipe, breaking Ash's arms.

The spell faltered and failed. Sam could feel his hands again. He recovered his feet and stood upright.

Ash snarled. Smedge tried to punch Vengeabil. The old man struck him in the face with his staff.

"Don't raise your arm to me, boy."

"No magic, now," warned Flaxfold.

Vengeabil smiled at her.

"Always cautious, Flaxfold," he said.

Ash's arms grew back under her sleeves. Sam sighed. Nothing could stop her.

"Try this," said Smith.

He lunged at Ash and smashed his hammer down towards her head.

His words alerted her. She clicked her tongue. The hammer stopped, inches from her skull, and bounced off, out of Smith's hand and crashed through the window, clattering on the cobbled street below.

"Nothing," she said. "Nothing can stop me. Nothing."

She smiled and leaned forward, confidentially.

"Do you know," she told them, "there was someone who could. Someone who had magic enough to work, even here, even with the mirror in the room. But he's dead. He's gone."

"Flaxfield," said Vengeabil.

"Of course. He's gone and his magic has gone with him."

Flaxfold put her hands on the shoulders of Sam and Tamrin and spoke to Ash. "Flaxfield sealed you in Boolat," she said. "Remember?"

"And I've escaped." She expanded in triumph. "Escaped."

"Seal her," Flaxfold said, in a low voice.

Ash heard.

"What?"

Vengeabil hurried towards Flaxfold.

"What? You have the seal?"

Flaxfold indicated the weight tied around Tamrin's neck.

"This will stop her," he said.

Vengeabil grabbed it.

"Don't," shouted Ash.

It wasn't there.

"I've got it," said Sam. He closed his hand around it.

It wasn't there.

Vengeabil tried again.

It wasn't there.

Sam felt the weight at his throat.

Ash laughed.

"The magic has left you," she said. "It's my turn. Magic has its seasons, and yours has gone."

Flaxfold steered Tamrin and Sam into the middle of the room.

"Your season died many, many years ago, Slowin," she said. "You stole another's."

"Perhaps I did." Ash looked delighted. "Or perhaps I only understood what it was to have a new season. But I won."

"Years and years in that filthy prison?" said Flaxfold. "Do you call that winning?"

"No," she screamed. "No. But this is. Freedom again. And you can't seal me back there. Not now. I'll kill you all and take the seal and then I'll be free to do as I please."

Taking care not be reflected in it herself, Flaxfold moved Sam and Tamrin in front of the mirror.

"And when I'm free," Ash hissed, "then you'll have to watch out." She pointed to them, one by one. "You, boy, and you, girl. And you, old woman. All of you. You'll wish you were dead when I get to you."

"You'll never escape," said Sam.

Ash snarled.

"I'm already out," she said. "And soon I'll be free to come and go. And your magic will be dead alongside you. Then the world will see what magic can do."

Ash reached out to grab the seal from Tamrin's throat.

But Tamrin wasn't there.

And Sam wasn't there.

"Flaxfield," said Vengeabil.

Just as sleep was folding its wings over Starback he snapped awake.

Flaxfield.

He rushed from the armchair, through the door and leaped into the air's embrace.

He could see a room, a mirror, a roffle, a schoolboy, Flaxfold, the smith and his daughter, Smedge and grey-gowned Ash.

He couldn't see Tamrin or Sam.

He could see himself, Flaxfield, reflected in the mirror, his hand at his throat, clutching the seal tied there with the leather cord.

He was Flaxfield reflected. But he felt Sam, and more than Sam, other than Sam.

No matter. He flew at full speed, through the late night and coming dawn to a village, a narrow street, a tailor's shop.

Flaxfield tore the seal from his throat, snapping the cord.

Ash sent a bolt of fire straight at him.

He brushed it aside with casual disdain.

Ash tried to turn and run out, and he took her arm, twisted her around and pushed the seal to her forehead.

Her face crumpled and became the face of an old man, tired, near to death.

"Slowin," he said. "You're going back."

He threw her across the room and she fell to her knees in front of the mirror.

The grey dress was smoke. It curled up, taking her with it. A draught from the mirror sucked the smoke in. In no time Ash had disappeared behind the shining surface. The room was itself again and seemed strangely crowded now.

"Flaxfield," said Smith.

Flaxfield had gone too. Tamrin and Sam stood side by side, the seal between them on the floor.

And so had Smedge and Tim, crept away while the others watched Ash leave.

Flaxfold veiled the mirror.

"I'll take care of this now," she said.

"I've been searching for it for years," said Smith. "It should go with me."

"Let the young ones decide," said Winny.

"It goes with Flaxfold," said Tamrin.

Vengeabil put his arm round her shoulders. From his other hand a dribble of stars fell from the finger ends to the floor. A small, old cat licked them up and rubbed its head against his legs.

"It's been a long time, Cabbage," said Flaxfold. "It's good to see you."

"I'm hungry," said Solder. He hitched his barrel on to his back. "Can we get something to eat?"

The window crashed inwards and a green and blue gale rushed through, swept over their heads and settled itself on the top of the mirror.

Tamrin felt a surge of exaltation and knew what it was to be dragon and boy.

Sam, in his delight to be Starback again, gave Tamrin the same freedom and received it back.

He looked at her.

She looked at him.

They looked at themselves in Starback.

"Go and eat," he shouted. "We'll see you later."

They ran out of the room and down the stairs. Starback soared through the broken window, out into the early morning.

"We're going to fly," said Tamrin, disappearing through the door.

"Breakfast?" said Solder.

Flaxfold and Vengeabil together made a strong spell of sealing on the door at the top of the stairs and at the front door; they sealed the broken window as well. Nothing could get in or out. Not a person, not a roffle, not a kravvin. ||

# Tamrin ran in first

and flung a garland of mushrooms on the counter top.

"These are all good to eat," she said.

Jaimar's shop was crowded already, and Sam and Tamrin added to the crush. Starback took one look and scampered up the shelves behind the counter.

"I can cook them," offered Tamrin. "You're all eating already."

Her face was glowing. She couldn't keep still. She scooped up the mushrooms again, so many that they spilled out from her hands. She threw the ones she had up into the air, spun round and clapped her hands. All of them, the ones that had fallen, and the ones that she had thrown, formed a circle in the air over the table and then, like a skein of geese, travelled in line to settle in a bowl on the counter.

Tamrin laughed. She looked at Flaxfold, and at Vengeabil, unsure which of them she should ask.

"That's all right, isn't it?" she said. "Just a little magic?"

They spoke together.

"Under the circumstances," said Vengeabil.

"Just this once," said Flaxfold.

"I'll cook them for you," said Jaimar.

"I can do it."

"Sit down," she said. "Take some bacon. I won't be long. There's wizard talk they're waiting to share and they need me out of the way."

Sam and Tamrin joined the others at the tables.

The bacon was thick and salty. The eggs were fresh. Solder offered them bread and made room.

Food had never tasted so good. Not even the lemon curd that Vengeabil made. Tamrin chewed slowly, relishing every mouthful. She knew that the storeman was watching her, trying not to. She avoided his eye as much as she could.

Sam began the talk.

"Is she beaten now, Ash?" he asked.

"Wounded," said Flaxfold.

"Weakened," said Vengeabil.

He pointed to the seal at Sam's throat.

"We've strengthened the magic that locked her up," he said. "It may last a hundred years. Or ten. Or one. I don't know."

Tamrin listened, but it wasn't the thing she was most interested in.

"Smedge," she said. "Where's he?"

"Back to Boolat, I suppose," said Vengeabil. "We shan't see

him back at the college."

For the first time since she had run in a shadow crossed Tamrin's face.

"I'm not going back there," she said.

"You will," he said. "Don't you know who you are?"

It was the question.

And now she knew the answer.

"I'm him," she said, pointing her fork at Sam. "And him," pointing it at Starback.

"You are," he agreed. "And you're my apprentice, remember? You signed an agreement. You're coming back to the college with me."

"I'm never going there again," she said. "Never."

"And you're coming back with me," Flaxfold told Sam.

"We're staying together," said Tamrin. She banged her fork on the table.

"You are," said Flaxfold. "You have no choice about that. But you're going your separate ways, just for now."

Smith had been eating steadily, paying close attention. Now he joined in.

"Was that really Flaxfield?" he asked. "In the room just then?"

"What?" said Sam.

"You don't know?"

"What are you talking about?"

Smith explained what they had all seen, that when Sam and Tamrin stood together, looking into the mirror, they had become Flaxfield. Sam argued and he questioned Smith and the others. They made him understand.

Jaimar came in with a dish of mushrooms fried in butter.

"I'll leave these here," she said.

"Stay," said Flaxfold. "Please."

Jaimar found another chair and joined them.

"What do you think it was?" Flaxfold asked Vengeabil.

"I've been thinking about it. Could it be this? I was Flaxfield's apprentice. Tam's mine. Sam was Flaxfield's apprentice, too." He looked at the old woman. "Were you?" he asked.

She shook her head and strands of hair fell loose.

"No. I wasn't."

"Well, anyway. An apprentice always keeps something of the wizard who trained him. And more than that, Flaxfield sealed Ash in Boolat with that very seal. There was a lot of Flaxfield in the room just then, and it looked to us as though he was there himself." He shrugged. "That's as good as I can do."

"It sounds very reasonable," agreed Flaxfold. She touched the seal around Sam's neck. "Is this where it stays now?"

Sam unfastened the knot and handed the seal to Tamrin. She tied it round her neck and it stayed there.

"It goes to either of us," said Sam. "I think."

Tamrin untied it and held it in her hand.

"May I hold it?" asked Dorwin.

Tamrin hesitated. She didn't want to hand it to anyone but Sam. It had become important to her.

"I was there when it was made," said Dorwin. "Would you

mind? I'd like to see it again."

"You can't have been," Tamrin argued.

"At my forge," said Smith.

Tamrin allowed it to pass to Dorwin.

"It's beautiful," she said, turning it in her hands. It was a dragon's head, with flames pouring from the mouth.

Smith touched it with his fingertip.

"I was there when it was made," he said.

Tamrin had to know.

"Tell me."

"The girl who made this," he said, "she was the one, the one Slowin stole the magic from. She came to me afterwards, and she made that."

He put his hand into his pocket and took out a small iron bird, the one Tamrin had liked.

"Here," he said. "You can have this. Have you still got the scissors?"

She nodded.

"Did they come in useful?"

She nodded again.

"Take it," he said. "It's yours."

Tamrin cupped the bird in her hands.

"Thank you."

"Now," said Smith. "The mirror." He stared at Flaxfold. "I should take it. Guard it."

"I think I'll look after it."

"Where?"

"At my house."

"You'll never get it there. It's too far."

"I think I'll manage."

Tamrin had never heard an argument carried out with such quiet voices, such polite words, such a friendly-seeming manner. She had no doubt it was a real fight.

"Now see here," said Smith. "I made that mirror. It belongs to me. I'm taking it back."

Tamrin needed to have the seal again. She took it, too quickly, not politely. She smiled an apology to Dorwin.

"You can't have made it," she said, when the seal was safely back in her hand.

He leaned back and smiled.

"And why not?"

She gave him a look that suggested he was mad, or stupid.

"Because it's the mirror. If you'd made it you'd be older than magic. That's why."

In the long silence that followed this, Tamrin felt the dragon seal in her hand move. The head turned. The flames grew warm. She looked at it and it was just the same. Nothing had altered.

At last, Flaxfold spoke.

"Solder," she said. "It's been very nice to meet you. We'll meet again, I think. You're going back with Smith now? And with Dorwin?"

"Yes," he said. He spooned some mushrooms on to his plate. "When breakfast's over."

Flaxfold stood up. "Jaimar, your food's better than ever. Thank you."

Jaimar hugged her and cried a little. Then she hugged Solder and cried some more.

"Vengeabil," said Flaxfold. "It's been a long time."

"It has."

"I don't think it will be so long before we see each other again."

"I think you're right. Look after Sam."

"And you look after Tamrin."

"I'm not going," said Tamrin.

Vengeabil faced her.

"If we forget the indenture," he said, "if we lay aside the fact that you're bound to me, do you want to leave me, before we've finished? Do you want to be a spoiled apprentice?"

Stars dribbled from his fingertips.

Tamrin watched them bounce against the floor and settle. She waited for the cat. It was old and thin. It moved slowly, as though with aching legs. Its rough tongue lapped up the stars. With a final, affectionate brush against his legs it faded and vanished.

"No," she said. "I want to finish my apprenticeship with you. I really do. But I can't go back there."

"You'll walk through empty corridors, read in a deserted library, eat your meals with me, practise your magic in secret. No one will see you. Frastfil and Duddle will never imagine you've returned. You'll walk in silence, like the night."

"And Sam?" she asked. "I'll still see Sam? And Starback?"

"How could you not?"

"All right. I'll come with you. Tomorrow."

He smiled.

"I'm leaving today," he said. "Catch me up?"

"Easily."

"We leave tomorrow as well," said Flaxfold to Sam. "With the mirror."

"With the mirror," Smith agreed. "It's pointless arguing with you. Mind you look after it this time."

Starback swooped down from the top shelf, circled once and sped through the open door.

Sam raced after him.

Tamrin paused.

"Thank you," she said. "All of you."

She ran out into the sunlight and up and over the house-tops. ||

# "Well what am I?"

asked Tamrin.

She stood on a hilltop outside the town.

Sam held her hand and they looked up into the blue sky.

And they looked down from dizzying height to see themselves, tiny on the green slope, heads tilted back, mouths open in laughter.

Sam squeezed her hand.

"That's easy for you," he said. "You always wondered who you were and now you've found out. I never wondered who I was, and now I don't know any more."

"You're you. You're me. You're us. We're him," she said, pointing up to the swooping dragon.

"Like a tree," said Sam, "that's leaf and branch and root and trunk and all at once, and all different and all the same."

"Acorn and dry twig, beginning and end, start and finish," she said.

"And all that's in between."

"All that."

Starback dived and hurtled towards them, only veering off at the last moment and rising high again as swift as sunlight.

Tamrin's stomach churned with the sudden movement.

"I've never been so happy," she said.

She waited for Sam's answer, fearful it would be different.

He let her see his mind and she was content.

"Will it last?" she asked. "The happiness."

"For ever?" said Sam.

"Yes?"

He made his hand tight on hers and they sprang again to fly with dragons.

## envoy

It was night when Smith arrived at the small house by the river. There was no moon, but he knew the road well enough not to need light. Sharp stars watched him approach and Sam was in the doorway when he arrived.

"You're late," said Sam.

"If I'm late, you should be in bed. Where's Flaxfold?"

"You know she's away for the night," said Sam. "That's why you're here."

Smith closed the door.

"I'm not stopping long," he said.

"You'll stay the night?"

"No."

"I won't let you see the mirror except by daylight."

"Then I'll stay. But I'm up early. All right?"

Sam gave him supper and stayed reading after Smith had

gone to bed.

When Smith got up the next day Sam was in the same chair, reading.

"Have you been up all night?"

"No."

"Come on, then." ·

Sam led Smith to Flaxfield's study. He unlocked the door and held it open for Smith to pass.

The mirror was veiled.

"If you stand there," said Sam, "you can't be reflected. I'll stand here."

Sam pulled the green damask from the mirror.

"What do you see?" he asked.

"The room."

"Good."

"Does Flaxfold know that you look at the mirror?" asked Smith.

"I don't tell her."

"What do you see?"

"Wait," said Sam. "And don't speak."

The ash tree in the garden tapped against the window. The river chanted to the willows. The house creaked.

"See?" whispered Sam.

A woman in a grey gown put her face to the mirror and looked at the room. Sam and Smith were out of her sight.

"Does she see us?" asked Smith.

"I don't think so."

"Does she see this room?"

"I don't think so."

"What is she looking at?"

"She's not looking at," said Sam. "She's looking for."

He veiled the mirror and they left the room.

"I'll give you some food to take," said Sam.

"No. I don't need any."

Smith shook Sam's hand.

"Tell Flaxfold I called," he said.

"She'll know anyway."

"Yes, but tell her all the same."

"I will."

"Come and see us. Dorwin misses you. And she likes to share stories about Flaxfield."

"Flaxfield," said Sam. "Yes, those are the good stories."

He watched Smith until the man was out of sight. And then he kept watching.

It was a Friday and they would eat trout later. ||

**Acknowledgements:** No names. No pack drill. You know who you are. I'm hugely grateful, and please accept my apologies for all the times I've not been easy to help and support. I'm trying [as you know].